THE BONE FOREST

A WOLF LAKE THRILLER

DAN PADAVONA

GET A FREE BOOK!

I'm a pretty nice guy once you look past the grisly images in my head. Most of all, I love connecting with awesome readers like you.

Join my VIP Reader Group and get a FREE serial killer thriller for your Kindle.

Get My Free Book

www.danpadavona.com/thriller-readers-vip-group/

1

His breath rasped through the forest, in concert with the songs of a million insects.

The man never would have believed that hauling a petite woman through the woods could be so difficult. His arms trembled from exertion. Adjusting her weight over his right shoulder so her face brushed the middle of his back and her hair hung past his hips, he struggled onward, cursing when prickers tore his flesh.

Tonight a canopy of clouds blanketed the stars and the September moon. It wasn't cold enough to see his breath, but it would be soon. In another week, Wolf Lake would experience its first killing frost. Then the leaves would shrivel and tumble from the trees, soon to be suffocated under five months of snow and ice. When the cold arrived, the water would freeze, as would the ground, forcing him to find alternative ways to dispose of the bodies. He hoped it wouldn't come to that.

He loved Alena, but she hadn't reciprocated. She'd failed him, and for that reason she'd paid the ultimate price. After he was rid of her, he would find a suitable replacement, a woman who returned his affection and understood he was her master.

Balancing Alena's dead weight on his shoulder, he stepped over a log. A tree sprang out of nowhere, and he stopped before he walked into the massive trunk. It was dangerous to walk through the woods in the dark. He didn't dare turn on the flashlight. Even in the forest, the lone beam would be visible from a mile away and draw unwanted attention.

Inside the deeper shadow of the oak, he stood and drank in the darkness. He felt larger than life, at one with the night. Here he was master of his domain, holding ultimate power over life and death.

A backpack containing a towel and a change of clothes hung off his shoulders. He'd need both after he completed his task. The man kept reminding himself that it was only a task, a job, something he needed to complete before he moved on to the next woman. Yet his heart ached with loss. Alena was special to him, and until she betrayed him and tried to escape, he'd believed she was the one.

He started walking. Another cursed thorn ripped his forearm and drew blood. The warmth dripped from his elbow to his wrist, wetting the cuff of his jacket. No time to tend to the wound. He forced himself to keep moving. The sooner he completed his task, the quicker he could find the love of his life.

Indecision brought him to a stop. A stand of evergreens loomed ahead, their jagged points like the sawtooth pattern of distant mountains. By now, he should have located the pond. With Alena draped over his shoulder, he spun and looked back the way he'd come.

Nothing but forest as far as his eyes traveled.

At the base of the hill, the country road snaked through the valley and angled toward Wolf Lake. Every second the man wasted increased the slim chance of a witness spotting his vehicle and alerting the sheriff. He'd hidden his truck behind a clump of trees. At night, someone traveling down the road would never see the truck, unless the driver stopped and parted the brush. But it paid to be careful.

In his mind, he tossed a coin. Left or right? He might wander until the sun rose if he chose wrongly. Fatigue spreading down his shoulder and back warned him not to linger. Pretty soon his strength would give out.

He drew a deep breath, inhaling the crisp night. Crickets sang through the forest. Placing one foot in front of the other, he angled up the hill, then turned left when the distant gurgle of the creek told him he'd chosen correctly. The land leveled out here, then dipped into a tiny bowl. Centuries of drainage fed the forest pond, where a few adventurous souls fished on summer days. Though one needed to walk a mile uphill through dense forest, the fishing made the effort worthwhile.

The trickles grew louder. He was close now. A mosquito lighting on his neck confirmed the water was just beyond the tree line.

Buoyed by the pond's proximity, the man forgot his exhaustion. He strode with renewed vigor, his body humming with adrenaline. Another few minutes, and he'd arrive.

The snap of a branch brought him to a stop. Bracing himself against a tree, he held his breath and listened. Probably just an animal trudging through the woods. What if he stumbled upon a bear? That thought quickened his heart. The chance of encountering another human at this time of night was too slim to consider. But that didn't stop him from fingering the knife hilt inside his pocket.

The forest fell silent again, save for the night sounds accompanying the man on his journey. Emboldened, he swung Alena onto his opposite shoulder and muscled through the underbrush, intent on reaching the pond before midnight. As though in a sign from above, the clouds parted and revealed a sliver of moonlight. The pond glimmered like a beacon.

All strength abandoned him when he reached the edge of the water. On his knees, he allowed the dead weight to slide off his shoulder and splay across the wet ground. Already the marshy earth seeped through the knees of his denim jeans. He spared the woman a glance. The moonlight turned her pallid flesh silver and blue. A black strand of hair dangled over her eyes. He brushed it away and caressed the gelid flesh of her cheek with his thumb. Why had she betrayed him? Hadn't his undying love been enough? The possibility that he would never again possess a woman as perfect as Alena shrouded him with doubt.

"It didn't have to be this way. You never should have run."

A lump formed in his throat. This was the last time he'd see her. Only photographs would preserve her beautiful face.

One at a time, he pried off his shoes, then stripped off his socks. The man grabbed Alena's ankles and tugged her through the grass and weeds. Another mosquito bit his arm, while more buzzed hungrily beside his ears.

Alena's arms caught on a tall stand of grass. A tug freed her body, and she slid down the terrain as if she'd been greased.

His foot landed shin deep in the pond. Though he'd expected the water, the chill shocked his body and pulled his nerves taut. His other foot plunged downward, kicking up murk and mud as trapped air bubbled to the surface. Somewhere in the night, a frog croaked. He swatted at the swarming insects and waded deeper. Alena's hips descended into the pond, followed by her head. Her body submerged now, except for her legs, which he grasped by the ankles. It was too risky to leave Alena along the bank, where the next person to cast a line into the pond would spot her body in the shallows. He needed to drag her to the deep center. Easier said than done. The sticky mud swallowed his feet to the ankles and tried to drag him under. He wrestled his legs free and pulled the woman along, her hair skimming the surface and collecting scum and plant life.

The moon vanished behind the clouds again. It was as if he'd turned off a light in a windowless room. He swung his head around, estimating the distance to the bank. When the water was deep enough, he turned on his side and swam, one arm pulling him across the pond.

Far enough.

The man paddled to stay afloat, the water engulfing his frame beneath his chin. Goosebumps rippled his skin, and the heat fled his body at an alarming rate, setting his teeth to chattering.

With a groan, he let go of Alena's ankle. One last burst of air bubbles, and she disappeared into the pond.

He hoped luck was on his side. Even if he weighed Alena's body down with rocks, she'd float to the surface after a few days of decomposition. Cattails and tall grass formed a natural fence along the banks, concealing the woman. Timing was everything. Another two or three days, and she'd drop back to the bottom of the pond. Provided nobody came along and spotted her inside that forty-eight to seventy-two-hour window, he'd get away with murder.

His work finished, he searched for the bank. The frigid water shocked him into action. Worried about leeches and the biting insects that called the pond home, he swam. It was too dark to be sure he was heading in the right direction. Eventually, he'd find the backpack and his change of clothes. A moment of panic set in when he realized how tired he was. Carrying a hundred-and-ten-pound woman through the forest had turned his arms into rubber. The pond spilled over his mouth and nostrils, clogging his air passages with filthy water. He coughed and hacked, kicking his legs, refusing to surrender to exhaustion until his palm thwacked down on the marshy earth. He lay upon the bank, facing the black sky. Laughter careened through his chest and set off another coughing fit.

He'd done it.

Off to his right, he spied the mute glow of his white socks amid the weeds. He pushed himself onto his hands and knees and crawled to his belongings. First, he peeled off his pants and wrung them out, careful not to drizzle water over his shoes. His hands slid up and down his thighs and calves, fingers probing for any devilish leeches, draining his lifeblood. He found one on the back of his knee. With a wince, he worked his fingertips beneath the leech and pulled. It popped free with a trickle of blood.

His shirt came next. There was a second leech on the underside of his arm, just above the elbow. This parasite had dug itself deep into the man's flesh, requiring him to use the knife to work the leech free. He shivered as much from the parasites as from the cold. After he toweled his body dry, he slipped into his clothes and shoes. His bodyweight had left an impression on the spongy soil, matting down the grass. With a rake of his arm, he rustled the grass until it stood tall again. Soon any sign that he'd visited would vanish beneath the cattails and weeds.

He limped through the forest as strength returned to his body. Still unwilling to shine the flashlight, he wandered down the hill, doubling back three times after he lost the path. At each stride, the sadness constricting his throat eased as though a noose unraveled.

She could be replaced. The right woman was out there, waiting for him to show her the way.

He just needed to find her.

2

Private investigator Chelsey Byrd studied the dingy Cape Cod at 42 Meadow Brook Lane. At eight-thirty, the neighborhood was quiet, except for the meter reader beginning her rounds at the end of the block. Most everyone had left for work or school, and it was too chilly for a morning walk. Two homes flew autumn flags. Mums embellished porches, and one family had already placed a pumpkin beside their door. A few backyards contained lacrosse nets and tree forts. Colored by the first orange leaves of September, this could have been any neighborhood in Wolf Lake, New York.

Urban Hammond's Cape Cod stood out from its neighbors. The overgrown brown lawn, sagging porch steps, and missing shingles suggested Hammond hadn't maintained his property. Too bad. Slap a fresh coat of sunshine-yellow paint on the house, fix the stairs, spruce up the landscaping, and the home might look adorable.

"You sure he's in there?" Raven Hopkins asked from the passenger seat.

Chelsey swept the dark curls off her shoulders and zipped

her leather jacket. "His truck is in the driveway. Maybe he hasn't woken up yet."

Hammond's black Toyota Tundra crouched in the driveway like an enormous guard dog. Raven eyed the dashboard clock. Her breath puffed condensation clouds, despite the dappled sunlight beaming across the windshield.

"Can't you turn on the heater? It's freezing in here."

"I can't," Chelsey said, her teeth chattering. "The motor and exhaust fumes will draw attention. So far nobody has bothered us, and I intend to keep it that way. Besides, it's supposed to hit sixty degrees this afternoon."

"It's only thirty now." Raven searched the backseat for snacks and found two apples. She bit into one and chewed, then tossed the other to Chelsey. "Eating raises your body temperature."

"Okay, but if we run out of food before break time, we're out of luck."

Dark-skinned and muscular, Raven Hopkins was Chelsey's best friend, as well as her top investigator. Raven had grown up in a broken household in nearby Harmon. Her father had walked out on the family when she was seven, and her heroin-addicted mother had kicked Raven out of the house after she turned eighteen. During the last year, Raven's mother, Serena, had turned her life around, but Raven remembered her upbringing. Having battled depression during high school, Chelsey empathized with Raven.

Chelsey's green Honda Civic sat beneath a maple tree three houses down from Urban Hammond's Cape Cod. Every few minutes, she wiped the inside of the windshield with a cloth. Her breath kept fogging the glass.

"What do we know about Hammond, other than he's a dirtbag?" Raven asked.

"He works at a hardware store in Wolf Lake and has four

assaults on his record, including striking a police officer five years ago while he lived in Orlando."

"Classy."

"I never promised we'd spend our days pursuing choir boys."

"And you're positive he's keeping the girl in the house?"

"Have you ever known Scout to be wrong about these things?"

Raven laughed and shook her head. Scout Mourning was Chelsey's teenage intern, a girl fast-tracking toward college and a career with the FBI. Scout, who'd regained the ability to walk after a successful spinal operation two months ago, possessed a knack for tracking fugitives online. Chelsey's target was a fifteen-year-old girl named Holly Doyle, who'd run away from home six weeks ago. Convinced their daughter was in Wolf Lake, the Doyle family had hired Chelsey's firm, Wolf Lake Consulting, to find Holly, and Scout had tracked her to this address.

"Tell me again how you intend to get Holly out of the house," Raven said, picking up the binoculars and glassing the front windows.

"We're not rushing inside, guns blazing, if that's what you're asking. I doubt Thomas would approve."

"Thomas will cut you slack. Dating the Nightshade County Sheriff has its benefits."

"I'm pretty sure he draws the line at armed home invasions. All I want is proof that Holly is inside. Visual identification will be enough, but I'll take a photograph if I can get one."

"You don't intend to knock on the door and ask for Holly, do you?"

"Not unless I want my head blown off," said Chelsey.

"Does Hammond own a gun?"

"Not legally."

"Which means he probably owns a gun."

"Yup."

"Great," said Raven, resting her head on her palm, her elbow propped against the door. "And he goes for underage girls, I take it."

"That's the rumor on the street."

A station wagon whipped past, causing the Civic to shake. The driver turned into a driveway beside a split-level house halfway down the road. Raven finished the apple and wrapped the core in a paper towel, which she stuffed into a plastic bag. She shrugged out of her jacket and stretched her arms, cracking her knuckles above the dashboard. Pulsing with energy, Chelsey's partner appeared ready to break her bench press record or tackle someone on a football field. Raven's sense of humor always set Chelsey at ease. But during an investigation, Raven was pure bad-ass and all business.

"You complained about being cold," Chelsey said.

"I'm limbering up. All this sitting around is locking up my muscles."

"But I'm the one meeting Hammond."

"Isn't it a better idea if I go? What if Hammond turns violent?"

"I'm prepared." Chelsey patted the bulge along her hip, where she hid a gun beneath her leather jacket. "But violence doesn't need to be the first option."

"I don't like this."

Chelsey reached over Raven and opened the glove compartment, from which she removed a bottle of perfume. A quick check of her hair in the mirror, and Chelsey sprayed the perfume on both sides of her neck, then added a sweet-scented burst to her wrist.

Raven cocked an eyebrow. "Now, what are you up to?"

"A little female persuasion never hurts. We know Hammond is a creep. I'm appealing to his sleazy side."

"He's into younger girls."

"He's had his share of legal-age girlfriends over the years."

"I wish you'd reconsider."

"Stick to the plan. I knock while you circle the house and peek through the windows. Don't forget to take pictures."

"I won't forget. But I'll watch you the entire time, Chelsey."

"I wouldn't have it any other way."

Chelsey took a deep breath and released her pent-up tension. A glance around the car to ensure nobody was on the sidewalk, then Chelsey popped out of the Civic with Raven trailing a step behind. The grass held morning dew, sparkling like gems. Chelsey shivered until she walked into the sunlight. Without a cloud in the sky, it wouldn't take long for the temperature to rise.

Chelsey waved a hand. Raven sneaked around the side of the Cape Cod, staying under the windows while she waited for Chelsey to ring the doorbell.

A man with a violent record would turn hostile when cornered by the police or a private investigator. How would Hammond explain concealing an underage runaway? Hammond's background check had revealed nine addresses over the last six years, not counting the jail cells he'd called home. It seemed he was forever fleeing to stay one step ahead of the law.

Chelsey paused when a warped step jiggled beneath her weight, as though one end might rocket upward and launch her through the air like a maniacal teeter-totter. The next three steps shrieked and groaned. At the front window, a curtain fluttered. Someone was inside.

Chelsey pressed the bell and waited. Nobody approached. Straining her ears, Chelsey heard a television in the background. Next, she rapped her knuckles against the door.

The door whipped open, making her flinch. Dressed in sweatpants and a tank top that showed off muscular, tattooed arms, Urban Hammond stood a head taller than Chelsey. He looked her up and down, apparently disappointed that she wasn't wearing a leather miniskirt to match her jacket. Judging by the reek pouring out of his mouth, Hammond hadn't brushed his teeth. She craned her neck to see around him, searching for Holly Doyle. Hammond blocked the doorway with his imposing frame.

"Who the hell are you?"

Chelsey cleared her throat. "Chelsey. I'm your new neighbor."

Hammond stepped outside and closed the door behind him. He peered left and right. "I don't have a new neighbor."

"Not right next door, silly." She pressed her index finger against a dimpled cheek and grinned. "I bought that cute little house for sale on the corner."

"Didn't realize it was on the market. Why are you here?"

"It seems everyone is gone for the day, but I heard the television on in your house. I wanted to introduce myself. You're Mr. Hammond?"

He scowled. "Who told you my name? You're not a saleswoman, are you?"

"Nope. I'm only a single mom looking to make friends in my new neighborhood."

"Yeah? Well, make friends with someone else. I'm a busy man."

When Hammond turned back to the door, Chelsey's eyes locked on the gun-shaped lump beneath the man's tank top and sweatpants. Her breath caught in her chest. Last year, a bullet fired by fugitive kidnapper Mark Benson had grazed her scalp. Chelsey shuddered to think what would have happened had the bullet struck her an inch lower. She wasn't taking any chances with Hammond.

Raven stuck her neck around the corner of the house.

Chelsey shook her head, imploring Raven to stay back. Raven pressed her lips together and edged backward, returning to the side windows, hopefully to photograph Holly and prove the girl was inside.

Chelsey hurriedly said, "It's just that I live alone with my fourteen-year-old daughter, and I'd feel safer if I had someone like you looking out for us."

He swung back to her. "Fourteen-year-old daughter, you say?"

"That's right. Perhaps you've seen her riding her bike. She's pretty and has black hair like mine. I'm so proud. She's a cheerleader this fall."

Hammond licked his lips.

What a sleaze bag.

"That's different. You should have told me about your girl from the get-go. You can't be too careful these days."

"That's what I say."

"Perhaps you can bring her by after school to say hello," Hammond said.

"She's kinda shy about meeting adults."

"My teenage niece is visiting this week. I'm sure they'd hit it off."

"Wow, what a great idea! With Joanna in a new school, she'd love to make a friend."

"Then it's settled. Come by after school."

Just then the door drifted open, pushed by a breeze moving across the porch. Hammond made to slam the door shut, but he was too slow. A golden-haired teenage girl in a T-shirt and pajama bottoms waltzed past the entryway.

"Did my Amazon order arrive?" the girl asked.

Chelsey put her arm out to prevent Hammond from closing the door. "Holly Doyle?"

With a growl, Hammond whipped around to Chelsey. "New neighbor, my ass. You're a bitch cop!"

Before Chelsey could react, two meaty hands encircled her throat and squeezed. Her sneakers rose off the porch. Chelsey swung her elbows down and broke his grip, but the tattooed man grabbed her around the waist and tossed her like a rag doll. Her back felt on the verge of snapping as his arms constricted.

She grabbed Hammond in a headlock and wrestled him down. His hip blasted against the top step. In a tangle of limbs, they tumbled down the stairs and struck the walkway, the air driven from Chelsey's lungs. From the doorway, Holly screamed at Hammond to stop, but his face was a mask of rage, teeth bared, spittle dripping off his lower lip. He clutched Chelsey's neck again. She pushed her legs against the concrete and fought for purchase. Gasping, she bridged him off her hips when his grip weakened. Chelsey lashed out and kicked Hammond's jaw, stunning him and snapping his neck sideways.

From the corner of her eye, Chelsey glimpsed Raven rushing toward the battle. But Hammond saw her coming.

He reached for his gun.

3

Chelsey had to save Raven.

As Hammond lifted the gun, Chelsey threw herself at her attacker and grabbed his arms, directing the weapon downward. The gun popped out of Hammond's grip with Chelsey astride him, trying to keep the bucking bronco down. He flung her sideways, and she landed hard on her shoulder. Before Hammond could regain control of the weapon, Raven barreled into the man. She reached for Hammond's gun, but he popped up and swung, clipping her behind the ear. Raven wobbled on her feet, dazed.

Chelsey kneed Hammond in the groin. He doubled over with a moan. A thrust to the chest knocked Hammond back on his heels, his arms pinwheeling as he fought to stay upright. She threw her shoulder into his midsection. It was like trying to wrestle a mountain. He shrugged her off and lashed out. Chelsey ducked the blow and landed a punch to his ribcage. The blow stunned Hammond long enough for Raven to kick the backs of his knees. He pitched forward, chin bouncing off the sidewalk.

Blood poured from Hammond's nose as Chelsey and Raven

fought to keep him prone. Chelsey was sure they'd lose control of the man until Raven wrenched both his arms behind his back and secured his wrists with a zip tie.

"You can't do this," he said, thrashing and kicking. "I'm not guilty."

"You hid a runaway child from her parents," Chelsey said, catching her breath.

"Holly was here of her own free will."

"She's fifteen, you sicko. Did you force her to have sex?"

"Bet you'd love to prove that, wouldn't you?" Hammond spat. "I don't even think you're cops. You never read me my rights."

"Ding, ding, ding," said Raven. "You win the prize for guessing correctly. We're private investigators with Wolf Lake Consulting. Tell him what he won, Chelsey."

Chelsey set a knee between Hammond's shoulders. "Well, Raven. Urban won a free ride in a Nightshade County sheriff's cruiser."

"And don't forget his box of Rice-A-Roni."

"Wait until my lawyer gets a hold of you bitches," Hammond said. "Posing as a neighbor and lying to my face. Ha! You're both going to jail."

"From what I saw, you attacked Chelsey without provocation. That makes you guilty of assault."

"I have a right to defend my property."

Chelsey massaged her neck. Raven looked over at her.

"You all right?" Raven asked, fishing the cell phone out of her pocket. She dialed the sheriff's department.

Chelsey winced and nodded.

After a brief phone conversation, Raven said, "The sheriff is on the way."

Only a minute passed before the first siren rose in the distance. A second cruiser followed. Two sheriff's vehicles stopped in front of the house. Sheriff Thomas Shepherd climbed out and adjusted his hat over an unruly mess of sandy hair. His lead deputy, Veronica Aguilar, hurried to his side. Thomas lifted a hand, indicating the other two deputies should stay back and keep any looky-loos at bay, though no one had ventured outside to check on the commotion.

"What do we have here?" Thomas asked.

"Urban Hammond," said Chelsey. "He was harboring a fifteen-year-old runaway."

Hearing her name, Holly Doyle stepped into the house and closed the door.

"After we identified Holly Doyle, Hammond attacked Chelsey and drew a gun."

"That's bullshit!" Hammond barked. "The gun fell out of my waistband. I never aimed it at anyone."

"You have a habit of storing a firearm in your sweatpants, Mr. Hammond?" Thomas asked.

"I have a license."

"That's not true," Chelsey said. "There are no licensed firearms under Urban Hammond's name."

"Are you injured?" Thomas asked Chelsey, concern drawing a V between his eyebrows.

"I'm fine. Just a little shook up."

Raven said, "She needs a doctor."

"I agree," Thomas said. "As soon as we're done here, you need to visit the hospital. Better safe than sorry."

"She's being a drama queen," Hammond said, a nasty, purple shiner coloring his right eye. Chelsey wondered if she'd landed a punch to Hammond's face, or if Raven had caused the damage. Either way, Hammond would be in a world of hurt for a few days. "I barely touched her."

Thomas read Hammond his rights and replaced the zip tie with a pair of handcuffs. Together, Thomas and Aguilar lifted

Hammond to his feet and walked him to the cruiser with Chelsey following.

The moment Thomas forced Hammond into the backseat, the front door of the house flew open, and Holly leaped off the porch and sprinted across the lawn.

Rolling her eyes, Aguilar said, "I've got her."

Chelsey wanted to help, but there was no chance Holly could outrun Aguilar, and Chelsey's neck throbbed as though she'd just been in a car crash. She already felt a mound rising off her cheek, another bruise she'd gained during the scuffle. Pulling a tissue from her pocket, she wiped her nose and discovered she was bleeding. Wonderful. As much as she loved Thomas, she didn't want him playing the role of a mother hen. Private investigative work carried its share of risks, but she was tough enough to handle them. She took another look at the bloody tissue and sighed.

"Maybe I should go to the hospital, after all," Chelsey said.

"Don't worry, I'll make sure you get there," said Raven, implying Chelsey had no choice.

Thomas said, "An ambulance is on the way."

Chelsey's back straightened. "What? I don't need an ambulance. I can drive to the hospital on my own."

"It's just a precaution. The paramedics will look you over . . . both of you . . . and if you're all right, you can drive yourselves." Thomas closed the back door of the cruiser, locking Hammond inside the vehicle. "We already have Hammond on assault and child endangerment. Throw in possession of an unlicensed firearm, and he'll need a helluva lawyer."

A hundred yards down the sidewalk, Aguilar caught up to Holly. The girl leaned over with her hands on her knees, shoulders rising and falling with a combination of breathlessness and sobs. Aguilar put a hand on Holly's shoulder and said something to the teenager. The brief exchange convinced Holly to accompany Aguilar back to the cruisers, though the deputy kept a hand on the girl's elbow, anticipating another chase.

Now that Holly was close, Chelsey overheard the girl pleading with Aguilar to let her go.

"You don't know what it's like. I hate my parents. They won't let me have friends or go out. I swear, they're trying to destroy my life. You can't make me go back."

Aguilar walked Holly to the second cruiser and helped her into the backseat. Thomas motioned for the deputies to transport Holly back to the station. The deputies knew enough to keep Hammond as far from the teenager as possible, but just picturing the tattooed maniac in the same building as Holly sent a chill down Chelsey's back.

Raven huffed. "I don't know what gets into teenagers' heads. It's one thing to hate your parents, but why would you shack up with a lowlife like Urban Hammond?"

"What's next for Holly?" asked Chelsey.

Thomas set his hands on his hips and watched the cruiser pull away. "I'll call the parents and have them meet me at the station. No doubt the county will involve itself. Let's hope the girl gets the help she needs and doesn't run off a second time."

He ran his eyes from Chelsey's bruised cheek down to the tissue.

"You're giving me that look again. Like you think I'm too fragile to be a private investigator."

"Not at all. Hammond is a monster. I'd have ended up with just as many bruises if not more. I trust you to keep yourself safe, but I reserve the right to care."

"Duly noted."

"I need statements from both of you," Thomas said, his gaze taking in Chelsey and Raven. "Tell me everything that happened and leave nothing out."

As Chelsey and Raven recounted the attack, Thomas used

his phone to photograph their injuries. He wasn't taking any chances. Hammond's lawyer would argue that the private investigators had instigated the fight, and he'd fought back in self-defense. Thomas's thumb brushed Chelsey's neck as he pushed her hair out of the way. Warmth traveled through Chelsey's body.

Upon seeing the red imprints of Hammond's fingers on her neck, Thomas's shoulders stiffened. Chelsey knew Thomas wished he'd been there when she knocked on Hammond's door. The sheriff lifted her hand and assessed her scraped knuckles, almost with admiration.

"You're one tough woman, Chelsey Byrd," Thomas said. He studied Raven and grinned. "And I wouldn't mess with you if my life depended on it. All right, a few more pictures."

When the sheriff finished taking their statements, he waved to Aguilar, who sat inside the cruiser with Hammond stuffed in the back. The arrested man hung his head, sulking.

"I'd better get back to the station. And you two need to visit the hospital. That includes you, Raven."

"Yeah, yeah," Raven said, kicking a stone on the sidewalk. "I wish I had another five minutes alone with Hammond."

"I didn't hear that." Thomas hugged them both, but he held Chelsey a few seconds longer, his hand rubbing the small of her back.

Raven's phone rang. Chelsey recognized the ring tone for Darren Holt, the ranger at Wolf Lake State Park and Raven's boyfriend. He must have heard about the fight. Raven stepped away to take the call.

Thomas caressed Chelsey's cheek, careful not to touch the bruise. "Call me after the doctor checks you over. You scared me this morning."

Chelsey realized she'd frightened herself. If she'd been a second slower lunging at Hammond, the psycho would have shot her. And Raven. What was Hammond thinking, attempting to shoot two private investigators because they'd caught him harboring a fifteen-year-old runaway? Was keeping Holly Doyle worth two murder charges?

Chelsey didn't want to let go of Thomas. Her heart rate had come down, and she felt safe in the sheriff's arms. Nudging him away, she set her hands on his shoulders and held him at arm's length. "Tell you what. After the doc clears me and you get off work, we'll toss that steak on the grill and take the boat out at sunset."

"Twist my arm, why don't you?"

"It will be nice to put this fiasco behind us. Plus, the sunsets this week have been out of this world."

He took the tissue from her hand and dabbed it against her nose, soaking up another drop of blood as the ambulance turned the corner and headed in their direction.

Raven was still on the phone with Darren when Thomas's radio crackled. He fielded the call along the curb, pacing while he spoke to the dispatcher. A moment later, he pocketed the radio and returned to Chelsey.

"That was the station," Thomas said. "I might need to take a rain check on that boat ride."

"What's going on?"

"There's a man waiting to speak with me. He says his wife is missing."

4

Thomas stopped his cruiser in the parking lot behind the Nightshade County Sheriff's Department. With Deputy Aguilar's aid, he led a surly Urban Hammond into the station and handed him off to Deputy Lambert for booking. At that moment LeVar Hopkins pushed through the front door and stopped to speak with Maggie, the administrative assistant. Built like a linebacker, LeVar tied his dreadlocks back whenever he entered the station, though he wasn't dressed for duty today. Beyond the glass frontage, LeVar's black Chrysler Limited waited curbside.

A little over a year ago, that car had been the most-feared vehicle in Nightshade County, back when Raven's brother ran with the Harmon Kings gang. So much had changed after Thomas saved Serena Hopkins from a heroin overdose. LeVar had moved into Thomas's guest house, sworn off gang life, and enrolled at the community college, where he studied criminal justice.

"There he is," LeVar said, striding to Thomas. "Shep Dawg."

"I'm surprised to see you here today. You're off until the weekend."

"Yeah, but I was in the neighborhood and needed to stop in. Something is all jacked up with my tax withholdings. Maggie is helping me figure out what I did wrong."

In her fifties, the orange-haired Maggie Tillery had served the Nightshade County Sheriff's Department for two decades, long before a shy high school senior named Thomas Shepherd walked through the door as a student intern. Sheriff Stuart Gray had never balked over the boy's Asperger's Syndrome. The encouragement and support from the sheriff led Thomas to a detective's position with the LAPD before he returned to Wolf Lake. After Gray retired, Thomas ran unopposed and was elected sheriff.

"Maggie will fix whatever you did. I'm sure it's something minor."

Sitting at her desk, Maggie gave Thomas a meaningful look and tilted her head at the interview room, where a man with short blond hair scratched nervously behind his ear, his eyes refusing to sit still.

"I had better get in there, LeVar," said Thomas.

"What did he do?"

"Mr. Weir? He's not under arrest. His wife is missing."

LeVar bounced on his heels. "Mind if I sit in on the interview?"

"Are you keeping up with your courses? You're in class today."

"I had class this morning. No worries. I'm acing my courses this semester."

"I'm sure you are, but it's only September. Two months from now, you'll be hip deep in papers and exams. I don't want you to fall behind." Maggie cleared her throat. "I guess that's my cue. If you want to sit in, you're welcome to join me. Afterward, I'm meeting with a teenage runaway's parents."

"What's that about?"

"Long story, and it involves Chelsey and your sister. They found Holly Doyle, and I arrested Urban Hammond. I'll tell you everything later."

Seated across the table, Lance Weir jerked upright and stood when the door opened. Weir's haircut was a shade longer than a buzz. His untucked shirt girded the waist of his jeans, as though he'd rushed here before he finished dressing. Weir gave LeVar a curious look.

"Sheriff Thomas Shepherd," Thomas said, extending a hand. "And this is Deputy Hopkins."

LeVar grinned. He'd only been a part-time deputy for a few weeks and was still getting used to the title, wearing it like a fancy new jacket.

"Lance Weir. Thank you for agreeing to meet with me."

"Can I get you a bottle of water?"

"No, I'm not thirsty."

The sheriff gestured for Weir to sit. Beside Thomas, LeVar already had a yellow legal pad in front of him, pen in hand.

"You say your wife is missing?"

"I can't find Karley anywhere, and she isn't answering her phone."

"How long since you last spoke to her?"

"Yesterday evening. About sixteen hours ago. Karley left after dinner. She was meeting her friends at a concert in Syracuse, but they said she never showed up."

"That would have been about seven or eight o'clock?"

"Karley and her friends agreed to meet in the parking lot at six-thirty, then walk into the show together. But she never arrived."

LeVar met Thomas's eyes and turned his attention to Weir.

"You never noticed your wife was missing until now?" LeVar asked.

Weir looked down and ran a hand across the top of his head.

"I meant to stay up and wait for Karley, but I fell asleep on the couch while watching television. The next thing I knew, the sun was shining through the windows. I thought Karley had returned and let me rest—the last few weeks at work have been brutal—but she wasn't in bed. No missed texts or calls, but I didn't expect she'd phone me unless there was a problem."

LeVar set an ankle on his knee. "Wouldn't your wife call to tell you the concert was over and she was heading home?"

"I told Karley to contact me if she drank and didn't feel safe driving. She swore she wouldn't drink, that she just wanted to watch the show and have fun with her friends. I messaged her all morning. She hasn't replied. I knew I never should have agreed to her going."

"Karley's friends knew she was missing last evening?" asked Thomas.

"That's right."

"Weren't they worried enough to contact you?"

"They tried last night. My ringer was off. I swore I'd kept it on." Weir clenched his hands into fists. "It's not my fault. I've been under a lot of pressure at work. These damn phones. I feel like I'm tied to mine. There's never time to rest."

"Okay, the ringer was off, and you never received their calls. What did you do when you woke up?"

"After I realized Karley wasn't home, I wondered if she'd stayed in a hotel last night. She was due at work at eight this morning, but when I called, they said she never came in."

"Where does Karley work?"

"The federal credit union in Treman Mills," said Weir. "She's an account manager."

"I'll need the names of the people Karley was meeting."

"Sure. Hannah Mickley and Leigh Park."

"How long has Karley known them?"

"Karley and Hannah went to Wolf Lake High School

together. She met Leigh last year at a cafe in town. What was the name of it?"

Weir closed his eyes and pinched the bridge of his nose.

"The Broken Yolk?" asked LeVar.

"That's it. The Broken Yolk."

"I'll need phone numbers for Hannah and Leigh," Thomas said, "and for anyone Karley might have seen last evening."

Weir scrolled through his missed calls and recited the numbers for Thomas.

"You'll find her, right?"

"We'll do our best. Have you fought with your wife recently? Any disagreements or tension?"

"I hope you're not suggesting she ran off. Karley loves me."

"I have to ask," said Thomas.

Weir's face reddened. "My wife and I have a strong marriage. She wouldn't leave. It's insulting that you'd make such a suggestion."

"What do you do for a living, Mr. Weir?"

"I work at Bryant Media Group. I'm sure you heard of us."

Thomas glanced at LeVar. They both shrugged.

Lance Weir released an exasperated sigh. "We're only the top-performing media group this side of New York City."

"What do you do there?"

"I handle public relations, web content, advertising, anything that needs to be done."

"Sounds like a busy job."

"You don't know the half of it," Weir said. "I work the evening shift this week. When Wallace isn't in the office—that's Wallace Bryant, the company founder—I run the show."

"But you didn't work last night."

"Yesterday was my day off. My hours change all the time, but I don't mind. I'm good at my job, and our client list grew a hundred percent over the last year."

"Mr. Weir, can anyone verify you were home last night?"

"What? No. Just Karley, but she left before six." Weir narrowed his eyes. "You don't think I had something to do with my wife's disappearance, do you?"

"Maybe a neighbor saw you last night?"

"My car was in the driveway."

LeVar scribbled a note.

"Do you share a credit card account?" asked Thomas.

"Damn right. If I let Karley have her own account, she'd run us into bankruptcy. Why?"

"Can you access the account now?"

"I suppose so. What's this about?"

"Call up the account activity for the last twenty-four hours."

Weir grumbled something under his breath. He turned his phone to face Thomas and LeVar. "There. Happy?"

Thomas scanned the account. There was a pending charge from a gas station, but it was two days old. No Uber or Lyft rides, no airline transactions that suggested Karley had left town without telling her husband. More importantly, Thomas couldn't find a transaction that pinpointed Karley's location after she'd left the house.

"Any other credit or bank cards?"

"We both have bank cards, but they're only for withdrawals."

"I'll need that account information as well."

Weir nodded.

"I also need to see your bedroom," Thomas said.

"That's my private space. What's so important about looking inside our bedroom?"

"Karley might have left something behind that will tell us where she is."

"Fine. This search of yours won't take long, will it?" Weir asked.

"I don't see a reason it will."

Thomas finished questioning Weir and told him he'd visit the house in an hour. He couldn't decide if Weir was more upset over his wife missing or someone invading his personal space. The door closed behind Weir, and Thomas shifted his chair to face LeVar.

"What do you think?"

"I wouldn't want that guy for a neighbor," said LeVar. "What a hothead. And what kind of husband goes an entire night without realizing his wife isn't home?"

"He claims he fell asleep."

"If it was after midnight and Chelsey hadn't returned from an investigation, wouldn't you sense something was wrong and wake up?"

"Without question."

"That tells me their marriage isn't as strong as Weir says."

"You think Karley left him?" Thomas asked. "I couldn't find an airline transaction on their credit card statement. Then again, if Karley planned to leave her husband, she wouldn't put it on a shared credit card. Perhaps she opened an individual account and didn't tell him."

LeVar looked toward the ceiling in thought. "I doubt Karley left town. Why would she go through the trouble of purchasing concert tickets and worrying her friends?"

"That's a good point."

"What's our next step?"

"*Your* next step is to drive home and study," said Thomas. "This weekend, I'll put you on the case with Aguilar and Lambert."

"Shep, you know I'm gonna head over to Wolf Lake Consulting, and I assume you'll bring them into the investigation."

"True, but I don't want you to overextend yourself. College classes, an internship, and a part-time job—that's a lot of work to juggle."

"I'll keep up. Getting back to the case, I don't trust Weir. He should have known his wife was missing. Falling asleep on the couch is a lame excuse, and it's damn convenient that he forgot to turn his ringer on and missed those calls from Karley's friends."

Thomas agreed. Lance Weir struck him as brash and uncaring. If Chelsey drove to Syracuse to meet friends, Thomas would stay awake until he knew she was safe.

"Statistics show the spouse is usually to blame when someone goes missing," LeVar added.

"If Lance Weir lied to us, we'll catch him."

5

Karley's head throbbed. She touched her temples, flinched, and rolled onto her side.

Her first thought was she'd had too much to drink at the concert, but that made no sense. She would never drink and drive, and come to think of it, she remembered nothing about the show. Had she pulled into a rest stop and fallen asleep? Were her friends expecting her? A musty scent tickled her nose.

Opening her eyes invited a splitting migraine. She pulled the pillow from under her head and laid it over her face, shutting out the harsh glare.

A pillow.

She couldn't be home in bed. The mattress felt wrong—lumpy and hard with no give.

One blink.

Another.

This wasn't her bedroom. And a cushion lay below her, not a mattress.

Confusion and panic twisted Karley's insides as she took in her surroundings. She didn't recognize this place. Various explanations fluttered through her brain—she'd gotten sick at the concert and gone home with Leigh or Hannah. Wait, wasn't she supposed to be at work?

She dug through her pockets. No phone, no wallet. Car keys gone.

Her head sprang off the pillow, and she sat upright, a shudder rippling across her flesh. A concrete-floor basement spread out before her with a water heater in the far corner. Three bare wooden shelves jutted off the wall, and a staircase ascended into darkness. Across the room, one washer and one dryer perched in a vertical stack, everything utterly unrecognizable.

Lance.

At the concert, Karley had intended to tell Hannah and Leigh that she was leaving Lance. Just thinking of separating from her husband tied Karley's throat into knots. Karley and Lance never spent time together—when Karley returned from the credit union, Lance was working at Bryant Media Group and didn't come home until after seven. To make matters worse, Lance volunteered for weekend shifts, leaving Karley alone on her days off. They argued over meaningless topics. On the rare occasion when they ate dinner together, Lance stared at his phone the whole time, his free hand shoveling food past his lips while he ignored anything she had to say. When was the last time they'd made love?

They both knew the marriage was over. It had taken Karley a year to muster the courage to leave her husband. She'd found a cute efficiency apartment between Treman Mills and Coral Lake, a short commute to work and perfect for her budget. She only needed to sign the lease.

Lance suspected. He shouldn't have, for Karley had hidden the breadcrumbs well. She conducted all her apartment searches on her work computer, guarding her secret. Yet somehow he'd read the tea leaves and figured it out.

One glimmer of hope kept Karley sane. Lance would search for her and involve the police. Or at least she hoped he would. What if Lance didn't care and assumed she'd already abandoned him? No. All her belongings were at the house. Lance wasn't stupid enough to believe she'd walk out on him without packing a bag.

Please, Lance. You haven't paid attention to me in years, but I'm sure there's some love remaining in your heart. Call the authorities. Tell them I never made it to the concert.

Asking the man she intended to divorce for help made her cringe. Not that anyone heard her begging.

Even if Lance sat on his hands, Karley's parents would contact the police. Karley spoke to Mom every other night. When she didn't call tonight to tell her about the show, Mom would worry. Someone had to be looking for her.

Karley massaged her forehead, fighting to span the memory gap. She couldn't be certain how long she'd spent in the cellar. Since last night? Longer?

On her way to Syracuse, she'd stopped at the grocery store for snacks. She strained to remember what had happened next. Didn't even recall paying for the energy bars and water, yet she must have, or the cameras would have caught her shoplifting. Why was there a hole in her memory?

As if viewing a dream, she pictured the automatic doors parting, the paper bag tucked under one arm, a stray shopping cart rolling across the parking lot in an escape attempt. Her car was at the rear of the lot—Lance always made her park near the back, insisting careless shoppers would open their doors and ding the vehicle.

The wind had tossed Karley's hair across her eyes, temporarily blinding her.

A shadow converged on Karley, followed by a pinprick against her neck, almost like a bee sting.

At some point, she'd awakened to total darkness, claustrophobia squeezing her until she wanted to burst. Her body jostled back and forth as a motor rumbled. Someone had thrown her inside a trunk. She'd struggled to stay awake, but bricks weighed down her eyelids. She recalled the hum of wheels over blacktop, the ticking of a blinker before centrifugal force whipped Karley around and rolled her.

Then nothing.

Ice congealed over Karley's heart. She covered her mouth and moaned.

Kidnapped.

But who would abduct her?

Another horrible thought: Had the kidnapper raped her while she lay unconscious? Her hands groped her body in search of an answer. No, she didn't believe anyone had raped her. But what could be more violating than tossing Karley into a locked basement and confining her like a misbehaving pet?

Karley's eyes traveled to the lone window in the room, a rectangle cut into the wall six feet off the ground, the opening smaller than her hips. Daylight beamed through the glass and drew a circle of white heat on the floor. Bars covered the window.

She slunk into the corner and hugged her knees to her chest. Until now, she hadn't realized the bed was a futon. One white sheet, one comforter adorned with blue and yellow flowers.

A thump brought her attention to the ceiling. Someone was upstairs. Her kidnapper.

She swept her gaze across the basement and searched for a weapon. The man who'd taken her must have removed all the objects from the basement. There wasn't even a jug of detergent for the washer.

A television played upstairs. Hoping the sound would mask her movement, she crawled off the futon to explore her cell. Her legs gave out, and she grabbed the wall before she toppled. It was clear she'd been drugged. Her clouded brain and unsteady gait made it obvious. She shook her head to clear the cobwebs.

A door stood ahead of her. Was there a way out of this place?

She limped along the wall, willing her legs to respond. The door opened to a half-bath with a sink, toilet, and a medicine cabinet. Bars covered another window. Nothing else, except the roll of toilet paper affixed to the wall and a tissue box. She tested the faucet, and water flowed into the sink. Ravaged by thirst, Karley placed her lips beneath the flow and drank until her stomach hurt.

Footsteps moved across the ceiling. She needed to hurry before the kidnapper came downstairs and found her awake. Opening the medicine cabinet, she prayed for a razor blade, anything she could use to defend herself. But the cabinet was spotless. No toothpaste, no pill bottles, no deodorant.

Nine weeks had passed since the last time Karley enjoyed a night out with Hannah and Leigh. Though Lance was never home, he forbade her from going out with her friends, perhaps because he suspected her plans. She'd looked forward to the concert for so long. And now she was held against her will by a madman.

Moving in silence, she crossed the basement. A stairway led to a closed door at the top. With the windows barred, the door was the only way out of this prison. She crept up the steps, listening for the man who'd abducted her. She tested the knob and found it locked. Shouldering her way through the stout door wasn't an option. In the next room, a faucet ran.

She retraced her steps to the basement, panic raising the hair on her neck as she searched for a way out of this place. Water gurgled through a long black pipe against the wall. Her eyes stopped on the water heater. If she kicked the connections and dislodged the pipe, she'd cause a flood. Someone would need to bail out the basement.

Bad idea. She might drown or electrocute herself in a knee-deep flood.

Karley returned to the window and leaped, glimpsing blue sky and a residence in the distance. Grabbing the bars, she lifted herself and crawled her sneakers up the wall, hoping for a better view.

The lock clicked open at the top of the stairs.

She dropped and scurried to the futon. Maybe if he thought she was asleep, he'd leave her alone. She tucked her legs under the sheet and dragged the comforter past her shoulders and over her head. Tremors wracked her body.

His footsteps descended the staircase and stopped beside the wall. She felt him watching her, assessing.

Karley didn't hear him cross the room so much as she felt his shadow drift across her body like a December wind. Her white knuckles clutched the comforter over her face, an ostrich burying her head in the sand at a predator's approach. Terror prevented her from peeking at him.

A heavy silence fell over the room. She almost believed he'd lost interest and left the cellar.

His hand ripped the cover back. She looked up and screamed.

He wore a sheer stocking over his face, distorting his features and preventing Karley from recognizing him. He spoke in a raspy whisper to disguise his voice. Did she know him?

"You slept a long time, Karley. Are you feeling better now?"

She sat up and grabbed the comforter, but he yanked it out of her grip. The wall stopped her from scrambling backward, trapping her with the leering kidnapper.

"Don't wish to talk? That's fine. In time, you'll open up and come to trust me. May I get you something to eat or drink? You must be starving."

A whimper escaped her throat. Someone had to know she was missing. She prayed the police were trying to find her.

The disguised man sat on the edge of the futon and placed a hand on her thigh.

"You've always been the most beautiful woman to ever grace my life. Why are you nervous? I won't hurt you."

He spoke as if they knew each other. Karley's mind sifted through names and faces. Who would do something like this?

"Look at you: afraid and unsure of yourself. It has been too long since you made love. Am I wrong?" He tossed the cover onto the floor. "I'll prove to you there's nothing to fear."

His hands groped beneath her shirt and slid along her chest. By the time he'd yanked the shirt over her head and unbuttoned her jeans, her screams were ringing off the walls.

6

Chelsey was filing paperwork at Wolf Lake Consulting when Scout Mourning arrived from school. The girl sported plaid shorts that appeared comfortable for the mild afternoon but must have chilled her to the bone this morning. Scout's legs had filled out after weeks of jogging and weightlifting, and no longer showed signs of atrophy. To Chelsey, the successful operation was nothing short of a miracle. Scout had a new lease on life and lived every day to the fullest.

Working beside Raven, Darren Holt glanced up from the computer and asked, "How was school, Scout?"

"Awesome," Scout said, setting her backpack on an empty desk in the corner.

Chelsey said, "There's a smoothie with your name on it in the fridge."

"Ooh, thanks. What kind?"

"Protein, greens, frozen berries, and fresh ginger."

"My mouth is watering already. I'm starving."

Scout's training regimen demanded nutrition, and Chelsey was determined to keep her on track. The teenager hurried from the office to the kitchen and returned seconds later with a smoothie in a mason jar.

Chelsey closed the drawer on the filing cabinet. "Meet any interesting people this year?"

Chelsey remained concerned over Scout's ability to assimilate. Fate had dealt the teen two devastating blows when a tractor trailer struck her parents' car from behind—Scout lost movement in her legs, and she moved from Ithaca to Wolf Lake, where nobody knew her.

"Actually, yes. There's a girl in my social studies class named Liz. She's really into those ghost shows on television, the ones with the EVP recorders and crazy people walking around in the dark. And I guess she likes crime documentaries."

"Sounds like your type of friend."

"Liz is coming to my house for a sleepover next weekend."

Scout had made a few friends after moving to Wolf Lake, but none had invited her to parties or sleepovers. They'd treated Scout as if she were made of glass, too fragile to be a normal teenager. Now that she was out of the wheelchair, her classmates viewed her in a different light. Chelsey wished the students had given Scout a chance last year, but she understood what it was like to be young. Accepting Scout was an important first step for teenagers not used to interacting with people different from them. Hopefully, they had learned a valuable lesson and would embrace the next wheelchair-bound student.

Scout did a doubletake when she noticed Chelsey's bruised face. "What the heck happened to you?"

"I was on the wrong end of a punch this morning."

"Geez, are you all right?"

"For the most part," Chelsey said, touching her swollen cheek. The red markings had faded from her neck, yet she still felt the ghosts of Urban Hammond's fingers strangling the life out of her. "The doctor gave me a clean bill of health and told me to take it easy for a few days."

"Which means she'll wait an hour or two before fighting another ex-con," Raven said, smirking.

"Hey, I've behaved all day. Give me credit."

Scout glanced around the office. "Where's LeVar? I swear I saw his car in the parking lot."

"In the bedroom at the end of the hall, studying. He has a quiz Monday morning."

After Chelsey had returned to Wolf Lake and founded the investigation firm, she'd purchased a two-bedroom house in the village center and converted the living room into an office. The furnished bedrooms proved handy whenever the investigators worked late hours and didn't want to drive home. A stocked refrigerator in the kitchen held enough food for everyone, and the central location provided the investigators with a short commute.

As Scout logged on at her workstation to begin her after-school internship, Chelsey slid into a chair beside her.

"Here's some amazing news," Chelsey said.

"What's that?"

"We found Holly Doyle, thanks to you."

"Seriously? Is she all right?"

"She seemed pretty shook up, but she's unhurt. Last I heard, Holly was at the station with Thomas while they waited for the parents to arrive."

"Wait, did Urban Hammond do that to your face?" asked Scout.

"He did, but you should have seen what he looked like after Raven and I finished with him."

"I should have been there," Darren said, shaking his head. Though the state-park ranger didn't hold a private investigator's license, he'd worked as a police officer in Syracuse. Besides wanting to spend time with Raven, he remained interested in solving cases. "If you had called me, I would have found someone to watch the campground this morning."

"You and Thomas are two peas in a pod," said Raven, grinning. "Both of you believe only a big, strong man can keep us safe."

Darren raised his hands. "I never said you couldn't handle yourselves. Just that asking an extra investigator to watch your backs is a wise decision when pursuing a suspect with Hammond's assault record. You didn't even call the sheriff's department until the surveillance spun out of control."

"It's not as if we could have predicted he'd attack us," Chelsey said.

"You didn't assume after viewing his record?"

"That was my mistake. Next time, I will request an extra investigator."

"I'm just happy both of you came out of the fight with your health. And you found Holly Doyle. How did Scout work her magic this time? Nobody ever explained to me how she found your runaway."

"Simple," Scout said, pulling up an enhanced photograph on her computer and turning the monitor toward Raven and Darren. In the image, an envelope sat on a kitchen table littered with crumbs. "After Holly ran away from home, she opened new social media accounts. I guess she wanted to stay in touch with her friends. To fool everyone searching for her, she used a fictitious name—Heather Drew."

Interested, Darren sat forward with his elbows on his knees. "Very clever."

"That's right. I wouldn't have figured it out, except she used her fake account to connect with her old friends. Then she started posting selfies."

"How did you determine she was still in Wolf Lake?"

"EXIF data, like I used to track Jeremy Hyde." Serial killer Jeremy Hyde had evaded the authorities for weeks until Scout caught his trail on the internet last year. "The data won't tell you the photograph's exact location, but you can narrow the radius down to a mile or two. That got me close. Then Holly made a mistake."

"This is my favorite part," said Raven, winding her hand and encouraging Scout to continue.

"Holly . . . or Heather . . . photographed herself inside a kitchen. There was a window behind her and a water tower in the background, which told me where in Wolf Lake to look. But here's the kicker: I spotted envelopes scattered across the table. They were too blurry to read until I loaded the image into Photoshop and sharpened the print. It took some manipulation, but I brought out Urban Hammond's address."

"And that's how we found Holly," Chelsey said.

"Only she wasn't happy to see her parents," said Raven. "Holly tried to run again, but Deputy Aguilar caught the girl and brought her back to the cruiser."

"Teens blow things out of proportion, but something tells me Holly doesn't have the best home life."

"How bad?" Scout asked.

"Though Holly might be making mountains out of mole hills, it sounds like her mother and father are overprotective."

"That's no reason to run away. I hope it's not worse than that." Scout lifted her palms. "Isn't there anything we can do to help?"

"It's up to the county now."

"That doesn't give me much confidence."

"They see cases like this all the time. I'm sure they'll do what's best for Holly. At least she isn't living with a sexual predator."

LeVar poked his head around the entryway and said, "Did someone say Scout Mourning had arrived for duty?"

"Aren't you studying?" Scout asked.

LeVar waved her concern away. "I put in an hour this morning and another hour this afternoon. If I don't pull a perfect score on Monday's quiz, I'll lose my—"

"No swearing," Chelsey said.

"Lunch. How about that?"

"I'm sure that's what you meant to say."

LeVar joined Scout at the desk in the corner. "Isn't that the photograph that caught Urban Hammond and brought Holly Doyle home?" He turned his attention to Chelsey's bruises, then eyed the scrapes across Raven's face. "I could have helped you this morning after I finished class."

"Don't go there," Darren said. "I already got the big-strong-man lecture."

"Fight club tip number one. Don't block punches with your face."

"Funny, LeVar," Raven said, elbowing Darren for laughing.

"*Aight*, enough with the jokes. What are we doing this afternoon? Just so you're aware, I sat with Thomas during the Lance Weir interview."

"The Weir disappearance is our new investigation," Chelsey said, printing copies of the case notes. She passed them to each investigator. "To bring Scout and Darren up to speed, Karley Weir, age twenty-nine, disappeared on her way to a concert in Syracuse last night. Twenty-One Pilots. Right up your alley, Scout?"

Scout smirked. "They're cool."

"Karley planned to meet her friends, Leigh Park and Hannah Mickley, but she never arrived."

"The husband claims the friends called and messaged him

last night," LeVar said. "He says he silenced his phone and took a nap, but ended up sleeping through the night."

"And he didn't worry when his wife never made it home?" asked Darren.

"That didn't sit right with me, either."

"Scout and LeVar," said Chelsey, "you're our internet tracking experts. Find Karley Weir's social media pages, including her professional accounts. She works for the federal credit union in Treman Mills. Tell me everything she's been up to over the last month and make a list of her friends."

"On it."

"Darren and Raven, I want you to help me sift through news articles."

Raven scrunched her brow. "News articles?"

"Focus on any women who've gone missing over the last three months. There is no evidence that someone kidnapped Karley, but I want to cover all bases in case the person who abducted her has done this before. The sheriff's department will interview Karley's friends and family."

"What do we know so far?"

"LeVar?"

LeVar cleared his throat. "Lance Weir said his wife left the house a little before six. Karley was scheduled to meet her friends at six-thirty, which means she vanished inside a thirty- to forty-five-minute window."

"That narrows the search area," said Chelsey. "If we assume she traveled the interstates between Wolf Lake and Syracuse, we might figure out where she disappeared. She didn't charge anything to her credit card last evening, but she might have paid cash. We need a list of likely turnoffs, places she might have stopped for a bite to eat or to gas up."

"If she bought fast food," Darren said, "there are dozens of options along that route. That's not counting the gas stations, grocery stores, and convenience markets. This won't be easy."

"Each of you has a digital image of Karley Weir in your email. Circulate that photo. Someone must have seen her last evening."

7

As Sheriff Thomas Shepherd hunched over his desk and reviewed the charges against Urban Hammond, Deputy Tristan Lambert knocked on the open door to announce his presence. In his early forties, Lambert stood a few inches over six feet and still possessed the fit physique he'd forged in the army.

"Sheriff, Urban Hammond's attorney is here."

"All right, Lambert. Bring Hammond out of the holding cell and sit him inside the interview room. I'll meet you there in a second."

Lambert departed, and Thomas gathered the paperwork and clicked the edges together against his desk. From the corner of his eye, he glimpsed a lanky, blond-haired man in a silver suit, shoes polished and shining. Thomas groaned. Heath Elledge was a notoriously aggressive attorney with a track record of winning cases for unsavory clients. He predominantly handled white-collar crimes, which made Thomas wonder why Elledge would represent Urban Hammond. He would have doubted Hammond could afford Elledge. The attorney appeared to be reading Maggie the riot act while Thomas walked down the hallway.

"Mr. Elledge," Thomas said.

"Sheriff Shepherd," Elledge said, disdain tainting his voice.

"If you will join us in the interview room, we'll get started."

Elledge sat across the table from Thomas and set his briefcase on the desk. He snapped open the locks and pulled two sheets of paper from a folder, then fixed a pair of reading glasses on the end of his nose. Lambert led Hammond into the room. Elledge swung his head around, stood, and gestured at the handcuffs.

"Are those necessary?"

"Your client assaulted two people this morning and resisted arrest, so yes, I believe they're necessary."

Elledge waited for Hammond to sit before settling into his own chair. The attorney tugged the tip of his tie and smoothed his hair. Thomas instructed Hammond to sign the Miranda agreement, acknowledging he understood his rights. Hammond glanced at Elledge, who nodded. The convict lifted his cuffed wrists onto the table with mock distress and scribbled his name. Lambert joined Thomas, opposite Hammond and his attorney.

"I'm recording the interview," Thomas said, pressing the button on his digital recorder.

Elledge reviewed the signature, passed the paper back to Thomas, and said, "You don't intent to hold my client on these charges, do you?"

"Mr. Hammond endangered a minor," Thomas said.

"I fail to see how."

"Let's start with Holly Doyle's age. She's fifteen, and she ran away from home. If Mr. Hammond had any sense of decency, he would have returned the girl to her family or notified the sheriff's department."

"Mr. Hammond didn't know Ms. Doyle's age. She

approached my client outside McPherson's Bar on Second Street and claimed she was twenty-one. The girl even had a fake ID that she used to purchase alcohol. How was he to know she'd lied about her age?"

"Holly Doyle doesn't look a day over fifteen."

"That's your opinion."

"Do you often pick up underage girls?" Thomas asked Hammond.

"Don't answer that," Elledge snapped.

"Did you buy Doyle drinks at McPherson's?"

"Don't answer that, either."

"So Mr. Hammond took Holly home and allowed her to live with him for six weeks, just because they hit it off outside McPherson's?" asked Thomas.

"That's not a crime."

Thomas shifted to face Hammond. "Did you have sexual relations with Holly Doyle?"

"Don't answer that," Elledge said. "There's no proof my client did anything but put a roof over Ms. Doyle's head."

"He also possessed an unlicensed firearm."

"A simple mistake. Mr. Hammond purchased the pistol five years ago, but the license expired last month. As New York State didn't notify my client of the impending expiration, he wasn't aware. Every state has different gun laws, and they are always changing. It's too much for a working man to keep up with."

"If I call the state, I assume their office will tell me they contacted Mr. Hammond about the expiration."

"Even if they did, my client never received the notice," Elledge said. "Letters disappear in the mail all the time, Sheriff. Unless the state required a signature upon receipt of the letter, you can't prove he received it."

"Mr. Hammond is responsible for ensuring his firearms are licensed, letter or not."

"It's not enough to hold my client." Elledge tapped an index finger against the table. "Two assault charges?"

"Mr. Hammond attacked two private investigators—Chelsey Byrd and Raven Hopkins—after Byrd knocked on his door and spotted Holly in the entryway. After strangling Byrd, Hammond aimed his unlicensed handgun at Hopkins."

"Lying bitches," Hammond growled.

Elledge held up a hand to silence his client. "Mr. Hammond tells a different story. Byrd lied, pretending to be a neighbor so she could peek inside the house. When Mr. Hammond asked her to leave, she threw him out of the way and tried to grab Holly. Mr. Hammond, believing Holly was in danger, subdued Byrd and told Holly to call your department, but Hopkins attacked him, knocking his gun loose. Byrd mistook my client for brandishing a gun. He only retrieved the weapon to keep it from the two hostiles attacking him."

Lambert continued to eye a furious Hammond, as if he expected the convict to leap up and overturn the table.

Thomas couldn't stop himself from laughing. "That's not what happened."

"Oh? Did you witness the conflict?" Elledge adjusted his reading glasses and scanned his notes. "Your report states you arrived on the scene five minutes after Hopkins and Byrd unlawfully constrained my client with a zip tie."

"Yes, but—"

"And isn't it also true that you're dating Chelsey Byrd? She lives in your home, and the sheriff's department uses Ms. Byrd's private investigation business, Wolf Lake Consulting, to solve crimes. In fact, you consider Raven Hopkins a close friend. Do you deny these claims?"

"That doesn't recuse Mr. Hammond."

"What it demonstrates, Sheriff, is you have relationships with the accusers. You have a biased opinion."

"The bruising on Ms. Byrd's neck proves Hammond strangled her."

Elledge waved an unconcerned hand across his face. "Those bruises could have happened any time during the scuffle, which, I'll point out again, the accusers instigated. Two private investigators attacked my client, Sheriff. Mr. Hammond was within his rights when he defended his property, and he had every reason to believe Ms. Doyle was in danger. Do you still intend to file the assault charges?"

"Yes, I do."

"It seems to be my client's word against those of your friends. Can you produce an unbiased witness? Certainly, someone must have viewed the scuffle if it was half as harrowing as Ms. Byrd and Ms. Hopkins claim."

"Not yet," Thomas said, shifting his jaw.

"I thought not. Before your department turned Ms. Doyle over to her parents, did she tell you what happened? Your report states Ms. Doyle watched the altercation from the entryway. When I ask her, she'll say Byrd and Hopkins attacked Mr. Hammond, and he acted in self-defense."

"Self-defense?" Lambert chuckled. "Mr. Hammond has multiple assaults on his record, including an attack on a police officer in Florida."

"That has no bearing on this case. I demand you release Mr. Hammond immediately."

"There's not a chance of that happening," said Thomas, sitting back and crossing his arms over his chest. "Mr. Hammond concealed an underage girl from her parents, threatened Chelsey Byrd and Raven Hopkins with an unlicensed handgun, and assaulted both, resulting in Byrd and Hopkins each seeking medical care."

"Your charges won't stick. Mr. Hammond will walk free by this time tomorrow."

Hammond swung around to face his attorney. "What the hell does that mean? I have to sleep in a cell?"

"It's only for one night," Elledge said, patting his client's arm.

"You promised you'd get me out of here."

"And I will, but these things take time. Patience is a virtue."

The discussion concluded. Elledge swept up his briefcase, as though he had a pressing engagement elsewhere. Lambert grabbed Hammond by the forearm and helped the convict to his feet. Hammond shrugged free of Lambert's grip, drawing a grumble from the deputy.

"Drop the charges," Elledge told Thomas from the doorway. "Don't force me to make an example of you and your department."

8

Lance and Karley Weir's house was a red-brick ranch with a rock wall curling along the driveway. The blacktop appeared recently sealed, the yard mowed in crisscrossed diagonals like a baseball field. In front of the house, a woman walked a child down the sidewalk. The child sat on a bike with no training wheels, the woman—probably the mother—holding the back of the seat to keep the bike from toppling.

At four o'clock, the neighborhood kids had returned from school, and adults rushed home from their commutes. Most of the houses were upper middle class. The Weir home was among the smallest on the block, but the landscaping and manicured lawn made it appear almost grand.

Thomas and Aguilar exited the cruiser and approached the home, the sheriff doublechecking the mailbox to ensure they had the correct address. He didn't see Lance Weir. A man and a woman, each in their sixties, sat on the porch and hooked elbows, the woman's head upon the man's shoulder as he ran a consoling hand through her hair. Their red, swollen eyes told Thomas they'd been crying.

"Is this Lance and Karley Weir's home?" Thomas asked.

The man stood and offered his hand. "We're Karley's parents. I'm Rocco Sinclair, and this is my wife, Clare."

Gray-haired, Rocco wore brown khakis and a short-sleeve collared shirt, while Clare appeared comfortable in black yoga pants, sandals, and a bulky gray sweatshirt.

"Sheriff Thomas Shepherd," Thomas said, shaking Rocco's hand, then Clare's. "And this is Deputy Veronica Aguilar."

After the brief introduction, Thomas asked where Lance was.

"Lance ran out for sandwiches," said Clare, tugging the fabric on her yoga pants. "We're not hungry, but I suppose we should eat something. Lance will arrive home in the next five minutes. You're welcome to wait inside with us."

Before Thomas answered, a white Audi veered into the driveway and jerked to a stop. Lance Weir stepped out of the vehicle, holding a paper bag with "Tim's Sandwich Shop" emblazoned across the front. Weir wore the same clothes he had at the station, but he'd tucked in his shirt and slicked his hair with gel.

"Got you an Italian deli sub on whole wheat, Mom," Weir said, leaning over to kiss Clare's cheek.

She didn't return his smile. Rocco buried his hands in his pockets, tapping a foot.

"Who is ready to eat?" asked Weir.

"Perhaps you should speak with the sheriff first," Rocco said. "Finding Karley is the priority."

"Of course. It's just that . . . Never mind. I only wanted you to be comfortable. Neither of you have eaten since breakfast. That's bad for your blood sugar."

"Mr. Weir," Thomas said, "why don't you go over last night's events with Deputy Aguilar while I speak with Karley's parents and check out the bedroom?"

"I answered all your questions at the station this morning."

"I'm aware, but I want to ensure we didn't miss anything."

Weir shrugged and handed the bag to Rocco. "Can you put this in the fridge, Dad? We'll eat after the sheriff finishes."

Rocco opened the door for Clare and directed the sheriff toward the kitchen. After standing in the bright sunshine, Thomas's eyes struggled to adjust to the dark interior.

"Please," Rocco said, pulling out a chair for Thomas after he seated his wife.

Weir's voice traveled through the screen door. Clare glanced down at her hands as Rocco rolled his eyes.

Not bothering to put the sandwiches in the refrigerator, Rocco slid the bag to the side. "Help yourself, Clare."

"How can I eat at a time like this?"

She teared up, and Rocco rubbed his wife's shoulder.

"Mr. Sinclair," said Thomas, "when did you last speak to your daughter?"

"Clare talked to Karley two nights ago. Isn't that right?"

Clare sniffled. "Karley is a good girl. She calls every other night to check up on us."

"Did she tell you about her plans in Syracuse?"

"She did, though I'm unfamiliar with the artists and wouldn't understand their music. Karley was so excited. She couldn't wait to go."

"If you ask me, she was just happy to spend time with Leigh and Hannah," added Rocco. "The concert was an excuse to get out of the house."

Thomas asked, "Does Lance object to his wife going out with friends?"

Rocco scowled. "He's a control freak."

"Don't say that," Clare said, patting her husband's hand.

Rocco forced his face to soften. "It's like he doesn't trust Karley. Our daughter would never cheat on Lance. I don't get what he's worried about."

"I take it you've met Leigh and Hannah," Thomas said, noting that the parents spoke of both as if they knew them.

"Nice women," Clare said. "We celebrated Karley's birthday at the Wolf Lake Steakhouse in May. Leigh and Hannah came. Lance had to work."

"The usual," Rocco muttered. "It was only his wife's birthday."

"I'm sure Lance did his best to make it. That Wallace Bryant only cares about money. He overworks his staff."

Thomas clicked his pen and wrote a note. "Have there been marriage issues between Karley and Lance?"

"They never see each other. Karley gets home from Treman Mills after five, and Lance works until six-thirty. Later, some nights. Anytime his boss offers a weekend shift, Lance takes it. I don't understand why. It's not as if they need the money."

"They paid off their mortgage in five years," said Rocco. "That's the benefit of having two steady incomes and no kids, though we'd love grandchildren."

Thomas set his forearms on the table. "Did Karley resent Lance for always working late and on weekends, and not letting her spend time with her friends?"

"If she resented Lance, she never said so," said Clare.

Rocco shook his head. "You know she resents him. Who wouldn't? He treats her more like a possession than a wife."

"Careful, Rocco. The door is open."

"I hope he hears me. Should have set him straight years ago."

"Was Karley angry enough to leave Lance?" asked Thomas.

"Without telling us? No, I don't believe she would skip town and worry her parents sick."

"I understand Karley works at the federal credit union. Has she been under added pressure lately?"

"They treat her well. Karley has had offers to work elsewhere, but she's been with the credit union for almost a decade and gets along with her coworkers."

Thomas passed them a business card. "If you think of anything else, please call. I realize you're not hungry, but try to eat."

"I'll regain my appetite when you bring our daughter home, Sheriff."

"If you don't mind, I need to search the master bedroom."

Clare rose, and Rocco held up a hand. "I'll show the sheriff where the bedroom is. Rest your feet and eat a bite of your sandwich."

Rocco led Thomas down a narrow, carpeted hallway, past the bathroom and what appeared to be a home office. The master bedroom stood at the end of the corridor, its door closed as if walling away secrets.

"Here you are, Sheriff." Rocco lowered his voice. "I didn't want to bring this up around my wife. She hasn't come to grips with Karley disappearing. Do you think someone took our daughter?"

Rocco's voice broke, and Thomas touched his arm.

"We're exploring all possibilities. Is there any reason to believe someone would hurt Karley?"

"No," Rocco said, scuffing the carpet with the toe of this shoe. "But does anyone need an excuse these days? Seems the world has turned vicious. People hurt each other over nothing. Please bring her home, Sheriff."

"I'll do everything I can to locate Karley. You should go back to your wife. She needs you."

Rocco pressed his lips together and nodded. The man's shoulders slumped in defeat, and Thomas wished he could offer comfort. Thomas watched Karley's father until he turned the corner and entered the kitchen. Finding Karley was the only solution to their pain.

The king-sized bed dominated the floor space. A nightstand held a half-empty glass of water on the right side of the bed, where the sheets were pushed partway down the mattress. Didn't Weir say he'd fallen asleep on the couch?

Thomas opened the closet door. Clothes hung from two bars, and someone had tucked two suitcases and a pair of travel bags into the corner. It was possible Karley owned another bag and had packed it before leaving her husband, but Thomas doubted it. As Rocco had said, Karley wouldn't skip town without notifying her parents.

The sheriff snapped photographs with his phone, then moved to the dresser. There wasn't a speck of dust anywhere. Sliding open the drawers, he discovered Karley's belongings on the left, the husband's on the right, all clothing items folded and without a single wrinkle. A full inch separated the clothing piles, as though neither could bear the idea of their belongings touching.

Thomas thought about how much he loved Chelsey and cherished sharing his home with her. He no longer saw his lakeside A-frame as his but *theirs*. The Weir relationship felt cold and uncaring. What would drive apart two people who'd once loved each other?

Raised voices outside warned Thomas that Weir had lost patience with Aguilar's questions. He needed to hurry. The top three drawers held clothing, and the bottom drawer contained an iPad, looseleaf paper, one stapler, a staple remover, plus two books about fertility and adoption.

As Thomas closed the drawer, Weir stomped down the hall.

"That's enough, Sheriff. As I stated, Karley didn't leave any clues behind. She's just gone."

"I'd like to continue looking around if you will allow me to do so," Thomas said.

"You've taken too much of my time. My in-laws are upset and

need normalcy, not the sheriff's department pawing through the house."

Without a warrant, Thomas couldn't search the house if Weir didn't want him to.

"Very well, but I hope you reconsider. If you want me to find Karley, you need to let me do my job."

"If I find anything of note, I'll call you."

Thomas turned to leave and stopped. "One question: You said you slept on the couch last night."

"Yes, and?"

"I noticed the covers weren't made on your side of the bed."

"Oh, right. After we spoke at the station, I took a nap."

If Chelsey vanished, Thomas wouldn't sleep until he found her.

"Is that all, Sheriff?"

"For now," Thomas said.

Thomas touched the brim of his hat when he passed Rocco and Clare in the kitchen. They'd unwrapped their sandwiches, but neither had eaten anything.

Aguilar awaited Thomas in the driveway. She painted on a smile and waved to Weir, who watched them from the porch, arms folded over his chest.

"Pleasant guy," Aguilar said, sliding into the passenger seat. "I've met my share of control freaks over the years, but that guy takes the cake."

Thomas started the cruiser. "He didn't want me poking around the house. Learn anything new?"

"Nothing. He repeated all the answers he gave you and LeVar this morning. What about you? Find anything inside?"

"Maybe. I found two books tucked inside the bottom drawer of the dresser, one on fertility and another on adoption."

"Sounds like they tried to have a baby and failed," Aguilar said.

"I got the distinct impression that their marriage isn't as close as Weir pretends. While you were outside, the parents mentioned Karley and Lance weren't getting along. The father had nothing positive to say about his son-in-law."

"Are their problems bad enough that Lance Weir might have harmed his wife?"

Thomas pressed his lips together.

"That's what we need to find out."

9

At six-thirty, the sun hung low over Wolf Lake, and there was enough of a chill in the air that Thomas donned a sweatshirt before leaving the house. Squeezed between his arm and hip, Thomas hefted a paper bag of snacks and soda. A couple fishing off a motorboat wore windbreakers, the woman cupping her elbows with her hands. She appeared to be convincing her husband to call it a day and return to their dock. Soon the recreation season would end, and the weather would prevent anyone from venturing out on the water. The lake rarely froze before late January, when the ice-fishing season commenced.

Thomas could see the familiar faces of his friends through the windows fronting the guest house, where LeVar Hopkins lived beside the shore. The savory scent of pizza greeted him in the entryway, as did Jack and Tigger, who'd arrived home with Chelsey after Wolf Lake Consulting closed for the day.

"Thomas!" someone called. Maybe Raven. It was difficult to hear over the clamor of voices.

"I'll take that," LeVar said, holding out his arms for the bag of snacks. "I picked up two pizzas on the way home."

"Perfect. We could all use a little comfort food tonight."

"Everyone is in the front room. Make yourself at home. What am I saying? This is your property."

"It's your house for as long as you want it," Thomas said. "You know that."

LeVar handed Thomas a stack of plates and cups. "If you don't mind, take these with you and pass them around."

The front room of the guest house offered a pristine view of Wolf Lake and the coming sunset. Sunlight bronzed the crashing waves, and the few remaining boaters still on the water motored toward safe harbor. When the wind gusted, the spray off the lake dotted the window, obscuring the sunset.

Most people couldn't wait to get away from their jobs after leaving for the day, but the crew crowding the room and taking up all available seating never got enough of investigating. Together with Raven and Darren, Scout and LeVar had formed an amateur investigators group, which worked independently of Wolf Lake Consulting and the sheriff's department. This evening, everyone focused on Karley Weir and teenage runaway Holly Doyle.

Even Scout's mother, Naomi, had joined the party.

"Yes, I acknowledge Holly is better off at home," said Scout, accepting a slice of cheese pizza as LeVar held out an open box. "But she obviously needs help. If Holly's parents suffocate her, she'll run away again."

"We can't prove Holly's home life is half as bad as she claims," argued Chelsey. "Regardless, the county is handling the case. Just be thankful she isn't living with a psycho who is into younger girls."

Thomas glanced around the room, noticing one missing member. "Where's Ms. Hopkins?"

"She's cleaning the house. Apparently, she's inviting Buck

Benson to dinner tomorrow," Raven said, sighing. "I don't understand what she sees in that man."

"As long as she's happy," Darren said, putting an arm around Raven's shoulder.

She didn't appear convinced. Thomas kept a close eye on Raven. Post-traumatic stress disorder was a crippling affliction, and only a year had passed since two kidnappers locked Raven in an old farmhouse outside Wolf Lake. One of those kidnappers had been Mark Benson, and now her mother was cozying up to Benson's second cousin. Were they dating? Raven had a right to worry. This was her mother. Serena Hopkins valued her independence since completing rehab and purchasing Raven's old house on the west side of the lake. It comforted Thomas that Serena lived a quick drive down the road, in case Buck Benson turned out to be trouble. After the abduction, Raven had suffered from anxiety whenever she was alone. Thomas hoped their latest kidnapping case wouldn't reincarnate old ghosts for Raven.

As the chatter continued, LeVar handed out pizza slices and passed the soda bottles around. He'd set up a card table in the center of the room with four chairs squeezed around the perimeter. Raven sat with Darren and Naomi on the couch, while Thomas pulled a folding chair into the room and claimed the last three feet of floor space.

"What's our first item of business?" Raven asked.

"The Karley Weir disappearance," said LeVar. "Since we don't have another gripping mystery to solve, we should concentrate on the same case we've been researching at the office." Nobody objected. "Raven, you and Darren had something to share."

After the conversation ceased, Darren spoke. "We searched all missing persons reports for the last thirty days, restricting ourselves to a hundred-mile radius."

"Of the four missing people on the list," said Raven, "two were men. If we assume a man abducted Karley Weir, statistics suggest our kidnapper is only hunting women, not men."

"Who are the two women?" asked Thomas.

"Bianca Holland, age thirty-two, went missing from Coral Lake twenty-nine days ago. Alena Robinson, disappeared sixteen days ago from the Syracuse suburbs."

"Both women are similar in age to Karley Weir, but it's a little premature to jump to conclusions," said Darren. "I suggest we focus on Karley Weir and link her to the two missing women. The best place to start is on the internet. She opened multiple social media accounts."

LeVar pointed at Scout, who sat beside the computer. "Scout, give everyone an update on Karley Weir's social media profiles."

Scout frowned. "Unfortunately, I've made little progress. Karley protects her accounts and keeps her posts private. Short of hacking her profile—which would be highly illegal—I can't follow her activity unless I find who among her friends opened their accounts to public viewing. Karley has almost five hundred people in her connections, so it will take time."

Thomas raised a hand. "I'll ask each company to give the sheriff's department access to her profiles. They're not obligated to help, but sometimes they cooperate in matters of life and death."

"I have a list of forty-seven fast-food restaurants, gas stations, convenience markets, and grocery stores Karley might have visited on her way to Syracuse," said Darren. Chelsey blew out a breath. "It could be worse. If I expand the list to include stores two miles from each exit, things get crazy. Put it this way: most people visit the quickest, most convenient stops on their way to Syracuse. Since Karley needed to meet her friends at six-thirty, she didn't have time to waste."

"Makes sense," Chelsey said. "Tomorrow morning we'll run

down that list and call every place where she could have stopped. Many will have security cameras, but let's not request footage until we narrow the list down to a handful of likely candidates."

"Thomas, you and LeVar interviewed the husband and searched his house. Is Lance Weir a suspect?"

"He's abrasive and aloof," said Thomas, "and I gather Karley's parents don't like or trust him. Despite what Weir told us during the interview, their marriage isn't strong. That's according to the parents. For a supposedly worried husband, he makes curious decisions. After Weir spoke to us, he claims he drove home and took a nap."

"He should be searching for his wife, not resting," said Chelsey, drawing nods from the others. "That's a red flag."

"For now, we'll give him the benefit of the doubt. Grief affects everybody in different ways. Perhaps the gravity of the situation hit Weir all at once and overwhelmed him. But I agree. Napping after your wife goes missing is unusual to say the least."

"You said Lance Weir works for Bryant Media Group?"

Naomi, who had busied herself with reading her phone, sat forward. "Bryant Media Group? We work with them. Shepherd Systems, I mean."

Thomas had inherited Shepherd Systems, a company that provided collaboration and project-management software to small businesses, from his late father, Mason Shepherd. Thomas's mother, Lindsey, still held an upper management position there. Though Thomas's parents had begged him to take over the company, he considered himself ill-equipped for the job. Instead, Naomi ran day-to-day operations, and Serena Hopkins led the sales department.

"Have you ever met Lance Weir?" asked Thomas.

"Now that you mention Bryant Media Group, Weir's name sounds familiar. Serena will know who he is."

"I'll call her," Raven said, removing her phone from her pocket. "She can't be too busy cleaning. There's never an item out of place when I visit."

As the others discussed the case, Thomas focused on Raven. After waiting for Serena to answer, Raven ended the call and dialed again. A worried frown formed on her face.

"Is everything all right?" Thomas asked.

Raven set the phone on her lap and stared out the window. Shadows spread off the lake shore and bled across the water.

"I don't know. My mother isn't answering, and that's not like her."

"Do you want me to drive over and check on her?"

"No, no. I should go, Thomas. Stay here in case she drops by."

"I'll go with you," Darren said, rubbing Raven's back. "I'm sure she's okay."

The possibilities flickered across Raven's haunted face—a prowler had broken into the house, Buck Benson had attacked her, Serena had relapsed.

"Call me as soon as you find your mother," Thomas said.

Darren and Raven hurried out the door.

10

Raven couldn't hear the motor over her pounding heart. She was thankful Darren had volunteered to drive his midnight-blue Silverado 4x4. As the truck rumbled down the lake road, Raven redialed her mother over and over, each call going to voicemail.

The sun disappeared when Darren turned into the driveway and parked behind Serena's car. Before he shut off the engine, Raven hopped down from the cab and hurried to the door. Three loud knocks. Nobody answered.

"Is anyone inside?" Darren asked when he caught up with Raven. "Maybe she turned up the television."

"I don't hear a damn thing." She pounded on the door again. "Ma? You in there?"

Darren stuffed his hands inside his pockets and wandered to each side of the house, peering around the corners. Raven pictured Benson's boathouse as she remembered it—ramshackle and unkempt, the windows perpetually dark, his rusty pickup truck dominating the driveway with a skull and crossbones sticker on the back and a confederate flag flying off the cab. And the dog. Raven almost never saw the dog, but its booming, wall-rattling barks warned her to keep her distance.

Raven raised herself up on tiptoe and stared at Buck Benson's home, which stood a hundred feet down the incline. Benson's truck was in the driveway, but no dog barked, and there wasn't any light shining through the boathouse windows.

"I'm worried," she said.

"There must be a logical explanation. Doesn't your mother take walks along the lake?"

"Not after dark." Raven dug a key out of her pocket and inserted it into the lock. "I still have my house key."

"Raven, what if she's inside with . . . someone. This could get embarrassing."

"I don't have time to worry about that. Something is wrong, Darren."

Unwilling to wait a second longer, Raven unlocked the door and rushed into the kitchen. "Ma? Where are you?"

While Darren checked the living room, Raven ran down the hallway, pushing the doors open as she called out. Last year, Mark Benson had broken into the house while Serena hid inside the closet. Raven shuddered to think what would have happened had Mark Benson caught her. It seemed all too convenient that Mark's second cousin, who lived on the neighboring property, was showing an unhealthy interest in Raven's mother. Had Buck Benson aided Mark while the fugitive busted the lock and stalked Serena?

Raven shoved the bedroom door open and flicked on the nightstand lamp. Hands on hips, she gazed around the room. Blue gloaming oozed between the blinds. She eyed the closet and ran to the door, peeking her head inside. Empty.

"Ma, it's Raven. Answer me."

A shadow swung into the bedroom. Raven held a hand over her heart until she recognized Darren.

"Anything?"

"No," she said, lowering her hand.

Her mother wasn't out for a walk, and her car was in the driveway. That left one place to check. Buck Benson's house. Raven's pulse thrummed as she led Darren back to the kitchen. Through the window, she spied Benson's boathouse, the lake waters like black ink as they lapped the shore.

"What do you propose we do?"

Before Raven answered, footsteps scuffed along the driveway. Someone was coming.

Then Raven discerned a woman's content humming as someone wandered lazily toward the steps. Serena Hopkins slipped her key into the lock and opened the door. She jumped and yelled out, not expecting two people inside her kitchen.

"Raven, Darren. What are you doing here?"

Raven stomped across the floor and faced her mother. "Where were you? I tried calling you for the last hour."

"Oh, I left my phone on the counter," Serena said, picking it up and scrolling through the missed calls. "Child, what's so important that you called me seven times? Not every fool walks around with her phone. It's nice to have quiet time."

"You still haven't told me where you were."

Serena arched a brow. "Since when do I tell you my whereabouts 24/7? Have you forgotten I'm the mother and you're the daughter?"

"You were with that man, weren't you? That Buck Benson."

"What if I was? That's no concern of yours."

"He's a racist. And for goodness' sake, his cousin tried to kidnap you."

"Second cousin, dear."

Raven threw her head back. "As if that makes a difference."

"Buck is a righteous man, Raven. Perhaps if you'd give him half a chance—"

"No, no, no." Raven waved her hands. "Every day I lived here, I had to look at that flag."

"We had a long talk about the flag, Raven. He doesn't fly it anymore."

"Don't make excuses for him. You know what the Confederate flag means."

Serena shuffled past Raven and touched Darren's arm, as if saying she didn't blame him for her daughter's breathless outbursts.

"Most of Buck's family lives south of the Mason-Dixon line. To him, the flag is a sign of southern pride, nothing more. I explained what that flag represents to minorities, and he was honestly taken aback. The next day he removed the flag from his truck, and I haven't seen it since."

"He's quite the humanitarian."

Ignoring Raven's sarcasm, Serena opened the refrigerator and removed an apple pie. "How about dessert and a tall glass of milk?"

"I'm not hungry," Raven said, glowering.

"What about you, Darren?"

"Uh, I could eat," Darren said, wearing a sheepish grin as Raven gaped at him.

"Then sit yourself down. Raven, you can pretend you're not hungry and pout."

Raven stomped a foot. "I'm not pouting. Don't blame me for worrying about my mother."

Serena carved a slice of pie and plated it in front of Darren. Then she joined him at the kitchen table. To Raven's consternation, Darren shared a look with her mother and fought to keep from laughing.

"You never explained why calling me was so important," Serena said, pointing at Raven with her fork.

In truth, Raven wanted to join them for dessert, but foolish pride stood in the way and denied her stomach the best apple pie in the Finger Lakes.

"We're working on a missing person's case. Do you know a man from Bryant Media Group named Lance Weir?"

Serena set the fork down, finished chewing, and swallowed. "What's that fool gone and done now?"

"His wife vanished last evening. Karley Weir was on her way to Syracuse to join her friends at a concert and never arrived."

"And you believe the husband had something to do with her disappearance?"

"We're not sure. Naomi said you've dealt with Lance Weir through work. Is that true?"

"He's a horse's ass." Serena touched Darren's hand. "Pardon my French, Darren."

"Not at all," he said, scooping another morsel. "This is amazing pie, Ms. Hopkins."

"When are you gonna start calling me Serena . . . or Ma? Ms. Hopkins is far too formal. No need to be bashful."

"Ma: Lance Weir," Raven said, getting her mother back on point. "I take it you don't think highly of him."

"Full of himself, that one. I caught him in the waiting area, screaming at Janie just because he had to wait five minutes to see me. Thinks he's the center of the universe, and everyone should set their watches to his time."

"Any reason to believe he'd hurt his wife?"

"I couldn't tell you about that. Never met his wife, though I pity the woman. He has a temper. That much seemed clear, given the way he treated Janie."

"Weir never reported his wife missing until the next morning. Says he slept all night on the couch without realizing she wasn't home."

Serena snapped her fingers and pointed at Raven. "Now that

sounds like Lance Weir. So conceited. What would any woman see in that man?"

"All right, that helps. Weir didn't impress Thomas or LeVar, either."

"Speaking of your brother, how does he enjoy being a deputy?"

"He's fitting right in," Raven said.

"I had no doubts." Serena huffed. "Stop being dramatic and have a seat. I see your mouth watering, girl."

Raven didn't argue. Her mother's dessert was worth an extra hour at the gym tomorrow.

But she still didn't trust Buck Benson.

11

In the quiet solitude of the living room, he sat in absolute darkness. Night blanketed the windows, and an owl hooted outside. This was the time he felt most alive—when the last usable light seeped out of the sky, and the stars and moon shone like stage lights upon the earth, tainting the land blue and silver. He longed to join the night and run amid the shadows, like a beast on the prowl. This was his domain.

The cellar lay below the living room and kitchen. He'd locked his beauty away for safekeeping. Remembering their time together made him curl his hands into fists.

Karley had resisted when they made love. While he touched and kissed her, she'd pushed at him and squirmed, crying and begging him to stop.

In time, she'll come to love me.

He rose from the chair and strode to the window. The neighboring farm loomed a hundred yards down the road. Mr. Shorts had spent all afternoon on that damn tractor, the engine loud enough to rattle the windows. Not that he minded the noise, but it gave Karley hope. As long as she knew someone was nearby, she wouldn't surrender and stop fighting.

From the closet, he removed the shredder. He fed Karley's driver's license into the machine and grinned as the teeth chewed her identity into tiny pieces. Too bad the shredder didn't work on her phone and keys.

Catching Karley had been easy. Once he'd learned about the concert tickets, he'd followed her, anticipating she'd stop for gas or food along the way. She'd made the job simple by parking at the back of the grocery store lot, where the security cameras, if any existed outside, wouldn't record him. After abducting Karley and locking her in the basement, he'd walked two miles from his house to a bar and grill in the middle of the country. From there, he'd called for a taxi, pretending to be too drunk to drive, and ordered the cab driver to take him up the interstate to a suburban neighborhood a mile from the grocery store. Then he walked back to Karley's car and drove it home, concealing the vehicle in the woods behind his house and covering it with brush. He'd need to rid himself of the vehicle eventually, but this would do for now.

The shredder finished devouring the license and shut off with cold finality. He emptied the contents into the garbage, tied the bag, and tossed it beside the road for tomorrow morning's trash pickup.

In the kitchen, he stood beside the basement door. When she had first awakened, he'd caught Karley trying to escape. She'd feigned sleep after he hurried down the stairs, but he'd spotted her legs dangling off the wall, hands gripped around the bars, as though she thought herself strong enough to pry them away from the windows.

Why did they always resist?

Karley fought him with every breath, as had Alena. In his mind, he pictured his hands curling around Alena's throat, the fish-eyed panic staring back at him, her beating limbs coming to rest before she fell limp in his arms. Afterward, regret had struck him like a semi barreling over his body. All hope had vanished after Alena died. But what option did he have? Alena refused to return his love.

Yet he needed to tame his rage. By now, Alena's body might have floated to the surface of the pond. No one had witnessed him carrying her through the woods with his vehicle hidden from traffic. But if the authorities found Alena, they'd know a murderer was loose in Nightshade County. Sometimes anger engulfed his body and forced him to hurt the ones he loved. It couldn't happen again.

He pictured making love to Karley, felt the warm touch of her bare flesh against his. She'd tried to scratch out his eyes. With no other choice, he'd bound her wrists to keep her from harming him. Karley needed to see how much he loved and cared for her. She must understand now, after the beautiful moment they'd spent together.

She hates me.

No!

The man whipped around and dropped to his knees, the linoleum cold beneath him. Clutching his hair, he ripped until full clumps popped out of his scalp. Was this his destiny? To be alone forever, unloved? He tore his hair again. Tears trickled from his eyes, and he wasn't surprised when blood colored the strands gripped between his fingers.

His body pulsed with rage. He wanted to throw the door open and strangle Karley. Teach her a lesson she'd never forget.

A deep breath. He regained control. No need to be hasty. Karley might come around if he remained patient.

An idea curled his lips into a grin. Removing a black windbreaker from the entryway closet, he stepped into the night. The basement looked out on the backyard, and as he rounded the house, he imagined the terror Karley would experience if she saw him staring at her in the night. Unlike Alena, Karley was fit and strong, a challenge to be conquered. Controlling Alena had been easy, but Karley would fight him until he taught her the meaning of surrender. He would break her down until she lost hope. She'd never attempt to leave him.

He'd secured the house well. Besides the bars covering the basement window, cameras aimed down from the roof. If Karley somehow pried the bars free—an impossibility—and broke the window, he'd see her on the cameras and catch her before she got far. He loved technology. Software allowed him to monitor Karley on his phone and computer. At work, he'd hidden from prying eyes and stared at Alena. No one suspected what he'd done.

If Karley broke through the barred windows and escaped his eye on camera, the land would work against her. One hundred yards of soft, plowed earth separated his house from the farmer's. Escaping across that field in the dark would be akin to slogging through quicksand.

Behind the house, he knelt beside the window above the cellar bathroom. A sliver of starlight divided the floor. Not finding Karley, he crept to the window overlooking the futon. This room was darker. He squinted his eyes in search of his love.

The man flinched when he spotted a huge bulk staring back at him from the shadows. With a relieved laugh, he identified the shape of the water tank. His eyes flicked to the futon and the body curled on top of the covers. Karley shuddered and drew her knees toward her chest, as though she sensed him spying. A rap of his knuckles against the wall brought her up, back erect with terror. He shifted his body away from the window, merging with the dark so she wouldn't see him.

Why had he wasted time with Alena? As long as he'd known Karley, she'd always been the perfect woman. Despite his best efforts, he'd never convinced her to love him the way he did her. That would change.

But was it too soon to remove the stocking from his face and reveal his identity? The shock might be too much for Karley to handle.

When she rolled onto her side and pulled the covers over her head, he slid closer to the window and pressed his face against the glass.

She was his forever. And this time, his love had no hope of abandoning him.

12

On Thursday morning, Thomas carried two cups of green tea from The Broken Yolk to the cruiser. Aguilar opened the passenger side window and accepted her drink.

"Thanks," Aguilar said. "I could use a little healthy energy this morning."

Thomas circled the vehicle and shifted into drive. "Didn't sleep well last night?"

She sipped her tea without answering, and Thomas warred with himself for asking. At the end of summer, Aguilar's best friend from college, Simone Axtell, had drugged and kidnapped the deputy after suffering a mental breakdown and believing they'd been more than friends during college.

"Sorry," he said, turning down a side street that would take them to the highway.

"For what?"

"After all you went through with Simone, it's understandable if you're having trouble sleeping. Do you want to talk about it?"

"What's done is done. Simone is in an institution again. They never should have released her in the first place. She's getting the help she needs. That's all that matters."

A woman in a muscle car sped past Thomas and cut in front of the cruiser, beating him to the on ramp.

"That was a close call."

"You want to ticket her?"

"I'll let it go this time. Maybe she's having a bad day." Thomas drummed his fingers against the steering wheel, searching for the right words. What did you say to someone who'd just been abducted by a friend? "Would you ever consider visiting Simone?"

Aguilar did a double-take. "You mean at the mental facility?"

"I guess so."

She scrunched her shoulders, as though someone had scraped fingernails down a blackboard. "I care about Simone, but that's not a bridge I'm willing to cross. She violated my trust, Thomas. Even though her head wasn't in the right place and she lost control of her actions, Simone burned a bridge. I can't invite that toxicity into my life. Perhaps one day, when she's better, we'll work through our differences. For now, visiting Simone feels like an unhealthy decision."

"You're handling this well, Aguilar, and I think that's the right choice."

She set the tea in the cup holder and sighed.

"Thank you. Sometimes I worry that I'm turning my back on her, but I have to care for myself."

"Simone isn't your responsibility. She has family and a team of doctors looking after her."

Aguilar lifted her chin. "I'm glad you said that. A weight just tumbled off my shoulders."

"Anytime you want to talk, Chelsey and I are here for you."

The deputy cleared the frog from her throat and busied herself with the case folder on her lap.

"So Karley Weir's friend, Leigh Park, age thirty, moved to Wolf Lake a few years ago. She's a sales manager at the Toyota dealership off exit two. I called her, but she's in meetings for the next two hours."

"Sounds like we should pay the other friend a visit."

"Hannah Mickley," Aguilar said, sifting through the notes. "Age twenty-nine. Grew up in Wolf Lake and graduated from Wolf Lake High School with Karley Weir. After college, she returned home and accepted an elementary school teaching position on North Street. She goes on her break in fifteen minutes and has two free periods in a row."

"Perfect. We'll stop at the school, then swing by the Toyota dealership."

"I ran background checks on Karley's friends. No red flags, nothing interesting. Park is single. Mickley married two years ago."

Children on their way to a field trip piled into a bus outside the nougat-brick elementary school on North Street. Thomas pressed the buzzer beside the entryway and announced his presence. The main office unlocked the door. Principal Seibold, a stout woman in her fifties with shoulder-length silver hair, greeted Thomas and Aguilar and escorted them down a busy corridor choked with kids hurrying between classes.

"Mrs. Mickley doesn't have an office this year, so I'm letting her use mine for the interview." Seibold gave them a wary look. "She's not in any trouble, is she?"

"Not at all. We're searching for a woman who disappeared Tuesday night. Hannah knows her."

Seibold placed a hand over her heart. "I knew she'd done nothing wrong. Mrs. Mickley is such a wonderful teacher. I just hope you find her friend." After cutting through the main office, Seibold stood aside and motioned them inside. "Here you are."

"Thank you, Principal Seibold. This won't take long."

Seated at Seibold's desk and fidgeting uncomfortably, Hannah Mickley wore her straight chestnut hair down to the middle of her back. Bifocals framed sea-green eyes. She rose when Thomas and Aguilar entered and straightened her skirt. Seibold edged the door closed behind them.

"Mrs. Mickley, I'm Sheriff Shepherd. This is my partner, Deputy Aguilar."

"Hannah, please," she said, shaking their hands.

Hannah waited for Thomas and Aguilar to sit before she lowered herself onto her chair. She moved the stapler beside the fountain pen, thought better of it, and slid it to the side. The teacher couldn't keep her hands still.

"Take a breath, Hannah," Aguilar said. "We're only here to ask a few questions."

"I can't help it. Ever since Karley disappeared, I've been a nervous wreck. I'm not eating or sleeping. About the only time I feel like myself is during the middle of class, when I'm too focused on teaching to think about anything else."

"You teach elementary school science?" Aguilar asked.

Hannah smiled. "Fourth through sixth grade. I love it. During college, I wanted to be a physicist, but I found out I couldn't handle all the calculus. One day my advisor suggested I sit in on an education class, and I fell in love with teaching." She wiped her hands on her shirt. "Anyhow, none of this is helping you find Karley. What can I do?"

"Let's start with your plans on Tuesday evening. Take us through the timeline."

"Okay. I picked up Leigh at five, and we grabbed dinner in Syracuse at the mall. Then we drove to the parking area off I-481. Karley was supposed to meet us there at six-thirty. We waited until seven, assuming she'd run into traffic because it's not like Karley to show up late. We called and got her voicemail. After an hour, we began to worry. That's when we called Lance, but he didn't answer, either."

"Did you and Leigh attend the concert?"

"Not really. I sent Karley a text and told her to meet us inside the show. But before the warm-up act started, I sensed something was wrong. Neither of us wanted to stay. We left and kept calling Karley and Lance."

Aguilar asked, "Is this something you normally do? Meet in Syracuse, that is?"

"Sometimes Leigh and I drive up, but not Karley. Lance doesn't like her leaving the house. I'm still shocked he let her buy a concert ticket."

"Would Karley stop any place in particular on her way to the show? A favorite fast-food restaurant or convenience store?"

"Not that I know of."

"We checked Karley's credit card activity," Thomas said. "She didn't purchase gas with her card, but it's possible she paid cash."

Hannah shook her head. "No way. Karley only chooses pay-at-the-pump gas stations. Remember two years ago when those guys held up the gas station outside of Barton Falls and shot the cashier? That made Karley paranoid. She says gas stations are prime targets for thieves. Oh, and you can rule out fast-food restaurants and convenience stores. I wouldn't call Karley a health nut, but she eats healthy and steers clear of chemicals. She's in fantastic shape. A lot better than me, I admit."

"Does Karley own a gym membership?"

"She rides one of those exercise bikes with the online trainers. Peloton, I think. No chance Lance would let Karley buy a gym membership and exercise beside sweaty guys. The crazy part is, Karley put on several pounds last year, probably because she was sick of her husband ruining her life. Lance hassled

Karley over her weight. Said she was looking fat. I suppose that's why he bought her the bike."

"Would you describe Lance Weir as controlling?"

"Very," said Karley. "They work a lot of hours and don't spend time together, but he's in charge and lets her know."

"How so?"

"As an example, on the rare occasion Lance allows Karley to meet us for dinner or drinks, he forces her to tell him how long she'll be gone. If we change locations, he demands to know, and he'll text Karley while she's out, checking where she is and who she's talking to. It's ridiculous. And he's the last guy who should worry about his wife cheating."

"Why do you say that?"

Hannah looked down. "Over the summer, Karley invited me to the house for dinner. Lance was scheduled to work, but he drove home and acted like I was his best friend or something. Claimed Wallace Bryant sent everyone home for the evening. Doubtful. This is humiliating, but every time Hannah turned around, I caught Lance staring at me, like if his wife wasn't there, he'd have invited me into the bedroom. He's such a snake."

"I understand Lance and Karley had trouble having a baby," said Thomas.

Hannah's mouth fell open. "How did you hear about that? Yes, they tried for two or three years."

"The problem was infertility?"

"Right. Lance, not Karley. I'll go to hell for saying this, but it's a blessing. Lance Weir should never father a child."

"Would Lance ever hurt his wife?" asked Aguilar.

The teacher wrung her hands. "I can't picture it. As much as I detest Lance, he doesn't strike me as violent."

"Given the way Lance treated her, would Karley leave him?"

"She might, but not without telling her parents. I can

imagine how worried they are. Karley wouldn't put her mother and father through that."

"Would she tell you if she was considering leaving Lance?" Thomas asked.

"I believe she would. Karley expressed her frustrations to me on many occasions, but if she intended to walk out on her marriage, she never said so." Hannah pushed her hair off her shoulders. "You'll find Karley, won't you?"

Thomas hoped they would.

But the chance of finding Karley alive diminished every hour.

13

At the Toyota dealership, Leigh Park recounted Tuesday evening's events, her story a perfect match for Hannah Mickley's. Though Leigh had never caught Lance Weir undressing her with his eyes, she verified the man ruled over Karley's social life and suffocated his wife with ridiculous rules and curfews. That is, when he let her out of the house.

Having learned nothing new, Thomas turned the cruiser toward Bryant Media Group, Weir's employer.

"Leigh and Hannah paint Lance Weir as the ultimate nightmare of a husband," said Aguilar. "I can't imagine what he's like to work with."

"Neither can I, but let's not allow his bullying attitude to color our opinions. He's a jerk, but that doesn't mean he harmed Karley."

Bryant Media Group took up a two-story charcoal-brick building with plenty of glass frontage. The modern architectural design made it appear as if the building rocked forward as Thomas approached from the corner. Bryant Media Group stood a mile east of exit four. Thomas wondered why he'd never encountered the stunning building before today.

A security guard at the door escorted them into a large eatery and cafe, where workers congregated during their breaks. The scent of coffee beans encompassed the interior. A mammoth television took up half of one wall and displayed financial news, stock prices scrolling along the bottom of the screen. The audio echoed off the tall ceilings.

At the far end of the eatery, a welcome desk guarded the elevator doors and staircase. Another security guard sat beside a diminutive, thirty-something woman with short black hair and glasses. Upon spotting Thomas and Aguilar, she rose from her chair and rounded the desk, her high heels clicking off the polished floor.

"You must be Sheriff Shepherd," the woman said. "I've read about you. I'm Rosa Fernandez, Mr. Bryant's administrative assistant. He's concluding a meeting and will speak to you soon." Fernandez touched his arm. "It's wonderful that you've accomplished so much. You give hope to disabled people everywhere."

The sheriff's cheeks flushed. Fernandez was just being friendly, but it embarrassed Thomas when people fawned over him. He just wanted to do his job and protect his county.

Fernandez punched a code into the keypad beside the elevator. Thomas wondered why a media and advertising group in the Finger Lakes needed security. After a lengthy delay, the doors opened.

"Right this way," Fernandez said, ushering them in and holding the doors open.

Inside the elevator, Fernandez flashed an ID card at an electronic reader. Yet another security measure. The elevator started moving. It seemed like a waste of time and effort. Had Thomas and Aguilar taken the stairs, they would have reached their destination by now.

"How many people work for Bryant Media Group?" asked Aguilar.

"Fifteen. Twenty-two if you count security and support. I can't tell you how lucky we are to work for someone like Wallace Bryant. Nightshade County is fortunate to benefit from his talent and vision. He could operate out of Los Angeles or New York City, but he calls Wolf Lake home. Did you know he graduated from Syracuse University's Newhouse School of Communications?" Aguilar gave Fernandez a blank look, and the administrative assistant concentrated on the floor number. "Well, here we are."

They passed an open floor space with desks every ten paces. The workers concentrated on computer screens without paying attention to the sheriff and his deputy. A door at the end of the second story opened to a waiting area with a couch, kitchenette, and another television, this one streaming a 24-hour news channel.

"Help yourself to coffee and croissants. Mr. Bryant will be in shortly."

Fernandez exited, and Thomas shared a look with Aguilar.

"This seems rather extravagant," Aguilar said, twisting her mouth. "Bet you they're out of business five years from now."

Thomas slumped against the soft cushions. The couch wanted to swallow him, before a knock on the door brought them to their feet. Thomas expected Wallace Bryant would be a distinguished man with hints of gray at his temples, but the man in the doorway had the smooth, boyish complexion of someone shy of his thirtieth birthday. He wore form-fitting blue jeans, loafers, and a black zipping sweater over a white button down, the collar open.

"Sheriff Shepherd? I'm Wallace Bryant. My apologies for keeping you waiting. Our meeting ran late."

"No worries," Thomas said. "This is Deputy Aguilar."

Bryant took her hand, and to Thomas's shock, the deputy blushed. Even Thomas had to admit Bryant looked more like a fashion model than an advertising and media mogul. Bryant had slicked his dark hair and parted it on the side, not a strand out of place.

"We'll want privacy. Follow me to my office."

Two glass walls inside Bryant's office offered sweeping views of the countryside and hills surrounding the valley. Squinting, Thomas discerned the ridge which housed Wolf Lake State Park several miles in the distance. Bryant motioned at two chairs beside his desk, and Thomas sat beside Aguilar.

"What do you do here, Mr. Bryant?" Aguilar asked, opening a notepad and clicking a pen.

"Call me Wallace. Everyone here does. We do a lot of everything. Bryant Media Group's bread and butter is public relations for businesses, including Fortune 500 companies interested in growing their market share. But we're far more diversified than simple PR. Our advertising division runs campaigns for companies who aren't comfortable doing it themselves, and we have a technology division that will build your website and maintain it, install e-commerce software, and design your custom storefront."

"Impressive. How long has Lance Weir worked for your company?"

"Four or five years. I'd have to check my records to give you an exact date." Bryant frowned and set his elbows on the desk. "We're doing everything we can to support Lance in his time of need. Paid leave, counseling. Bryant Media Group will provide Lance with anything he needs, no charge."

"That's generous of you."

"Family means everything," Bryant said, looking down at his hands. "I lost my brother to a stroke six months ago. He was only thirty-two."

"Sorry for your loss."

"Thank you. Losing Gerald forced me to focus on what's important. All this only means so much," Bryant said, sweeping an arm across the room. "Family is the priority here and will be as long as I'm alive. We all hope Lance's wife shows up soon."

"So you've met Karley Weir?" asked Thomas.

"Karley stops by the office to eat dinner with Lance. A striking woman. You've seen pictures, of course. But her beauty isn't skin-deep. She always has a kind word for anyone she encounters."

Thomas shifted his back. Rosa Fernandez had told them Bryant Media Group employed twenty-two people, and it sounded as though Karley Weir had spoken to many of them. That was a lot of potential suspects.

"Did Karley ever have a problem with someone here?"

"A problem? You mean like an argument?"

"Anything. Perhaps someone paid her too much attention, and she took exception. You mentioned her beauty."

"Sheriff, anyone who mistreated a worker's spouse would land in counseling and receive a written warning. If it happened again, I'd find someone to replace them. But I promise you that isn't a problem here."

"Any issues between Lance and Karley that you're aware of?"

Bryant stared out the window and ran a hand along his hair, careful not to mess it up. "Once, I heard raised voices from Lance's office. Karley wasn't here, but I heard her name and assumed Lance was yelling at her over the phone. But all couples argue. It's part of marriage."

"When did this occur?" asked Aguilar.

"Three or four weeks ago."

"Has Lance been under added stress lately?"

"Not that I've noticed," Bryant said. "Account reports were due last week, but those come up every month. Business is booming, and Lance is among our top managers. He lives for his work. I doubt we'd survive a week if we lost him."

"Did Lance work Tuesday evening?" asked Thomas.

Thomas already knew the answer to the question, but he wanted to test Bryant and see if Weir's boss was covering for him. Bryant raised his eyes to the ceiling in consideration.

"No, Lance was off Tuesday evening."

"Is he normally off on Tuesdays?"

"Our hours constantly change, depending on workload. But Lance has had problems with headaches since summer. I granted him sick leave."

"Are you in a relationship?"

Bryant blinked. "I was engaged until eight months ago. Didn't work out. We went our separate ways. What does that have to do with anything?"

"Where were you Tuesday afternoon and evening between the hours of five and eight?"

The perpetually easy demeanor melted off Bryant. His shoulders stiffened.

"Why?"

"Please answer the question."

"Here," Bryant said, rocking back in his chair and drumming a pen against his palm. "I filled in for Gene Digby, my top account manager. Gene got called out of town on a family emergency. I picked up his work. As I stated, family is of the utmost importance here. I always support a friend in need. You're asking because you think I had something to do with Karley disappearing."

"We need to rule out all possibilities. I'm sure you understand."

"I do, and I appreciate your thoroughness."

"Can anyone corroborate that you were here Tuesday evening?"

"Sales and tech had left for the day."

"What about security?"

"Not after hours."

"No one can confirm you were here?" Thomas asked.

"No."

A tone sounded on Bryant's phone, and he picked up the receiver.

"Yes, Rosa," Bryant said. His eyes moved from Thomas to Aguilar as he listened. "All right, thank you for telling me." Bryant set the phone down. "I'm afraid I must cut the interview short. If you need to speak with me further, Rosa will arrange a time."

"We'll contact your office," Thomas said, rising with Aguilar.

When Thomas and Aguilar turned around, a security guard was waiting at the door to escort them from the building. After the guard watched them exit, Thomas wheeled the cruiser out of the parking lot.

"Bryant kicked us to the curb rather suddenly," Aguilar said.

"As we were leaving, I overheard something about a CEO from some New York City firm flying in."

"Do you buy all that family-friendly talk from Wallace Bryant?"

"I'm not sure what to believe," Thomas said, rubbing his chin as he merged with highway traffic. "It seems convenient that Bryant doesn't have an alibi for the night Karley vanished."

Aguilar groaned. "And Lance Weir was asleep at home with no one to verify his whereabouts."

14

Halfway down the lake road, outside Scout and Naomi Mourning's house, Raven pulled her black Nissan Rogue onto the shoulder.

This was a terrible idea.

She checked the time and drummed her legs beneath the steering wheel. With fifty minutes remaining before she was due back at the office, she considered turning around and driving into the village for food. Anything except following through on her foolhardy plan.

Along the west side of the lake, she could see her old house —her mother's house now—jutting above the trees, where the land rose to meet the road. Her jaw pulsed. If Darren knew what she intended, he'd be furious.

Clouds blotted out the sun, and the breeze rippling the lake warned of colder days ahead.

It was now or never. She exhaled and shifted the SUV into drive.

Outside her mother's house, she stopped the Rogue and stepped onto the driveway, hands rubbing the goosebumps off her arms. She spied Buck Benson's home along the lake, the boathouse windows dark, the pickup truck parked out front—the same pickup that had flown the Confederate flag for years.

As soon as she approached the boathouse, the thunderous barks began. More grizzly than dog, Buster could take her arm off and swallow it whole.

Her mother was at Shepherd Systems, running the sales department. Nobody knew Raven was here. Benson could swipe a knife across her throat and dump her body in the water, and no one would ever find out.

She almost turned back before she reached the door. This was stupid.

But she had to set Benson straight. His second cousin had kidnapped and attempted to murder Raven before he broke out of prison and targeted her mother. The apple never fell far from the tree. If Raven accomplished anything today, besides surviving an encounter with the no-good redneck, she'd convince Buck Benson to stay the hell away from her mother.

Before her knuckles tapped the door, the dog threw itself against the other side, buckling the wood. Raven stepped back and hissed. The windows rattled every time the mammoth dog barked.

Holding her breath, Raven knocked. It didn't take long before heavy footsteps moved toward the door.

Buck Benson parted the curtain, identified Raven, and scowled.

"Buster, heel," he said with a growl.

The dog's barking stopped as though Benson had put a gun to its head and pulled the trigger. A heartbeat later, the door parted just enough for Benson to squeeze his head through. Scratching the scruff of hair on top of his head, he eyed Raven.

"Oh, it's you."

"I'd like to talk," Raven said.

Benson rubbed his mouth, glanced back at Buster, then held the door open. "Come in, I guess."

Raven wasn't sure what she'd expected to find inside the boathouse—a hoarder's worth of garbage jutting toward the ceiling like stalagmites, crushed beer cans strewn about the floor, cigarette butts littering the carpet—but it wasn't this. There was an order to the home that caused her to gape for a moment. Frilled, translucent curtains framed a window overlooking the lake. A gourmet coffeemaker sat on the kitchen counter. Half the size of Raven's old house, the boathouse delivered superior views.

Buster padded to Raven and sniffed her hand. One snap of the dog's jaws, and Raven wouldn't have a hand anymore. She stood ramrod straight, trying not to display fear. Thomas's dog, Jack, had been the largest dog she'd ever encountered, but Buster made Jack look like the runt of a Chihuahua litter.

"Come, Buster," Benson said. The dog sniffed Raven for good measure before obeying his master. Buster returned to sit beside Benson, but never took his eyes off Raven. "You said you wanted to talk."

Raven's mouth dried up. "I'd like to discuss this relationship you have with my mother."

He folded his arms over his chest. "That's none of your business."

"I think it is. My mother means everything to me, and I want answers. What's going on between the two of you?"

"You and I were neighbors for years, and you never spoke to me. Not once. What gives you the right to pry into my personal business? Seems to me you could have asked your ma. In fact, I bet you did, and she told you the same. It ain't your business."

"Listen, Benson, you can pursue any woman on this lake. I don't know what you want with my mother, but I won't stand by and let you hurt her. You're up to something. I haven't figured it out yet, but I will."

"Listen to yourself," he said, stroking Buster's head when the dog tensed. "You're acting like Serena is your teenage daughter, and you caught her dating the bad boy from high school. Don't you think your ma has enough life experience to make her own choices?" Benson's gaze moved to the lake. "Besides, we ain't dating. I doubt she'd want anything like that. We're just friends."

Raven couldn't believe what she was hearing. This was the same reprobate who'd referred to LeVar as *blacky* and told Thomas that her brother was a murderer.

"Why would she want to be friends with someone like you?"

"What's that supposed to mean?"

Raven threw her head back and laughed. "You stuck your damn flag in my face while I lived next door. And I remember what you said about my brother."

Benson opened his mouth to fire back and stopped. He ran a hesitant hand across the top of his head.

"I didn't know LeVar was your brother. All I saw was some teenage gangster driving along the lake every day, hanging out near your place. That was the week they found that woman's body in the water."

"Yeah, murdered by a serial killer named Jeremy Hyde. My brother could have gone to jail because of what you said. Admit it, Benson. You accused him because he's black."

"I accused him because he was a thug with the Harmon Kings gang. Had nothing to do with skin color."

"Yeah, right. I think I know why you're cozying up to my mother. This is about your cousin Mark."

The color drained from Benson's face.

Raven leaned toward the man. "That's it, isn't it? I'll never forget what he tried to do to us. Now he's in jail, where he belongs, and you are his only hope of getting revenge on me and my mother."

The man lowered his eyes and shook his head. "That ain't it at all. You want to sit down?"

He motioned to the two lounge chairs in the living room. No, Raven didn't want to sit. Her instinct told her to run screaming from that house and never look back. But when Benson slumped dejectedly into one chair with Buster lying at his feet, Raven eased herself down in the other chair, keeping one eye on the door.

"Talk," she said, willing her voice not to tremble.

For a long time, Benson didn't speak. When he did, the man studied his sneakers. "You ever have a family member who disappointed you?"

Raven pictured her mother with a needle in her arm. Then her mind flashed back to the first time LeVar returned to the apartment with a gang tattoo.

"It ain't like Mark is my brother. He's my second cousin." Benson forced himself to meet Raven's stare. "And if you think I helped him kidnap you and attack your ma, you couldn't be more wrong."

"Convince me."

He spread his arms. "I can't. It's not like I've given you any reason to trust me. All I have is my word. I had nothing to do with Mark going after Serena. As far as I'm concerned, he's dead to me. And I'm not the only person in my family who feels that way."

"You're a racist."

"I won't pretend I'm a good man, that I haven't made enough mistakes for several lifetimes. Yeah, I flew a Confederate flag off my truck, and I figured my neighbor wouldn't care for it."

"Why did you leave it up?"

He shrugged. "No good reason. Maybe because we didn't see eye to eye."

"Because you knew it intimidated me."

"I can't tell you why. But it's gone now, and it ain't never coming back."

Raven's eyes flicked to a shelf along the wall, where she spied a model car from the *Dukes of Hazzard* television show, painted red with *General Lee* scrolled above the door and the rebel flag across the roof.

"You haven't changed," Raven said, tilting her chin at the car.

"Shoot. I forgot about that."

"You want to explain why *that* is sitting on your shelf? Can't get enough of seventies comedy nostalgia?"

Benson pressed his lips together. "I made that when I was eight. Took me a month, gluing all those parts together then painting it."

Raven sniffed. "Fancy yourself an artist?"

Something flashed in his eyes. Anger? Injury? She wasn't certain.

"No, I ain't no artist. Nobody would want to see anything a nobody like me created. But that car is the first thing I ever made as a kid that my daddy didn't laugh at."

She paused, unsure how to respond. He stared out the window, viewing another time and place.

Raven rose from her chair and walked to the shelf. Benson flinched, as if he expected her to hurl the model against the wall and shatter it into a million pieces. She didn't touch the car.

"You know, when LeVar and I were kids, we used to watch the *Dukes of Hazzard* reruns on TV. They made us laugh, and I doubt either of us gave the art on the car a second thought." He smiled and nodded. "But did you ever consider my mother's reaction after you invited her into the living room, and she had to look at this?"

"I forgot it was there. I'll take it down."

Raven scrutinized Benson.

"You don't have to take it down," Raven said, dropping her shoulders. "It obviously means a lot to you."

"No, no." He pointed at the model. "It's just a stupid toy. Should have gotten rid of it years ago."

"I hope you don't. You spent a lot of time on it."

"Yeah, when I was eight." Benson rubbed his eyes. "You don't have to believe me, but people change. I'm not the man I was last year, and I ain't an eight-year-old kid anymore. No issue cutting ties with the past. In fact, it's probably a good thing if I do."

Raven felt an unexpected pinch in her throat. Sympathy?

"I need your word that you'll treat my mother well."

"You have it, not that my word is worth much. Never has been. Something else I'm trying to change." He lifted his head. "I like your mother. Don't mean we're dating, just that it's nice to have someone to talk to. And that's all there is to it."

Did Benson mean what he was saying, and could she trust him? At a loss for words, Raven only hoped Benson didn't mean her mother harm.

He set his hands on his thighs and blinked the mist out of his eyes. "If you will excuse me for a moment."

Good lord, was he crying? Raven looked away as he moved down the hallway, ostensibly to the bedroom, with Buster following. A door closed.

A million emotions twisted Raven's insides. She moved to the window and studied the lake. The water appeared gray and murky beneath a blanket of clouds, and the wind drove white-caps over the shore. When she turned back to the chair, she glimpsed a white sheet covering a thin, rectangular object that was as tall as her hips. Silence hung in the hallway where

Benson had vanished. Her hand moved to the sheet and stopped. It wasn't right to snoop.

Yet she couldn't help herself. Something about the hidden object tugged Raven's curiosity. If Benson caught her peeking, he wouldn't be happy.

Checking around the corner, she saw a closed door at the end of the corridor. No sound traveled back to her.

Raven hurried to the sheet and pulled it back. Her mouth fell open. She gasped.

A painting of her mother stared back at her. The beauty stunned Raven and knocked her back on her heels. She never would have guessed Buck Benson possessed this level of talent, but it was the care, the respect for her mother that left Raven breathless. Tears welled in her eyes. If she'd only known Benson had—

"I think you should leave."

Raven jumped and found Benson glaring at her from the door. She tossed the sheet over the painting, but it was too late.

"I'm sorry. I didn't realize . . ."

"You went through my belongings, so you aren't welcome in my house. Go."

"Mr. Benson, I meant no harm. It's beautiful, really. You should—"

"Go!"

As Raven departed, she saw him staring at the covered painting, his shoulders slumped in defeat.

15

Ashen midday light spilled into the cellar and pulled Karley awake. The last several hours were a blank slate. One touch to her forehead confirmed the kidnapper had drugged her.

Had he raped her again? She didn't believe so, though she wondered why he insisted on sedating her.

To control her, Karley believed. To ramp up the terror that he could do anything he pleased while she lay unconscious. Splayed on top of the futon, she pushed herself up to her elbows. The basement whipped and twirled in a blur. Unless the nauseating motion stopped, she was certain she'd throw up.

Her gaze fell to what she was wearing. She squirmed into the corner. These weren't her clothes.

Yet they fit, as though he'd taken measurements while she slept. The yellow T-shirt looked like something a teenager would wear, the hem riding above her bellybutton, the V-neck dipping between her breasts. The black cloth shorts were just as gaudy. What had he done with her real clothes?

Staring at the ceiling, she listened. Quiet.

Her attention swung to the tank in the corner. The water

heater hadn't ignited since she'd awoken, and no water trickled through the pipes. It didn't mean the psychopath wasn't home. She pictured him on the other side of the cellar door, waiting for her to stir.

So he could have his way with her.

Karley's legs buckled when she stood. She grabbed the wall for support, and another wave of dizziness threw off her equilibrium. Beyond the bars, the window displayed silvery clouds and nothing else. She would need to climb higher to see if any houses stood in the distance. Yesterday the rumble of a tractor motor had come to her. Logic told her she was in the country. Perhaps her abductor owned a farm. The possibility of a neighbor rescuing her rejuvenated Karley and got her moving.

Placing an unsteady foot on the futon, she craned her neck toward the window. The angle was too low. If humanity existed outside, she wouldn't see it from here.

What day was it? Time warped and blurred from the drugs and the confinement. She thought it might be Thursday, but she wasn't sure if she'd spent two or three nights locked inside this prison. Wind tossed grit and dirt against the window. She concentrated on the sounds outside, hoping the tractor would come. Except she couldn't scream until she was certain the kidnapper wasn't upstairs. If he heard, he'd punish and rape her. Even if she called out, a farmer wouldn't hear her over the roar of the engine, and she had no way of knowing if the man on the tractor had snatched her in the grocery store parking lot.

She wandered to the base of the stairs and looked up. Window light seeped beneath the door. The kitchen must be on the other side since running water and banging pots had awoken her last night.

Maybe he wasn't home. If she broke out . . .

Too risky. He might be upstairs, expecting an escape attempt.

Karley craved privacy. Though she was alone in the basement, this was where he'd violated her. She would never feel alone in this room. Last evening she'd discovered a working lock on the bathroom door. An oversight? Or an olive branch? The lock didn't matter, she supposed. With the bathroom windows barred, she'd never escape the cellar.

Face it. I'll die down here.

No, she refused to give up. There had to be a way out.

Karley slipped inside the bathroom and softly closed the door before punching the lock. She tested the knob and issued a relieved sigh. This tiny space, about four feet long and five feet wide, offered her sanctuary. She lied to herself that she was safe here. He must own a key or some way of unlocking the door. He'd considered every eventuality to ensure she never escaped.

And she wasn't his first victim.

Karley wondered about Alena, the woman he muttered about and compared her to. Who was she?

Hunger doubled Karley over. The man hadn't fed her in twenty-four hours. Her stomach lurched, and she bent over the toilet and retched. After a minute of dry heaving, she straightened and panted in front of the mirror. The pale reflected face wasn't hers. It appeared she'd aged twenty years.

She twisted the faucet and cupped her hands, spooning water into her mouth until her stomach filled. At once, her energy increased.

Turning back to the window, she realized she could stand on top of the toilet and see outside.

Karley closed the lid on the seat and climbed up, grabbing the wall for balance. On the other side of a plowed field, a white farmhouse stood along a blacktop road. The lack of traffic confirmed that she was in the country. Behind the house, she spotted a red barn with its doors open. She searched for the tractor, the farmer, anyone who might get her out of here. With her arms extended, she leaned forward and grasped the bars. A hard tug got her nowhere. The thin space between the bars stopped her from squeezing her hand through and punching out the glass.

Don't give up. Safety is on the other side of this window.

Though she'd searched the cellar for anything she might use to defend herself or break out of the basement, she determined to try again. Karley popped the lock and opened the door.

And found her kidnapper leering at her.

She screeched and stumbled backward. He snatched her by the hair and dragged her through the cellar, her legs flailing across the smooth cement floor.

"I warned you. Never try to escape, I said. But you don't listen."

Hair ripped out of her scalp as he pulled her across the room. He let go, and she slumped on the floor, supported by the futon.

"The windows have cameras over them. I watched you. There's no hiding from me, Karley. The sooner you stop fighting, the easier this will be for you."

"What do you want from me?"

The stocking masked his face, but she was sure she knew this man, despite the way he disguised his voice by whispering. Until now, she hadn't noticed the camera hanging from a strap around his neck.

"We're going to have some fun, just the two of us," he said, his grin displaying teeth.

The man reached into his shirt pocket and tossed a handful of photographs at her feet. There was a woman in the pictures, stripped down to her underwear and bra. She had hair like Karley's.

"Get those away from me," she said, kicking the photographs across the floor.

He knelt and retrieved the pictures, this time placing them on her lap.

"This is Alena. Or *was* Alena. She could have had it all—love, togetherness, intimacy. In the end, she failed me. But as you can see, we had fun together."

"You're sick."

His hand shot toward her face, and she flinched. The kidnapper stopped short of slapping her and lifted her chin, forcing her to meet his gaze.

"You are my wife, my love, Karley. We belong together and always have."

Lance? No, this couldn't be her husband.

"But if you fail me, you'll meet Alena's fate." He rose and peered down at her. From her position on the floor, he appeared giant-like, a monster with a distorted face. "We can be happy here. I'll keep you safe, and you'll love me and obey, just as Alena swore she would."

At his insistent stare, she forced herself to sift through the images. In the first photograph, bindings held Alena's wrists behind her back. The woman slumped forward, mouth gagged, tears in her eyes.

"I don't know what you want from me."

To her horror, he raised the viewfinder to his eye and snapped a photograph.

"You will remove your clothes, as Alena did. Then you will pose, per my commands. Obey, and this will go smoothly. Deny me, and I will have no choice but to punish you."

He let the camera dangle from his neck and reached for her.

"Stop," she said, raising her knees to ward him off.

"I warned you not to fight me."

As she cried out, he yanked the shirt over her head.

16

The clouds parted as Thomas pulled into his driveway. No sooner did he shut off the engine than Chelsey's Honda Civic parked beside him with Jack and Tigger in tow. When Chelsey opened the door, Jack bounded from the backseat and raced to the front porch, while Thomas lifted Tigger's carrier. On the top step, Chelsey worked the key into the lock as Thomas held Tigger's cage in one hand, propped the storm door open with his backside, and fished the mail out of the box with his other hand. Jack's tail thumped in anticipation. As soon as Chelsey opened the door, Jack burst inside, ran two laps around the downstairs, and snagged a squeaky toy. Thomas released Tigger, who gave him a sidelong glance for keeping him locked up for an extra ten seconds while Jack ran free.

Thomas checked the mail; the electric and gas bill had arrived, and a notice announced that their internet access would cost an extra ten dollars per month starting in October. Before he complained about the increase, Chelsey threw her arms around Thomas's shoulders and pressed her lips against his. The kiss lasted a good ten seconds, but it seemed to end too quickly.

"Hi," she said, brushing the hair off his forehead.

"Thanks. What was that for?"

"Because I miss you, and it looks like you needed it."

"I miss you too," he said. "And you're right. I needed that."

"Long day?"

"You don't know the half."

Thomas turned his attention back to the bills.

As he tore open the energy statement, Chelsey said, "I heard about Heath Elledge raising hell over Urban Hammond. You don't think Hammond will get off, do you?"

"Elledge is friends with the district attorney. I wouldn't rule out the possibility."

"He tried to kill Raven and me."

"And if I have anything to say about it, the DA will push for the maximum sentence. But there's only so much I can do."

She planted a kiss on his cheek and entered the kitchen, where she washed the pets' dishes. There was dinner to prepare —theirs, as well as Tigger and Jack's. It seemed they never had a moment to sit and spend time together.

For Thomas, the last year had been a whirlwind. Reuniting with Chelsey was a dream come true, yet expressing his emotions remained a struggle, something he worked on every day. He was lucky they spent time together whenever Wolf Lake Consulting collaborated with the sheriff's department. But working on a case didn't compare to quiet time at home. Come to think of it, he couldn't recall the last time they'd eaten popcorn in front of the television, or talked about their days after dinner. It was always a race to complete one task before the next was due.

"I'll feed them and start on our dinner," Chelsey said, drying the pets' bowls.

"How about you grab their food, and I'll cook?"

"You sure? It looks like you'd be better off unwinding on the deck."

"I'll make a deal with you. Let me prepare dinner, then we'll watch the sunset from the backyard."

"You strike a hard bargain, Sheriff." She pressed a finger to his lips. "And you have a deal. Maybe after the sun goes down, we can—"

A knock on the sliding glass door stopped Chelsey. Naomi and Scout waved from the deck.

"Did we make plans to eat dinner with the Mournings?" Thomas asked.

"Not that I remember, but I can't keep track of anything these days."

Thomas unlocked the door and let Naomi and Scout inside. Naomi cradled a casserole dish. Whatever was inside carried a delectable scent. A towel covered the lid, making it impossible to identify the food.

"What did you make?" asked Chelsey as Naomi handed her the dish.

"Tuna noodle casserole," said Naomi. "Keep the towel wrapped around the dish until you set it down. Careful, it's hot."

"You cooked us dinner? That's kind of you."

Jack padded to Scout, who stroked the dog's head and tossed a ball for him to chase.

"Thank you, Naomi," Thomas said. "I'll grab four plates from the cupboard."

Naomi raised a hand. "Oh, no. This is for you. Scout and I will eat at home."

"It's no trouble."

"You two never stop running. Enjoy dinner, then spend the evening together. You deserve it."

Thomas smiled. "We owe you one, Naomi. This is a wonderful surprise."

"Considering what you've done for us, this is the least we could do. Come on, Scout. Let's give Thomas and Chelsey some privacy."

Scout winked at Chelsey, and Chelsey gave the teenager a quick hug. "See you tomorrow after you get out of school."

"I almost forgot," Naomi said from the doorway. "After you brought up Lance Weir, I looked him up on the Bryant Media Group website. I remember him now."

"What can you tell me?" Thomas asked.

"Only that he's a creep. I caught him looking down my shirt."

Scout blanched. "Ew, Mom. Did you have to bring that up?"

"I remember thinking, the guy wears a wedding ring, and the first thing he does when he visits Shepherd Systems is check out the women."

"We've heard similar stories about Weir," Thomas said. "Thanks for telling me."

"Anytime. And don't worry. We made a plate for LeVar."

The door closed, and it was suddenly quiet inside the A-frame. Jack, holding a ball in his mouth, watched from the living room.

Chelsey grinned. "Well, then. I guess it's just the two of us."

"And our four-legged friends."

Thomas retrieved two dishes from the cupboard and set the table. The casserole tasted even better than expected, and they sat side by side, enjoying the conversation while they ate, with Tigger curled beneath Chelsey's feet and Jack gnawing the squcaky toy on the couch.

Chelsey wiped her mouth with a napkin. "Didn't you say Lance Weir ogled his wife's friend?"

"That's what the friend told me. The way she explained the incident, it was more lechery than admiration. She took it as a violation." Thomas leaned back and clasped his hands behind his head. "Naomi Mourning is beautiful, so it's no surprise that she'd draw eyes. But with Weir, it sounds like there is more to the picture."

"Are you checking out Naomi, Thomas? She's my friend."

Thomas blinked. "No. I would never."

"I'm kidding. Relax." Chelsey reached below the table and removed her laptop from its carrying case. "Oh, and Bianca Holland, the Coral Lake woman who disappeared last month, showed up in Vegas this afternoon. Seems she is having an affair and walked out on her husband."

"So we can cross Holland off the list. She has nothing to do with Karley Weir vanishing."

"Speaking of Karley and Lance Weir, I need to show you something."

"I thought we were putting work aside and spending the evening together."

"We are. This won't take more than a minute." Chelsey tapped a fingernail against the screen. "As you discovered, there was no credit card activity on the evening Karley disappeared. However, I found a purchase from a Kane Grove gas station. It occurred Sunday afternoon. If I had to guess, Karley gassed up the car ahead of her trip."

"Makes sense. What else?"

"One charge caught my attention. It didn't register until this afternoon, because it was a pending charge and the credit card company flagged it. Last Wednesday, someone shopped at Lakefront Hardware. No telling if it was Karley or Lance, but guess who works at Lakefront Hardware? None other than Urban Hammond."

"I thought the store sounded familiar."

Chelsey sighed. "Not that it does us any good. Hammond is in jail, so there's no way he's holding Karley somewhere."

"Except he isn't in jail."

Chelsey's eyes shot to Thomas. "What do you mean, he isn't in jail?"

"That was part of my long day. Elledge raised enough hell that the judge granted bail."

"That lunatic is running free?"

"Make no mistake—Hammond will serve hard time for his attack. For now, he's out."

"And Karley vanished the night before you arrested Hammond. Thomas, what if he saw Karley at the hardware store and abducted her?"

17

In the last light of day, Raven climbed the ridge trail through Wolf Lake State Park, her hiking boots digging into the soft earth as she pushed through a tangle of branches growing across the path. The evening chill burned her lungs, and her legs throbbed from the long walk from Lucifer Falls. After arriving home from Wolf Lake Consulting, she'd dressed in hiking gear and hurried out the door before Darren arrived home from the welcome center. She couldn't face him after the afternoon's events. He'd be upset with her for visiting Buck Benson without backup.

Worse yet, how would she explain her actions and the damage she'd caused?

With every step, she fought to wipe her memory clean of Benson's face—that heart-clenching combination of anger and hurt after he caught her removing the sheet from the painting. The portrait was beautiful, and her mother deserved to see it. But that didn't excuse Raven from betraying Benson's trust.

What had she been thinking? She'd tried to apologize and repair the damage, but he'd kicked her out of the boathouse. If she knocked on Benson's door again, he'd slam it in her face before she could say she was sorry.

Had she misjudged Benson?

She reached the top of the trail, which opened to a clearing. Cabins formed a neat row and ended with the ranger's cabin, where Raven lived with Darren. Charcoal smoke from one of the grills touched her nose. She was surprised someone had wanted to camp before the weekend. Once summer concluded, weekday traffic at the state park declined until the holidays.

Across the clearing, light shone through the ranger cabin's window. Larger than the public cabins, Darren's open floor plan featured a small kitchen and enough space for a couch and television, as well as a bed and dresser. Darren and Raven entertained their unofficial investigation crew a few times per month.

She paused at the tree line and formed the words in her head. Hiding the Buck Benson incident from Darren wasn't an option. No matter how she worded the confrontation, she couldn't paint the encounter in a positive light.

As she approached their home, a shadow rounded the corner. She jumped and set a hand on her chest. It was only Darren, his arms full of firewood.

"You scared me half to death," she said, catching her breath.

"Where were you? I called, but you left your phone on the table."

"Yeah. I wanted to walk without being tied to the outside world, social media, and everything else."

"But if you'd hurt yourself on the trail and needed help, what would you do?"

"I'm a big girl, Darren. How often do you hike without your phone?"

"Point taken. Come inside. I put a pot on the stove for hot chocolate."

Darren set the pile of wood on a rack beside the door. It

wasn't cold enough to run the wood stove, but it would be soon. Most years, the state park ranger started burning firewood a week before Halloween, and the September nights had carried a bite this year.

Inside, a space heater kept the cabin comfortable, though neither trusted leaving the heater on at night, worried it might short out and start a fire. Raven blew on her hands to warm them while Darren grabbed mugs from the cupboard.

As she removed her hiking boots, headlights swept across the cabin's exterior. Raven moved to the window and parted the curtains.

"Are you expecting arrivals tonight?"

"The welcome center closed an hour ago," Darren said. "Nobody checks in this late."

The lights prevented Raven from identifying the vehicle until they shut off. A door opened, and her mother marched across the grass.

"It's my mother."

"I wonder what she's doing here?"

Raven bit her lip. She had a sick feeling this was about Buck Benson. Raven swallowed and opened the door before Serena knocked.

"Mom, why didn't you call to let us know you were coming?"

Raven stepped aside, and her mother stomped through the entrance.

Serena's eyes were red, her cheeks chapped from crying. "How could you?"

"I don't know what—"

"Don't give me that. What did you say to Buck? He's been upset all afternoon, and he said we can't speak anymore. You visited his house, right? Don't deny it."

"I did," Raven said, slumping onto the couch and burying her face in her hands.

"You did what?" Darren asked, turning away from the stove.

Darren was obviously upset with Raven for a different reason.

Serena rounded on her daughter. "Who planted this fool idea in your head and convinced you to knock on Buck's door without my approval?"

"Wait a second," Raven said. "Without your approval? Have you forgotten Buck Benson was my neighbor long before I sold my house to you?"

"Girl, whatever you intended, you got your way. Now he refuses to give me the time of day. For the life of me, I can't imagine what you said to upset him so. I've never seen him like this. You'd better give me a damn good explanation for your actions."

"I'm sorry, Mom, but I was only looking out for you."

"Excuse me? How many times should I remind you that I'm the mother and you're the daughter? You don't know better than me." Serena swiped a tear off her eyelid. "I'm furious, Raven. As much as I love you, you can be stubborn. It's time you backed off and trusted me to make friends. Nobody wants you staring over their shoulder all the time."

"All we did was talk. I swear."

"You drove to Buck's house to convince him to stay away from me, because you still think he's a racist and a crook like Mark. Raven, people have prejudged us our entire lives—you, me, LeVar. After all this time, after everything we've endured, I'd think you would have learned to give people a chance before jumping to conclusions. Well, you got your way. Now my neighbor won't talk to me, and I stare at his boathouse, knowing my fool daughter blew up our friendship."

Raven stood and placed a hand on her mother's shoulder. "I'll fix this; I promise."

"No, you won't." Serena raised her index finger and placed it before Raven's face. "Stay away from Buck. Don't make things worse."

Serena slammed the door on her way out. Mouth agape, Darren stared at Raven for a long time.

"Don't you say anything," Raven said. "I spent the day beating myself up and don't need anyone else piling on."

"Hey, this will blow over." He grasped her shoulders and planted his lips against her forehead. "Still, you shouldn't have visited Buck Benson alone."

Raven paced through the cabin. "You don't need to worry. I learned a valuable lesson today."

"I'm relieved you won't try anything like that again."

"That's not what I meant." Darren questioned her with his eyes, and she brushed her beaded hair off her shoulders. "I learned I was wrong about Buck Benson."

He handed her a mug of hot chocolate, and she slid beside him on the couch.

"Tell me what happened."

"It's a long story, and I can't go into it without divulging secrets Benson doesn't want anyone to know." Darren raised an eyebrow. "Nothing bad. He's a . . . deeper person than I'd expected. Perhaps he's grown since meeting my mother. Either way, I'm positive he's not a threat to me, my mother, or anyone."

"Did you say something you regret?"

"A lot of things, I'm sure. But he caught me snooping through his belongings."

"Raven, why?"

"Fair question. Because I'm an idiot? I just can't separate Buck from Mark Benson. It's unfair, and what my mother said about prejudice was spot on. How can I forget what Mark did?"

Darren hugged her against him. "Don't blame yourself for assuming the worst. The kidnapping was a traumatic event, and you had every reason to assume your racist neighbor was involved."

"He's not a racist. He might have been a year ago, but people change."

"Promise you'll talk to me before you do something like this again."

"I will, Darren." Raven sipped the hot chocolate and let the heat spread from her chest to her belly, softening her. "I have to fix this."

"Please don't."

"I remember what my mother said. Somehow, I need to make things right."

But how could she repair the damage after her mother demanded she never visit Benson again?

18

"We're out of milk and eggs," Thomas called up the stairs.

The shower shut off, and Chelsey, wearing a towel around her hair, poked her head out of the bathroom.

"Sorry, I didn't hear you."

"I said we're out of milk and eggs. Unless you want toast and stale cereal for breakfast, I'd better run to the store. Need anything?"

"Not that I can think of."

Thomas saluted Chelsey and grabbed his keys off the banister. Halfway to the door, he heard the bathroom door swing open again.

"I'm running low on green tea," she said.

"Got it."

He checked his pockets for his wallet.

"Oh, and almond milk. I drank the rest this afternoon." She started to close the door and stopped. "And a box of greens. Get the super greens—kale, spinach, and chard. Make sure you get the large container. The small ones aren't worth the price."

He sighed. "Anything else?"

"No, that should do it."

Thomas reached for the doorknob and paused, anticipating another request.

"Shoot, Thomas. I forgot to stock up on protein powder. It wouldn't be a terrible idea to grab some organic ginger too. I'm almost out."

"Why don't I just buy a week's worth of groceries?" Thomas asked with an air of sarcasm.

"Great idea."

He groaned.

Full dark had settled over Wolf Lake, and Thomas wished he'd donned a heavier jacket upon encountering the post-sunset chill. He half-expected frost on the windshield of his silver Ford F-150. Though no ice formed, the glass fogged until he turned on the defroster and cranked the heat.

He veered down the lake road and braked when a red fox scurried across the centerline. Lately, the animals seemed more active, hurrying to scavenge for food before the cold of winter set in. The lake road took him to the village, where he turned down the thoroughfare and passed through the shopping district, a smattering of eateries still open. In the village center, before he reached the municipal park, he swung his gaze to Wolf Lake Consulting. The windows of the converted house remained dark with no vehicles in the parking lot. Sometimes LeVar and Raven worked late at the office, but not tonight.

The supermarket stood a mile past the village near an outlet shopping center, built where a K-Mart had sold goods for decades before closing. Driving this far to purchase groceries rankled Thomas, but he and Chelsey preferred the supermarket's fresh produce and varied selection to the village stores.

As Thomas directed the F-150 past the park, the bright beams of a pickup truck ignited his mirror. He glared back at the driver, unable to see beyond the shining lights. The truck inched up on his bumper, close enough to knock Thomas off the road if he chose.

"You'll cause an accident," he said to the headlights in the mirror, as though the tailgater cared.

Instead of backing off, the offending driver revved the motor and sped closer. It always amazed Thomas when people hurried without regard for the dangers of speeding.

"Fine, have it your way."

He pulled to the side of the road and let the driver pass. The Toyota Tundra thundered by, shaking the F-150 in its wake.

A black Toyota Tundra.

Didn't Urban Hammond drive a black Toyota Tundra?

Thomas squinted to read the license plate, but the Tundra swerved down a residential street and disappeared. If it had been Hammond, the convict was taking a brazen risk by harassing the county sheriff. One misstep would place Hammond behind bars again.

"Maybe it wasn't him."

He doubted his own words.

The driver had done nothing except tailgate Thomas for two blocks. Technically, he could ticket a tailgater for riding too close to his bumper, but it wasn't worth chasing the vehicle through a residential neighborhood. He lifted the radio, which he carried with him at all times, and contacted the office. Deputy Lambert was working the evening shift until eleven o'clock.

"Hey, Lambert, it's Thomas. Do me a solid and grab Urban Hammond's license plate number."

"Hold on while I call it up."

Thomas idled on the side of the road and waited. What if Hammond sought revenge on Thomas, Chelsey, and Raven for the arrest? The sicko might pursue Holly Doyle as well.

After a short wait, Lambert said, "Got the information for you."

The deputy read the license plate number as Thomas fumbled in the glove compartment for a pen and something to write on. After Thomas recorded the information, he recited it to Lambert, who confirmed the numbers were correct.

"While you're at it, Lambert, send a deputy past Holly Doyle's house. Make sure Urban Hammond isn't causing problems for the family."

"Will do."

Curious, Thomas turned into the neighborhood where he'd last spotted the truck. He still wasn't sure if it had been Hammond's truck following him. The sting of Hammond making bail dug into Thomas. The man should be in jail, unable to hurt anybody, not free and roaming Wolf Lake. By now, the offending vehicle was long gone. When Thomas reached the end of the block, he circled around and headed toward the supermarket. Perhaps he'd overreacted.

While the sheriff filled his shopping cart inside the store, Lambert radioed Thomas and gave him the all-clear. Holly Doyle was safe, and Hammond was nowhere to be found. Yet the sheriff couldn't shake the worry that the convict had trailed him out of Wolf Lake, intent on revenge. He rushed to fill the cart and hurried to the checkout line. The teenage boy took forever to bag Thomas's groceries, and the sheriff bounced on his toes with pent-up anxiety. At any moment, he expected a radio report that Hammond had attacked the Doyles and kidnapped Holly.

When at last the boy finished bagging the groceries, Thomas pushed the cart into the parking lot. Two dead lights left a pool of darkness beside his truck. He circled behind the cab and stopped when his shoe crunched down on shattered plastic.

Someone had broken both taillights and dented the rear bumper.

Thomas's eyes flicked around the parking lot, searching for a black Toyota Tundra. Hammond must be the vandal, but he wasn't here now. The sheriff glanced at the storefront and searched for a security camera. Finding none, he clenched his jaw. He needed to report the vandalism. After contacting dispatch—Deputy Lambert was en route to survey the damage—Thomas photographed the back of the pickup.

His heart pounded. Though Hammond had reason to attack Thomas, the convict's targets were Raven and Chelsey. Dialing Chelsey's number, Thomas willed her to answer. The phone rang and rang.

Where is she?

After Chelsey's voicemail played, Thomas hung up and dialed again. No answer. Thomas picked up the radio and contacted Lambert.

"How far are you from the supermarket?"

"Five minutes out," Lambert said.

"Change of plans. Meet me at my house. Chelsey isn't answering her phone, and I'm afraid Urban Hammond is going after her."

"Turning around now, Thomas."

The sheriff hopped into the cab and fired the engine. He only hoped they would reach Chelsey before Hammond.

19

Through the front windows of the A-frame, Chelsey watched LeVar's Chrysler Limited back out of the driveway and turn toward the village with Naomi riding shotgun and Scout in the backseat. LeVar had invited Chelsey to join them for ice cream—their favorite homemade creamery would close for the season in three days—but Chelsey had declined. Now she kicked herself, realizing this was her last chance to enjoy ice cream until spring.

Tigger purred from his perch on top of the couch, flicking his tail back and forth. Jack sprawled on the cushions and held a chewed-up tennis ball between his jaws. When Chelsey turned back to the pets, Jack sat up and lifted his paw, a sign that he wanted to shake hands. She giggled and acquiesced. The dog jumped down from the couch and padded to the back door.

"You need to go out?"

Jack issued a muffled woof, the tennis ball thwarting his attempt at barking.

"Hold on. Let me grab something warm out of the closet."

She pulled a heavy sweatshirt over her head and added a light winter coat. It occurred to her that she hadn't worn the jacket since April. Now it held a musty scent from hanging inside the closet all summer.

Chelsey zipped the jacket and considered if it was cold enough for gloves. It probably was, but she refused to yield to winter in September.

"All right, boy. Make it quick so we don't freeze."

She drew back the sliding glass door. The cold slapped her face. Off leash, Jack bounded past and sprinted into the yard. Since Thomas had rescued the dog from the state park last year, Jack hadn't required a leash. He proved his loyalty to Thomas, Chelsey, and their neighbors every day. Chelsey never worried he might run off.

Jack did his business beneath the shadow of an oak tree bordering the Mourning's yard. Chelsey hopped in place, trying to stay warm, wondering how her friends could stomach ice cream cones with the temperature hovering in the forties. Condensation clouds puffed out of her mouth, and she regretted not donning gloves.

The dog raced back to Chelsey and dropped the ball at her feet.

"You must be kidding." Unable to resist the enormous dog's smile and lolling tongue, Chelsey knelt and retrieved the ball. "Okay, but just a few throws. We'll both catch pneumonia before Thomas returns from the store."

Which reminded her—Thomas should have arrived home by now. What was taking him so long? He'd probably wandered down the snack aisle and discovered some devious, unhealthy treat.

As long as it's hot chocolate or something warm.

Chelsey dug into her pocket for her phone and remembered she'd left it in the living room. Forgetting her phone raised goosebumps on her arms, and it wasn't because of the cold. She eyed the driveway, expecting Thomas's headlights to sweep across the house.

"I don't know where your daddy is," Chelsey told Jack. "Hopefully he shows up soon. What I wouldn't give to be inside the house with the heat blasting."

With a heave, Chelsey tossed the ball past the guest house and across the yard. The ball bounced twice before Jack snapped it out of the air and returned. As the dog set the tennis ball beside her sneakers, a branch snapped in the darkness. Jack tensed and spun toward the sound. It had come from a thin grove behind the Mournings' house, where the yard met the lake.

"Easy, Jack. It's just a deer."

But Chelsey didn't see a deer pawing through the trees. The sound didn't come again, and Jack pawed at the ball to coax Chelsey back to their game.

"One more, boy. Then we're going inside."

She studied the trees, her instincts warning her to call off the game and usher Jack inside. But all she saw was the lake shimmering with starlight and the trees throwing long shadows across the grass.

Jack took off running when the tennis ball left Chelsey's hand. Her body thrumming with tension, she threw the ball further than intended. It soared over the guest house, struck a rock, and ricocheted.

Toward the grove.

Jack hustled after the ball. But instead of snatching it between his jaws, the dog froze and stared into the trees. A growl rumbled out of his chest.

Chelsey stiffened. A dangerous animal might have wandered into the backyard. Without a leash, she had no way to pull Jack to the house if the dog refused to obey.

"Come, Jack."

He growled again. Even from the neighboring property, Chelsey could see the dog's fur standing on end.

She took a hesitant step forward and called again. Jack glanced back at her, then returned his gaze to the deep shadows. Leaves rustled. Something was hiding among the trees.

She'd left her gun in the bedroom. Not that she needed a weapon at the idyllic lakeside property.

Or maybe she did. Unwanted memories of a dead woman's headless corpse floating in the lake came unbidden to her. She hadn't been on scene when Thomas, then a deputy, had helped Sheriff Gray drag the murdered woman out of the water last year, but she'd seen the pictures and heard countless tales from those who'd witnessed the horror. Even paradise held unseen dangers.

"Please, Jack. Come to me."

Chelsey felt torn. She couldn't retreat to the house for the leash and gun and leave Jack alone. But until she had a means to force him to follow, the dog would defend the backyard from whatever lurked in the night.

Blowing out a breath, Chelsey crossed into the Mournings' yard. Her teeth refused to stop chattering, and her sweatshirt and jacket did little to ward off the cold. Each step brought her closer to the grove, closer to the unknown threat. When she was steps away, Jack looked over his shoulder and whined. The dog wanted Chelsey to retreat to the house. To safety.

"Not without you, boy. Never without you."

Chelsey had never met a dog as loyal as Jack. He was her child, in a way, and she his protector, as much as Jack defended her. Whatever evil awaited them in the darkness, Jack would not face it alone.

She reached for his collar. Just then, Jack leaped into the trees and disappeared. She ran after him, following his barks, which got cut off with a shrill yelp. Her shoulder struck a tree, and she spun past the trunk, heedless of the pain rocketing down her arm. Jack cried out again.

She stumbled over a log, fell, and pushed herself back to her feet, vaguely aware of her palms leaking blood. It sounded as though some animal larger and stronger than Jack—if that was possible—had sunk its fangs into the dog, refusing to let go.

Tires screeched down the lake road. She turned back in time to see a dark-colored pickup speed away. Urban Hammond's truck?

Right now, she didn't care about Hammond. She only wanted to locate Jack, who kept screeching and yelping somewhere beyond her vision. Bramble, the size of miniature knives, ripped her skin and shredded her clothes. She pushed on and struggled through the prickers.

Steps from the shore, she found Jack. He'd bounded into the deadly bushes and tangled himself in bramble. Thorns punctured the dog's fur and drew red, angry slashes from his neck to his belly and legs. The dog struggled to reach her, crying as the bramble's teeth sank deeper.

"Don't move, Jack. I know it hurts. I'll get you out of there."

Ignoring the thorns, Chelsey wrapped her hands around the canes and twisted them until they snapped. The razor-sharp points cut into her palms. In the summer, the wild blackberry canes produced a bounty of sweet fruit. Now the canes were serrated blades that tore flesh.

After she pulled the bramble off Jack, the dog crawled up to a standing position. That's when Chelsey spotted a darker blotch amid the shadows, an item someone had left behind. This is what Jack had pursued.

A ski mask.

And Chelsey would have bet anything that it belonged to Urban Hammond.

20

By midmorning Friday, Chelsey should have been looking forward to the weekend. But the missing person's case was heating up, and she assumed work would keep her busy through the forthcoming days. Inside the office at Wolf Lake Consulting, she hovered over her computer and used the forefingers of each hand to type. With her palms covered by gauze, it was the best she could do.

"You're making me hurt just watching you," Raven said over the rim of her coffee mug. "Why don't you dictate and let me type?"

"I'll tough it out. The pain isn't as bad as it was when I woke up. It didn't help that Thomas dumped half a bottle of iodine on my hands."

"Ouch."

"Yeah, he tripped over Tigger and spilled the iodine over my wounds. I may have cursed once or twice."

"I'll wager it was more than twice."

"You'd win that bet," Chelsey said.

"And Jack? How's he doing?"

Chelsey winced as she remembered the hot slashes across

the dog's coat. She and Thomas had coaxed Jack into the truck last evening and driven him to the veterinarian.

"By some stroke of luck, only one wound needed stitching. Jack will be sore for a few days, but the doctor expects he'll be up and running by Monday. He has to wear the cone of shame until the stitches come out."

"Jack must be thrilled."

"He's a holy terror with that thing around his neck, always bumping into furniture and knocking stuff onto the floor. Tigger runs for the hills when he sees Jack coming."

"Do you think the ski mask belonged to Urban Hammond?"

"No way to tell," Chelsey said. "But watch your back until Hammond winds up in jail. Thomas thinks he might go after us for rescuing Holly. And since Hammond works at the hardware store Karley visited last week, we can't rule him out as her kidnapper."

"Does that make sense? He's into underage girls, or so it seems."

"Guys like Hammond are equal-opportunity offenders. But I share your concern. The hardware store purchase might be coincidental. I can't allow recency bias to influence my opinion. Still, be on the lookout for Hammond."

"After you told us what happened, Darren checked the security cameras at the state park and ensured the feeds were working. If Hammond shows his face, we'll catch him."

"I hope so. This afternoon I'm meeting Deputy Lambert at Lakefront Hardware."

"Where Hammond works?"

"Right. You're welcome to join me."

"As long as I finish filing my case files, I'm down."

The front door opened in the hallway, and Chelsey glanced up. "Did LeVar get out of class early?"

Raven swung her eyes to the window. "His car isn't in the parking lot. Maybe a new client?"

Scout turned the corner, out of breath and red-cheeked. The girl wore sneakers, a sweatshirt, and a beige skirt that touched her knees. Her hair was tied back in a ponytail.

"What are you doing here?" Chelsey asked. "School doesn't release for another five hours."

"Water main break. The basement flooded, and the administrators sent everyone home."

"Bonus," said Raven. "You scored a long weekend. Did you run all the way here?"

Panting, Scout wiped her forehead with her sleeve. "Pretty much."

"Gee, I know some students love their internships, but they don't sprint across town to get there."

"You'll be happy I did."

"Oh?"

"I figured out where Karley Weir stopped on her way to Syracuse."

Chelsey pushed her chair back from her computer. "How did you accomplish that feat?"

Scout dropped her book bag on the corner desk and signed on to her workstation. "During study hall this morning, I kinda researched Karley's social media activity."

"Kinda? Scout, you need to focus on your courses while you're in school."

"I do, but since I'm caught up on homework and don't have any tests coming up, I wanted to work on the case."

"All right, but don't let your teachers catch you investigating."

"I won't."

Raven frowned. "Didn't you say Karley Weir protected her social media accounts and kept her profiles private?"

"Yes, but she comments on her friends' pages, and some of those are open to the public." Scout typed on her keyboard and connected her own laptop to the workstation with a USB cable. "Check it out."

Raven and Chelsey wheeled their chairs behind Scout.

"At four o'clock, Karley's friend Janice posted about the concert in Syracuse and asked if anyone else was going. Fifteen minutes before six, Karley responded with this picture."

Scout clicked on the image, in which Karley Weir, wearing a black Twenty-One Pilots T-shirt and blue jeans, stood in what appeared to be a grocery market aisle. The post read, *Got tickets in section B, row three. Can't wait. Hope to see you there!*

Scout gestured at the image. "Notice the pre-made sandwiches in the background?"

"I see loaves of bread to the left," Chelsey said, pointing at the picture. "That's a supermarket, for sure. The question is, which one?"

"That's where I come in. Remember when I used EXIF data to prove serial killer Jeremy Hyde lived in Nightshade County?"

"EXIF data lists the approximate location where the picture was taken," Raven said. "Is that correct?"

"That's right. Though I could only narrow the coordinates down to a two-mile radius, there's only one grocery store inside that circle." Scout called up a map. "Right here. The supermarket off CR-26."

"This is huge," Chelsey said. "Now we know where Karley stopped on her way to Syracuse."

Raven nodded. "Cross your fingers and hope the store cameras picked her up."

"And if anyone followed her, we'll catch the kidnapper on camera."

21

Thomas set the phone down and snapped his fingers. "We just got our first break in the search for Karley Weir."

Deputy Aguilar poked her head inside the sheriff's office. "What break?"

"Scout Mourning and Wolf Lake Consulting came through again. Karley posted an image on a friend's social media page. She took the picture inside the supermarket on CR-26."

"Is the picture from the evening she vanished?"

"Definitely."

"Want me to drive?"

"Sounds good."

For the first time since Lance Weir had reported his wife missing, Thomas was closing in on Karley. More than ever, he believed someone had abducted the woman. But who? Only three suspects came to mind—Urban Hammond, Wallace Bryant, and Karley's husband—and he'd yet to discover evidence implicating any of those men. In the lot behind the station, Thomas hopped into the passenger seat. Aguilar turned the cruiser toward County Route 26.

"The supermarket is about twenty minutes outside of the village," he said.

Sunlight streaked across the windshield; Aguilar lowered the visor. "Isn't that close to where Lambert and LeVar saved me from Simone?"

Thomas chewed his lip. He hoped the proximity wouldn't conjure ghosts for his lead deputy.

"That was about two miles west of the store. Aguilar, if you want me to drive, just say the word. This can't be easy for you."

"The location doesn't bother me. Simone did what she did, and I won't let everything remind me of the abduction."

Aguilar had experienced too much hardship over the last year. Thomas admired her resiliency, but he wanted to ensure she was keeping up with her therapy sessions. He wouldn't allow her to shut down, like she had after she shot and killed a corrupt police officer. The same officer had almost killed Thomas by pushing him into a ravine.

Like a smile that didn't reach the eyes, the bright sunshine belied the chill in the air. The weather forecast called for a high temperature of fifty degrees today, cool for September. A frost warning was in effect for tonight. Preferring to ride with fresh air streaming into the cruiser, Thomas kept the windows closed this morning, at least until temperatures climbed out of the forties. The brisk north wind rattled the vehicle as they left the village limits.

A crowded parking lot greeted Thomas and Aguilar when they arrived. Signs with sale prices filled the glass frontage of the supermarket entryway. Thomas paused and let a worker push a train of shopping carts into the corral. Inside, long lines of shoppers stretched into the store from every checkout counter. It seemed all of Nightshade County had chosen to purchase groceries today. Aguilar's jaw dropped.

"First time here?" Thomas asked.

"Yup. Last time too. I don't mind a crowd while I shop, but this is worse than Grand Central during the holidays." She swiveled her head left and right. "Which way to the manager's office?"

Thomas rose on tiptoes and pointed. "That way. Past the restrooms."

Aguilar dodged a harried man shoving an overflowing cart. The deputy looked back at Thomas. "If he drives his car like that, I'm ticketing him."

The manager's office stood behind the customer service and return counter. Better yet, the complaint counter, judging by the number of unhappy people waiting to voice their displeasure over a defective product. A woman with a sharp nose glared at Thomas and Aguilar when they skipped the line, as if their uniforms didn't matter.

Oswald Cummings, store manager, was a skinny man with a thick mustache. Sweat stains marred the underarms of his white shirt, and the threadbare tie hanging around his neck flopped like the tongue of a dehydrated animal. Cummings led Thomas and Aguilar into his office and showed them the computer, where he stored the security recordings. A hint of onion-like body odor tainted the tight confines, enough to make Aguilar wrinkle her nose.

"You said Tuesday between five-thirty and six?" Cummings asked.

"Correct," Thomas said.

The manager moved aside and gave the sheriff directions. Thomas listened politely, though he'd worked with similar software packages many times and was already familiar with the controls.

It didn't take long for Thomas to locate Karley Weir on the security feed. At fifteen minutes to six, just as the EXIF data suggested, Karley wandered into the bread aisle and posed for a picture in front of the sandwiches. The store appeared far less crowded than it was now, making it easy to pick out the missing woman's face.

"Scroll back," Aguilar said. "Follow her to the store entrance."

Thomas reversed the footage. He lost Karley in the current view but picked her up on another camera. Four separate views tracked her progress from the entryway to the bread aisle. He slowed the footage after she first entered the store.

"There's someone behind her," Thomas said when a shopping cart trailed Karley. The cart, pushed by an elderly woman, turned and headed up an aisle. "False alarm. That's not our kidnapper."

Together, Thomas and Aguilar followed Karley's progress through the store, reversed the footage, and watched again.

"If anyone stalked her through the store, he kept his distance so he didn't raise alarm," said Aguilar.

"Maybe he didn't enter the store. He might have grabbed Karley in the parking lot. Let's see if the cameras picked her up outside."

In the recording, Karley stopped at the checkout counter closest to the exit. She set a sandwich on the conveyor belt and gazed at the magazine covers. The clerk who waited on her appeared to be a teenager. As Thomas and Aguilar viewed the recording, the clerk talked Karley's ear off, almost seeming to flirt. After paying, Karley carried the sandwich through the automatic doors. Thomas switched views to an exterior camera positioned over the exit, studying Karley as she waited for traffic to pass.

"Come on, come on," said Thomas, willing the kidnapper to show his face. A second later, she disappeared from view. "Grab that manager. We need a different view of the parking lot."

Cummings returned and apologized. This was the only view

outside the store. The cameras covered the first ten rows of traffic, leaving a massive blind spot across the rest of the lot.

Thomas stopped the footage at the point Karley made her purchase. "Who waited on her at the checkout counter?"

The manager leaned toward the screen. "That's Kevin Mardonis."

"When does Mardonis work again? I'd like to speak with him."

"He's here now, bagging groceries at the front of the store."

"Can I print a still frame of this picture?"

"Of course." Cummings called up a menu, clicked the mouse, and an ancient-looking printer hummed to life in the corner.

Thomas and Aguilar found Mardonis as he loaded a cart with groceries. He was tall and gangling, his face pockmarked with acne scars. The scruff of a failed beard bristled on his cheeks. Cummings motioned for another worker to fill in for Mardonis.

"Do you remember this woman?" Thomas asked, handing Mardonis the printout. "She walked through your checkout line late Tuesday afternoon."

Mardonis held the photo up to his face. "I remember her. She bought one item. A sub or sandwich, I think."

"Anything stand out?"

"Nothing, except she paid cash. Everyone pays with a credit card nowadays, even for small purchases."

"You spent a long time chatting with her."

The teenager rolled his eyes. "She was the only person in line. After I saw her T-shirt, I asked if she was going to the show. I was just being friendly."

"Did you notice anyone following her, or did she complain that someone had bothered her in the store?"

"No, but I expect she'd complain to the customer service department, not the person bagging her groceries."

"How long have you worked here, Mr. Mardonis?" asked Aguilar.

He lifted a shoulder. "A little over eight months. I graduated from Kane Grove High, and now I'm a freshman at the community college."

"Do you live at home?"

"Yeah, why?"

"Just curious."

After speaking with Mardonis, Thomas and Aguilar returned to the cruiser.

"You don't believe that teenager is involved, do you?" Thomas asked.

"He lives at home. If Mardonis locked a woman inside his basement, his parents would ask questions."

"We're assuming Karley was kidnapped and not killed."

"Let's assume Mardonis is a cold-blooded killer and buried Karley in the middle of nowhere. How did he catch up to her? The security footage proves he was still working when she exited the building."

"True."

"It feels like we're spinning our wheels. What did we accomplish this morning?"

"We confirmed Karley visited the store," said Thomas as he unlocked the vehicle. "And we narrowed down the time Karley vanished."

"Do you think she stopped again?"

Thomas shook his head. "I don't. My guess is she intended to drive straight to Syracuse and eat her sandwich on the way."

"So where did she disappear?"

"Here." Thomas's eyes moved across the lot, uncovered by the security cameras. "Someone grabbed Karley before she left.

Unless we're dealing with a random attack, it must have been someone who knew Karley's plans. He could have followed her to the store and waited near her car, aware the security cameras didn't cover the rear of the lot."

"A local."

"That's my assumption."

Aguilar buckled her seatbelt. "Lance Weir knew Karley's plans."

But how could they prove Lance Weir had abducted his wife?

22

The man secured the storm door on the house. After months of keeping his home cool, he needed to conserve heat. With the wind pushing against the outer walls, it wouldn't be long before the furnace turned on. Even in rural New York, where winter lasted five months and summer passed in the blink of an eye, it was unusual for the weather to turn this cold in September. If today's temperature was any sign, it would be a never-ending, brutal winter.

Which sent quivers of anticipation through his body. He pictured snow piled against the house, a frigid gale whistling over the roof, a comforting blaze in the fireplace to drive back the chill. It would just be him and Karley. By winter, she'd accept her fate and return his affection. No longer would he worry about her escaping. She'd stay because she loved him as much as he did her. They would be a proper couple, a family.

For now, the man remained watchful. He tested the locks and drew the curtains over the window. Today, for the first time since he'd brought Karley into her new home, he would invite her upstairs. If she behaved, he might allow her to sit in the kitchen while he prepared dinner. It was important that she saw he was human, capable of empathy and affection. Sharing time together would quicken the process and chip away at the ice between them.

The digital camera lay on the kitchen counter. He couldn't wait to view the pictures he'd taken. Per his demands, Karley had submitted to him as he knew she would. Anytime he wished, whether at work, alone in the living room, or in bed, he could relive the moment. She'd learned more quickly than Alena. Good for Karley. Severe punishment awaited any woman who refused his advances. For too long, people had seen him as weak, impotent, incapable of pleasing a woman. No longer.

As he removed cold cuts and vegetables from the refrigerator, he hummed to himself. Every hour, Karley drew closer to him. She was the only woman he wanted.

It tore him apart that he needed to wear the stocking when he visited Karley. It was too soon to reveal his identity. The recognition might shock the woman and send her scurrying back into her shell, breaking the bond he'd worked so hard to build.

Better to gain the woman's trust and prove he meant no harm. Then, and only then, would it be safe to remove the stocking in her presence.

He set two slices of bread on a plate and loaded them with sandwich meat. On one piece of bread, he slathered honey mustard, then topped the cold cuts with lettuce and tomato. It was important that Karley consume nutritious foods. A healthy body equaled a healthy mind. Beside the sandwich, he shook a handful of pretzels out of the bag and added carrot sticks.

Before he picked up the plate, he considered his next move. Should he feed Karley and build trust, or force her to please him in exchange for lunch? His heart told him to show kindness. Yet his brain had other ideas. The more power he held over her, the faster she'd surrender.

Yes, he'd allow Karley to eat after she made love to him. A long time had passed since she'd last consumed food. She must be starving. Hungry enough to do anything he asked.

He almost forgot the stocking before he entered the basement. Setting the plate on the kitchen table, he searched his pockets and dragged the stocking over his head, turning his vision hazy, as though he viewed the world through a fogged window. The fabric made his face itchy and pulled his cheeks taut. As uncomfortable as the stocking was, it was a necessity. For now. Until she learned her place.

The stocking served an alternative purpose—invoking terror. Fear of the unknown. As long as he concealed his identity, Karley wouldn't know who he was, and her mind would fill in the shadowed details. The old saying in horror movies held true: the less you showed the monster, the scarier it became.

Picking up the sandwich, he turned for the door and stopped. A prickle of worry ran down his back.

What if she was on the other side of the door, waiting for him?

He'd removed from the basement anything she might use as a weapon. Still, he remained cautious. A cornered animal turned vicious and fought with desperate aggression. With his ear pressed against the door, he listened.

Nothing.

He moved his hand to the lock and contemplated snapping it open. A few weeks ago, Alena had hidden on the top step leading up from the basement and slammed the door into his face after he'd released the lock. That indiscretion earned Alena a beating. The next night, he'd admitted the awful truth—Alena would never love him. So he strangled the woman and dragged her into his vehicle, then carried her limp body through the woods until he located the pond. She would never disobey him again.

The man stood back when he unlocked the door. It didn't fly open and strike him. With a cautious hand, he opened the door, which creaked and groaned like old bones rising from the grave. The stairs were empty. If Karley planned an ambush, she was nowhere in sight.

By now, she must have heard the door. He stepped quietly down the stairs, her lunch balanced on one hand, the other hand drifting to the knife in his pocket.

When he reached the bottom, he spied Karley on the futon. She curled in a ball, shivering, despite the comfortable temperature inside the basement. The woman faced the far wall, her back to him. Without disturbing his true love, he placed the food on the floor beside the futon.

He sat on the edge of the cushion and moved a hand across her shoulder. At his touch, she quivered and drew her knees to her chest. The man stroked her hair and whispered that he meant her no harm. She was safe here.

Suddenly awake, she spun around and cried out. He muffled her scream with the palm of his hand.

"I brought you food, my dear." He picked up the plate and showed it to her before removing his hand from her mouth. "I'm sure you're hungry. Would you like lunch? It's a beautiful day. Cool but sunny. One day, when you're ready, you'll join me outside. The forest lies at the edge of our property. We can explore nature together."

Karley gritted her teeth. "That will never happen. You expect us to fall in love?"

"We will. I've cared for you since you arrived in my home . . . our home. Never would I dream of harming you."

"You're a coward who kidnaps women in parking lots. Remove the stocking. Show me who you really are. If you dare."

The man released a frustrated sigh. This wasn't going as he'd planned. Why did she insist on fighting him?

"Coward!" she yelled.

Anger blazed inside his chest. The backhanded slap knocked Karley's neck sideways. He wasn't aware he'd lost control and struck her until she started sobbing. Breath flew in and out of his lungs. It wasn't right to strike the woman he loved. But she frustrated him so.

Instead of cowering, Karley twisted her mouth in fury. Before he reacted, she slapped him back, twisting his head around. A moment after, she realized what she'd done and slunk into the corner, putting as much space as she could between them.

He could have strangled the life out of her as he'd done to Alena. Not yet. Not until he exhausted every option. Through the stocking, he smiled.

"You need to learn your place," he said, grasping her ankle.

She kicked free, but he grabbed the ankle again and dragged her into the middle of the bed. As Karley thrashed, he pressed the love of his life to her back and grinned into her horrified eyes.

"You will please me, Karley. Either that, or you will die."

23

Set on the eastern edge of downtown Wolf Lake, Lakefront Hardware occupied a two-story red-brick building with glass doors. The store was a throwback to the Ma and Pa hardware retailers that once existed in every village before the big box retailers moved in and ran their small business competitors into the ground. A bell over the door jingled when Chelsey and Raven followed Deputy Lambert inside. Chelsey's gaze moved to the paint cans taking up the wall to their left. The guest room in the A-frame needed a fresh coat of paint.

Herman Armstrong, proprietor of Lakefront Hardware, had a sun-bronzed complexion. He wore faded blue jeans and a red flannel shirt, a slight stoop to his back. Armstrong had owned the store since Chelsey was a child, and she recalled visiting with her parents frequently, even purchasing sparklers for the Fourth of July.

"No, Urban Hammond no longer works here," Armstrong said in answer to Lambert. "After I found out what he'd been up to, I fired the bastard. Why you let him out of jail, I'll never understand."

"How long did Mr. Hammond work for Lakefront Hardware?" asked Lambert.

"About two years."

"You were aware of his assault record when you hired him?"

Armstrong straightened his back. "I believe in giving people second chances, Deputy. What he did in Florida, striking that police officer, troubled me. But he seemed to have changed his ways. Prison has a way of doing that to a man. My brother-in-law ran afoul of the law some years back. Started a fight in a bar, and in the middle of the melee, he kicked an officer, who tried to pull the brawlers apart. He wasn't an evil man. People make mistakes. Perhaps I saw some of my brother-in-law in Hammond." The store owner narrowed his eyes. "But housing an underage runaway . . . that's unforgivable. Parents bring their children into my store. I can't have a man like Urban Hammond working for me."

"A woman visited your store last Wednesday. Karley Weir. I brought a photograph to jog your memory."

Before Lambert placed the photograph on the glass counter, Armstrong held up a hand.

"I know Mrs. Weir well. She visits often, and I recall her coming in last week."

"Do you remember what she purchased?"

"A leaf blower." Armstrong's eyes flicked to a stray newspaper blowing across the sidewalk. "Can't blame her. The leaves will fall any day if this weather is any indication. Mrs. Weir stopped in over the summer and asked me to look at her lawn mower. Not sure how she managed to lug the mower into her car. I assume her husband lent a hand for once. Good-for-nothing loaf."

"I take it you don't think highly of Lance Weir?"

"Any man who sits on his backside while his wife does all

the yard work isn't worth keeping around. But I'm an old man, and times change. Maybe I can't let go of the way things were."

"Was Urban Hammond working last Wednesday when Mrs. Weir visited?"

"I believe so. Let me check." Armstrong pulled a dogeared ledger from beneath the counter and ran a crusty fingertip down the page. "Hammond worked from ten until six. If memory serves, Weir purchased the leaf blower around four-thirty."

"Did Hammond have any interaction with Mrs. Weir?" Chelsey asked.

"He walked her to the back, where we keep the lawn equipment. Helped her pick out a model."

"Did he show an unusual interest in Weir?"

"Not that I recall. Why all the questions about Mrs. Weir?"

"She's missing," Lambert said.

"Missing? Are you suggesting Hammond took her?"

"We're exploring all possibilities."

Armstrong set his forearms on the counter and leaned toward them.

"Here's what I say. Mrs. Weir finally got sick of her husband and left town. That's what I would do were I in her situation. No sense slaving away for a husband who never appreciated her."

24

Inside the office at Wolf Lake Consulting, LeVar Hopkins stared through the window. The sky took on a bruised appearance, the darkness spreading out of the east like a vampire's cape, a chilling reminder of how long the nights were becoming. A gust of wind spilled icy air through the drafty window, making LeVar rub the cold off his arms.

His day wouldn't end until he closed out a background check he'd helped Raven complete for a law firm in Auburn. Putting the task off for another day wasn't an option. He worked weekend shifts as a deputy with the Nightshade County Sheriff's Department and wouldn't have time to file the paperwork for the background check during the next two days. Besides, the Karley Weir investigation held his interest, and he hoped Scout could find a connection between Weir and Alena Robinson.

Chelsey and Raven were gone for the day, leaving the interns alone in the office. At her computer, Scout clicked through Alena Robinson's Facebook profile, which remained open to the public.

"Any link between Alena and Karley?" LeVar asked.

"Nothing. Usually, I expect to find a shared friend or relative, a place the two missing people visited, but so far I keep striking out. Maybe these women have nothing in common."

"That could be the case," said LeVar, propping himself on the edge of Scout's desk. "We can't even prove either woman was kidnapped, let alone that the same man grabbed both."

"Yet it's curious. Two women, roughly the same age, both pretty, vanishing a few weeks apart. They didn't live far from each other."

"Alena Robinson is from the suburbs outside Syracuse, right?"

"Yes, about a forty-five-minute drive from Wolf Lake."

LeVar scratched his chin. Alena Robinson had been missing for too long. If she turned up in the future, there wouldn't be a happy ending.

The ancient furnace did little to drive back the chill. Wind rattled the glass, and Scout cupped her elbows with her hands.

"You as cold as I am?" he asked.

"I'm freezing."

"No sense suffering if we end up working another two or three hours. Chelsey keeps extra clothes in the bedroom, including sweatshirts. I say we pick out a pair and drag the space heater out of the closet."

"That's the best idea you've come up with all day, LeVar."

In the bedroom at the end of the hall, LeVar clicked the wall switch and spread light into the gloomy interior. He pawed through the dresser. Not finding what he sought, he opened the closet and discovered five hooded sweatshirts dangling from hangers. He snatched a size large gray sweatshirt with *Lake Ontario* written across the front and tossed it to Scout. For himself, he chose an extra-large Syracuse University sweatshirt and pulled it over his head.

"That's a good look on you," Scout said. "But I always pictured you as Ivy League."

"At least it fits."

As Scout adjusted the sleeves, which dangled past her fingers, she eyed LeVar.

"You know, if people find out we're working alone again, they might ask questions."

During the Simone Axtell investigation, Darren and Raven had advised LeVar and Scout to remain aware of perceptions. Though LeVar was much older than his fifteen-year-old friend, the time they spent together often gave others the wrong impression.

"I was just thinking the same thing."

"My mom knows I'm here."

"You told her Chelsey and Raven left for the day?"

"Yup."

"Then we should be fine. Either way, I'll text Chelsey and let her know the situation."

Despite the age difference, LeVar considered Scout as close a friend as he'd ever had, and he didn't wish to complicate their relationship.

LeVar searched the hallway closet and located the space heater, buried beneath a drop cloth and a vacuum cleaner hose that looked like a boa constrictor in the dark. He carried the heater under one arm and set it in the office between his desk and Scout's. After he plugged the cord into the wall, the vents swiveled left and right, spreading heat to both workstations.

"That's better," Scout said, turning her attention to the computer monitor.

"Chelsey needs to replace the windows. The January heating bill must be extraordinary." He rolled his chair to Scout's desk. "What do we know about Alena Robinson?"

"Nothing new on Alena's social media accounts. She disappeared eighteen days ago. As we already learned, the police found her wallet and cell phone in a ditch one mile outside of Syracuse."

"Karley Weir was heading to Syracuse for a concert. Coincidence?"

"Tough to say."

LeVar rocked back in his chair. "Concert goers park at the field house outside the city. But Alena lived seven miles in the opposite direction. Karley wouldn't have passed Alena's house on her way to meet her friends. The kidnapper—if one exists—might be opportunistic. It's possible he randomly came across Alena and Karley. They fit his preferred type, so he snatched them."

"Or he met them through a business relationship. Karley worked for a federal credit union. She met people every day. As for Alena—"

The phone stopped Scout and caused both to jump. Amid the otherwise quiet confines of the empty office, the ringing sounded deafening. LeVar read the screen.

"That's Chelsey." He pressed the button. "Hey, it's LeVar. You're on speaker with Scout."

Thomas's voice called out in the background. A truck door slammed, and LeVar heard a motor roar.

"I'm leaving with Thomas right now," Chelsey said, sounding as though she was running.

"What's wrong? Did something come up in the Karley Weir investigation?"

"Hurry, Chelsey," Thomas said. "We need to go."

"A fisherman found a dead body floating in a pond outside Wolf Lake," Chelsey said. "We're driving there now."

"Is it Karley?"

"It's a woman. That's all we know. I'll call as soon as we learn more."

A somber pall fell over the office. Suddenly, the darkness at the window felt dangerous, volatile.

Scout pushed her hair back. "We might not be dealing with a kidnapper, after all."

"You're right," said LeVar. "Now we're searching for a murderer."

25

Night hurtled at the window as Thomas pressed the gas pedal, hoping to make up for lost time. In the passenger seat, Chelsey spoke with Raven and Darren, who drove behind them. Deputy Lambert was five minutes ahead of Thomas and already at the turnoff, where the fisherman waited for the authorities to arrive.

Since learning of Karley Weir's disappearance, Thomas had dreaded this moment. Now he was chasing a killer, a madman who preyed upon the innocent.

The flashing lights of Lambert's cruiser spun reds and blues across the county road when Thomas stopped the F-150. A forty-something bearded man wearing an orange hunting vest stood with his hands in his pockets, answering the deputy's questions.

The chill hit Thomas when he opened the door. He hoped the lining of his sheriff's jacket would keep him warm during their climb into the forest. With Chelsey at his side, he joined Lambert. Darren and Raven hurried to catch up.

"This is Troy Stover," Lambert said. "He called in the body."

Stover shifted his feet. The fisherman's eyes darted to the

forest, as though monsters stalked through the dark. When he spoke, his voice quivered.

"I still can't believe it."

"Tell the sheriff what you told me."

The fisherman nodded, unable to hold eye contact. He rubbed the back of his neck.

"I drove out after dinner. There's a pond at the top of the ridge, about a twenty-minute walk through the woods if you know the way. Better fishing than at the lake. Much quieter."

"What time did you reach the pond, Mr. Stover?" asked Thomas.

"Six thirty, give or take ten minutes. It's a hard climb, but once you've done it a few times, you figure out where to go. At first, I didn't see anything in the pond on account of the cattails and weeds along the edge. I cast my line out. Half considered putting on waders and walking out several feet, but it's been so cool lately, and the wind had a bite to it. So I tossed the line into the water and enjoyed the tranquility. That's why people come out this way. To get away from the noise."

"When did you notice the body?"

"Not for a good fifteen minutes. Once the fish started biting, I reeled in my line. Had a big one on the other end, but I lost him because the line caught on something. I assumed it was a log or a clump of weeds, but as I struggled to bring in the line, I saw something floating on the surface. That's when I stepped around the cattails and saw her. A woman. Face down in the water, her hair all fanned out." Stover shuddered. "I tried to call your department, but my cell coverage sucks out here, and my plan isn't worth the paper it's printed on. It took me until I was halfway down the hill before the call connected."

"Was there anybody else in the forest?"

"No."

"Any vehicles parked along the road?"

"Just mine. But that woman . . . she's been in the water for days."

"How can you be sure?"

"You'll see. I'm no doctor, but a body doesn't change that much overnight."

"Mr. Stover," Chelsey said, "when was the last time you visited the pond before this evening?"

"Summer. Probably back in July."

"In July, did you come across anyone in the woods or at the pond? Someone who didn't look like they belonged?"

"Nobody. Again, that's why people fish here. It's quiet. You might go years before you run into another fisherman."

Thomas took Stover's information. The stars were sharp, and the cold deepened by the second. It would be a long night.

After Lambert released Stover, the deputy said, "The medical examiner and her assistant are on the way. I doubt Claire knows the way up to the pond. Someone should stay behind and lead her."

"Are you volunteering?" Thomas asked.

"As long as you can find your way without me." Lambert pointed at two pine trees jutting above their neighbors. "Head in that direction. About a hundred yards past those trees, you'll hear the creek. Follow the water up the mountain until the land levels out. That's where the pond is."

"I have a rough idea of the location," Darren added. "Been a few years since I came out this way, but I'm sure I can find it."

Lambert nodded. "I'll catch up after the medical examiner arrives."

Darren took the lead with Thomas. Raven and Chelsey followed a few steps behind.

"Everyone, stay together," Darren said over his shoulder. "Lose your way this time of night, and you'll wander until the sun rises."

"Are there animals I need to worry about?" asked Raven.

"Mostly deer and foxes."

"Bear?"

"Not usually."

"But sometimes?"

"Just stay close."

They struggled up the hill, undergrowth snagging their legs and branches popping out of thin air to poke at their eyes.

"Are those the trees Lambert mentioned?" asked Thomas.

"Yeah. We're heading in the right direction."

After they passed the pines, the wind carried the sound of water cascading over rock. The land flattened, and Thomas noticed the air had thinned since the climb began. If it was chilly along the road, it was frigid atop the ridge. Thomas half-expected to find the pond frozen over.

"There it is," Chelsey said.

Moonlight reflected off the surface of the pond. As the fisherman had said, they needed to walk around the cattails and gain a clear view of the body.

"Oh my God," Raven said.

Thomas stopped in his tracks. Even with the body face down, he could see how pallid and bloated the woman's flesh had become. Some of her skin had rotted off, the insects and animals taking their share. The putrid scent of death reached Thomas's nostrils, and it was all he could do to hold his ground and not double over.

"She's in the middle of the pond," Darren said, setting his hands on his hips.

"No choice but to wade in," said Thomas. "I wish I'd brought water gear."

Thomas stepped toward the pond. Darren set a hand against his chest.

"What are you doing?" asked Darren.

"I'm going in."

"Not alone, you aren't."

"That pond can't be thirty yards across. No reason for both of us to soak our clothes."

"It's dark, and you don't know how quickly the bottom drops off."

Darren peeled off his coat and set it on the ground. Next, he worked the boots off his feet.

"You don't have to do this, Darren."

"Like hell I don't. You're not going into the water by yourself. It's too dangerous."

The sheriff stepped out of his shoes and handed his jacket to Chelsey.

She narrowed her eyes at him. "You two aren't really going through with this, are you?"

Thomas raised his palms. "She won't float back on her own. What choice do we have?"

"Grab a branch or something. Drag her in."

"When you find a branch as long as the pond, let me know. Until then, I'm going in."

Thomas and Darren wore gloves, though the sheriff doubted any trace evidence from the killer remained on the woman's decayed corpse. The cold took his breath away when he stepped into the water. Even if he pulled the body out of the pond, his clothes would be drenched, and he still needed to walk back to the truck. Darren grinned at him, the ranger's teeth chattering as Raven muttered something about fools drowning in the dark.

"Can't you call in a diving team?" Chelsey asked behind them.

"No time," Thomas said.

The women replied with expletives.

Thomas was close now. The corpse bobbed atop the scum-slick water, only a few steps away. He reached for the woman's leg, and suddenly the ground wasn't beneath his feet. He sank like a stone.

Murky black surrounded Thomas, engulfing his body, suffocating his lungs as an unseen force dragged him deeper, as though a whirlpool spun at the bottom of the pond.

His body twisted and thrashed until he didn't know which way was up. The water claimed him, dragging him down until his consciousness began to fade.

26

An invisible hand, hidden inside the viscous water, grabbed hold of Thomas's shirt collar. That hand supported the sheriff and prevented him from sinking deeper, giving him a sense of direction within the black pond. He could almost imagine the swamp thinning above his head, the sound of muffled, faraway voices calling his name, as if from inside a dream.

Thomas paddled upward and exploded out of the water, coughing and hacking. Darren held tight to the sheriff's arm and pulled him back from the underwater ledge.

"That's what I'm talking about," Darren said.

"How deep does this pond go?"

"Deep enough to drown you. Breathe. You all right?"

Thomas coughed again. "I am now."

Chelsey yelled something Thomas couldn't make out. Pond water clogged his ears and gushed from his nostrils like twin waterfalls.

"Hold my hand," Darren said, extending an arm.

Thomas felt where the bottom dropped off again. Using Darren for support, he floated toward the dead woman and grabbed her ankle. It was like wrapping his fingers around spoiled meat. Bits of flesh tore away in his hand, and again he wanted to vomit. The waterlogged cuff of her blue jeans gave him something to hold on to that didn't disintegrate. Trying not to breathe through his nose, he dragged the corpse as Darren pulled their combined weight across the pond.

When it was safe to walk again, Darren released Thomas's hand and helped the sheriff pull the woman out of the water. Chelsey and Raven were there to help them climb out.

Trees rustled in the dark. Panting from the cold, Thomas eyed the service weapon he'd left beside his shoes. A flashlight swept across the ridge.

"It's Lambert," Thomas said, shaking the water out of his hair.

Chelsey rounded on him. "Never do that again."

"I'm all right."

"Because Darren was there to save you. Thomas, you could have drowned."

Claire Brookins and her assistant followed Deputy Lambert into the clearing. Russet-haired and in her late twenties, Brookins had served as an assistant to longtime medical examiner Virgil Harbough before he retired. Everyone had expected she would take Harbough's place, and it was no surprise when she won the position. Unlike a county coroner—an appointed official who rarely had a medical background—Brookins was a medical examiner, holding multiple degrees with a background in forensic science.

She took one look at the victim's bloated, rotted flesh and covered her mouth. Somehow, the stench had increased twofold since the woman left the swamp.

"I need light," she said, kneeling over the body.

Her assistant, a college-age boy in bifocals, unclasped the

hinges on a silver case and removed a portable light, which he set on a tripod. He angled the beam over the body.

The first thing Thomas did was check the woman's pockets for identification.

"Nothing," he said. "If she had a wallet, it might be at the bottom of the pond or somewhere in the forest."

Brookins adjusted the light and studied the woman's upper body.

"Hemorrhages along the neck. I wouldn't have expected the bruising to remain so obvious given the state of decay."

"Strangulation?"

"That's my preliminary cause of death."

From a smaller case, she removed an electronic device Thomas hadn't seen since his days as a detective with the LAPD.

"I'll scan the vic's fingerprints," said Brookins.

"Can you figure out who she is?" Raven asked, leaning over Thomas's shoulder.

"That's what I'm about to find out."

Brookins tested the woman's index finger; the scanner didn't respond. When she switched to the ring finger, the device emitted a beep. The medical examiner grinned.

"Did you get an answer?" Chelsey asked.

"We're in luck. She's in the system." Brookins bent closer to the screen. "Alena Robinson. That name mean anything to you?"

"She went missing almost three weeks ago," Thomas said, scrunching his brow. "That explains why she doesn't have ID. Syracuse PD found her phone and wallet in a ditch outside the city limits."

"Someone strangled this woman and tossed her in the pond. When enough gas built up inside her body, she floated to the surface. That's why our fisherman found her."

"How long has she been in the water?"

"Definitely not three weeks. I'd estimate four to seven days, based on the state of decay and the amount of bloating. I might narrow it down in the lab." The medical examiner inserted a temperature probe and assessed the results. "The swamp is running colder than normal for this time of year. That affects the body temperature. But these readings confirm my estimate. She's been dead longer than three days, but not more than a week." Brookins shook her head. "The insects found her, and it looks like the fish and animals fed on the body. We need to get her back to the coroner's office."

Among the medical examiner's belongings were a body bag and a stretcher. So far from the road, there was no chance of driving an emergency vehicle to the pond. With no other choice, they'd carry the woman down the hill, a tall task at night in the forest.

After Brookins examined the scene, Lambert and Darren hefted the stretcher and carried the woman down the treacherous slope. Raven led the way with a flashlight. Without light, Thomas wasn't sure they could find their way back. The sheriff took turns carrying Alena, giving Lambert and Darren rest when they needed it. The cold plunged through his soaked clothing and froze his skin. Physical exertion was the only thing standing between Thomas and hypothermia.

Halfway down the slope, Chelsey called to Thomas and pointed at two indentations in the dirt. Setting the stretcher on the ground, Thomas and Lambert circled around Chelsey.

"Sneaker prints," Chelsey said. "Looks like a man's size nine or ten."

Thomas measured the print with an evidence marker and confirmed Chelsey's estimation. Someone with a size-ten sneaker had come this way in recent days.

"Those might belong to Stover," Lambert said.

"Maybe," Thomas said, shifting his jaw. He photographed

the print. "It hasn't rained all week, and the ground is hard-packed. I wouldn't expect to find many prints out this way."

"Sure they aren't ours?"

"Negative," said Darren. "We climbed through the forest a hundred yards east of here, closer to the creek."

Lambert slapped at a mosquito. "And we followed your path."

"It would take a lot of weight to leave sneaker prints on this soil."

"Which means we're searching for a heavy man."

Thomas shook his head. "More like someone carrying a dead body."

27

It was only a matter of time before the authorities found Alena. Yet the discovery sent shock waves through the man.

With Karley locked inside the basement and the feed from the security camera displayed on his phone, he drove through the night toward the turnoff, where he'd climbed through the forest and dumped his former lover into the pond. A police band radio informed him of the sheriff's progress. They'd located the body a little over an hour ago, and now they were carrying Alena back to the cruiser. After, they would transport her body to the county morgue for evaluation. That didn't worry him. He'd left no evidence behind. Nobody would trace Alena's murder back to him.

They were searching for a killer. Little did the sheriff and his team realize they were now the hunted.

When the man reached the intersection of CR-26 and the interstate, he doused the headlights and backed his truck behind a tree. The radio continued to crackle and squawk, giving him a play-by-play account of the happenings in the forest. The sheriff was almost to the cruiser. With the village of Wolf Lake down the interstate, they'd have to come this way.

The engine was off. Cricket songs rang around his truck as some winged, sticklike insect crawled across the windshield. He divided his attention between the security feed and the view down the road. Even with a light shining inside the basement, he couldn't see Karley unless she approached the window. Perhaps he should place a camera in the basement and spy on her at his leisure.

A deputy named Lambert announced over the radio that the team was en route to Wolf Lake and would arrive at the morgue in thirty minutes. The man didn't have to wait long before a faint glow blossomed in the distance, increasing until the train of headlights cut through the darkness, racing in his direction. Excitement rippled beneath his skin. The authorities didn't realize he was watching them.

From his hiding spot behind the tree, he waited until the cruiser took the ramp to the highway, followed by the medical examiner's van and two pickup trucks. The man recognized Sheriff Shepherd inside the trailing vehicle. A woman sat beside Shepherd in the cab.

A brief second to glimpse her face, then the Ford F-150 turned onto the highway.

Patience.

If the man followed too closely, he'd draw attention.

He waited until the taillights became bloody cat's eyes on the horizon before he turned the key in the ignition. Glancing in both directions, he eased his truck out of hiding, the tires scraping on stones until the front tires bucked over the shallow ditch and carried him onto the road.

Driving with his headlights off, he closed the distance. He could see their silhouettes inside the cab. The sheriff drove with one hand on the wheel. Nothing new had come through the radio since they'd reached the highway.

A little closer.

Just ahead of the two pickups, the medical examiner's van carried Alena's corpse. But not her soul. That was his to keep. Forever.

He wondered what the sheriff would see if he looked in the rearview mirror. The man's truck was an invisible predator in the night. Would Shepherd sense the man's presence, the way the gazelle does the lion before the killer bursts out of the tall grass?

Faster.

His imagination conjured a vivid image—his truck shooting out of the darkness and taking them by surprise. Smashing their bumpers would knock both pickups into the median at highway speeds, flipping them end over end. The van would be easy pickings. But there was still the cruiser to deal with. He'd spied Deputy Lambert earlier—a tall, strong man who would be difficult to overcome.

He pressed the accelerator until he traveled a quarter mile behind their vehicles. Murder the sheriff, and he'd eliminate the one person who might catch him.

His fingers tightened around the steering wheel, foot pushing harder on the pedal. He was really going to do this.

As the man crept up on the sheriff's pickup, his eyes flicked to movement on his phone.

Karley at the window. One hand grasping the bars and tugging, the other trying to snake between the bars and shatter the glass.

Impossible. Her forearm couldn't fit between the bars.

Could it?

Karley's insolence enraged him. She was trying to leave him, just like Alena.

Cursing, he slowed his truck and took the exit ramp, letting the sheriff and his friends live for now.

Tires screeched as he turned toward home.

He would make Karley pay.

28

Karley gritted her teeth and squeezed her arm between the bars.

Ignoring the pain, she pushed harder, her sweat acting like grease. A little farther. The window stood an inch from her fingertips.

Then what? Even if she shattered the glass, there was no getting past the bars. But she had to try. If she broke the window, the farmer would hear her screaming and send help.

Karley's arms trembled from exertion, her body tired and malnourished. She didn't trust the food the kidnapper fed her, nor the glass of water he left on the floor. She'd taken to drinking straight from the bathroom sink. Filling her gut with water quelled the hunger pangs for an hour or two, before her stomach realized she hadn't eaten all day.

The psycho had stormed out of the house an hour ago. Karley considered his pattern of coming and going. Often he left during the day and didn't return for eight to ten hours, suggesting he had a job. That didn't tell her much about his identity, though she felt certain she knew the man. He spoke like he'd known Karley for years. This evening, he'd cursed upstairs and slammed the door on the way out. Something was wrong.

Good. She hoped whatever had upset him would ruin his life. If there was any justice in the world, the kidnapper would crash his vehicle and burn in the wreckage.

Karley needed to hurry. No doubt the man was watching her on camera. If he caught her trying to escape, he'd beat and rape her. Or kill her. Then again, she would gladly choose death over another rape.

Her sneakers scraped up the wall for purchase. The treads lost traction as her strength gave out, and she tumbled backward and struck the concrete floor with her hip. Agony rocketed down her legs. She clutched her hip and bit back a sob, climbing back to her feet. There was no time for tears or pain.

Karley limped to the stairs and climbed the steps. When she reached the door, a chilling thought struck her. What if this was a test? Maybe the kidnapper had tricked Karley into believing he'd left. He might be on the other side of the door, a cruel grin curling his lips.

Yet she'd heard an engine outside and the crunch of gravel before his vehicle drove off.

She reared back and kicked the door with enough force to rattle every bone in her body. Her teeth clicked together.

The barrier held strong. He'd installed a reinforced door, anticipating his victims would bash themselves against it. How many women had he abducted? She slammed the heel of her foot against the door. It budged a fraction of an inch, just enough to keep hope alive.

"Someone help me!"

Karley pounded her fists against the door. When she regained her strength, she rammed her shoulder against the barrier.

She prepared to try again when the engine roared into the driveway. Her lips pulled back in a terrified rictus, and she backed down the stairs, head swiveling left and right, eyes searching for an escape hatch that didn't exist.

She was trapped. He must have seen her hanging from the window.

The entire house shook when the front door flew open. Footsteps pounded over the basement ceiling.

Karley eyed the bathroom. Even if she locked herself inside, the kidnapper owned a key.

He gave her no time to decide. The lock on the basement door snapped. Light from the kitchen flooded the stairway a moment before his sneakers stomped down the steps.

She turned toward the window. The kidnapper charged like a bull, the stocking flattening and distorting his face, making him appear even more monstrous. His hand caught her hair as she leaped for the bars. With a snap of his wrist, he yanked her back and tossed her onto the futon.

"I warned you," he growled. "What are the rules? You must never fight me or try to escape."

He slapped Karley, twisting her head around. Blood trickled from her nose.

"Do you wish to end up like Alena? Is that what you want?"

Karley drew her legs back when he threw the pictures across the cushion. Photographs of Alena, bound and stripped, eyes welling with panic.

"Look at her," he said.

Karley turned her head away. He grabbed her chin, forcing her to stare at the pictures.

"When I order you to do something, you do it. Never disobey me."

He threw a picture of Alena onto Karley's lap.

"I don't want to," Karley said, sobbing.

"Why? Are you jealous of what Alena and I had? She's beautiful, isn't she?" Karley closed her eyes. "Answer me!"

His shouts reverberated off the walls.

Karley nodded and wiped her eyes. "Yes, she's beautiful."

"*Was* beautiful. Before she betrayed me. Now look at her."

The madman tossed another picture at Karley. She turned her head away and he slapped her again, making her ears ring and hot pain shoot through her cheek.

Her eyes darted to the photograph for a split second, just long enough for her brain to interpret the haunting image. The life had fled Alena's open eyes. Something was wrong with the woman's neck.

"Do you want this to be your fate?" he asked.

"What did you do to her?"

"I gave the ungrateful whore what she deserved."

"You murdered her?"

His deranged laughter curdled Karley's flesh.

"You're mad," she said.

All at once, the face beneath the stocking contorted. The kidnapper's jaw clenched, and his hands clenched into fists.

"You will return my love, or you will die like Alena."

"Stop saying that. I'll never love you!"

The maniac snatched Karley's hair and forced her to face him.

"You defied me for the last time. I'll teach you to love and respect me."

Before she covered up, his fists rained down on her head and shoulders. The madman lost control, screaming as he punched her. Spittle wet the inside of the stocking. He was a rabid animal.

The kidnapper grabbed Karley and hurled her across the floor. She skidded toward the water heater, the concrete burning and scraping a layer of flesh off her back.

She lay panting, her body refusing to respond when she tried to scramble away. He stalked forward.

"Obey me."

As he raised another fist, Karley lost consciousness.

29

On Saturday morning, the warm, rich scent of freshly brewed coffee pervaded Wolf Lake Consulting. A full cup sat before Chelsey, who worked on her computer as she willed herself not to yawn. She hadn't returned home until after midnight, and nightmares had filled her sleep. Whenever Chelsey closed her eyes, she pictured Alena Robinson's swollen, chewed corpse, the milky-white flesh dangling off her body. The odor of death took up permanent residence in Chelsey's nose.

It had been an even longer night for Thomas. He'd had the unenviable task of notifying Alena's parents and did not return home until four in the morning. By seven thirty, he was hurrying to the office to catch the killer stalking Nightshade County.

Usually festive, the office carried a somber weight this morning. Scout and Raven worked at their workstations, the conversation muted. Even Jack and Tigger appeared lifeless. Jack lay on the floor with his head resting on his paws, sorrowful eyes following Chelsey across the office. The cone of shame made Jack appear even more pitiful, though his wounds were healing faster than Chelsey believed possible. Tigger curled in a ball in the corner, when typically he bounced from one desk to the next, purring until someone scratched behind his ears. Everyone had been so focused on finding Karley Weir that they'd given the Alena Robinson investigation only a cursory glance. The case had belonged to Syracuse PD—another county and someone else's responsibility. But the fisherman had found Alena's body in Nightshade County, a short drive from Wolf Lake. Now Thomas and his deputies were involved, and Chelsey's team would research a homicide, as well as Karley Weir's disappearance.

And they still couldn't prove the cases were related.

"Okay," Chelsey said, sighing. Raven and Scout looked up. "This isn't our fault, so we need to stop blaming ourselves and focus on finding who did this."

Scout bit her lip. The teenager continued to trace Alena's life through her social media profile. Chelsey hoped the girl didn't harbor guilt.

"It just seems like we could have done more," Scout said, lowering her eyes.

Raven bobbed her head in sullen agreement.

"Here are the facts," Chelsey said, ticking off the bullet points on each finger. "First, the two cases might have nothing to do with each other. Second, Alena Robinson's name only crossed our screens because she vanished a few weeks before Karley Weir. Until last night Syracuse PD had full jurisdiction over the investigation. Third, Claire Brookins says Alena died four to seven days ago, before Karley vanished and we got involved. There's nothing we could have done to save Alena. She died before our investigation began."

"It still hurts," Raven said, tossing a pen aside. "Besides, we know the cases are linked."

"It adds up," said Scout. "Let's say the murderer killed Alena on Monday. Then Tuesday evening, Karley Weir vanished while driving to a concert in Syracuse, close to where Alena lived."

"Circumstantial," Chelsey said, not because she doubted Scout or disagreed with the teenager's logic. She didn't want the members of her team to blame themselves.

"He tired of Alena, or she angered him somehow. So he strangled Alena and threw her body in a forest pond. But he needed a replacement. The next night, he kidnapped Karley."

"Allow me to play devil's advocate. We last saw Karley at the supermarket on County Route 26. Chances are she never made it to Syracuse. Plus, you found no overlap between their social media connections. We can't link Alena and Karley."

"But Scout's theory rings true," Raven said. "Karley replaced Alena. Similar ages and facial features. Even if the victims didn't know each other, it's likely the killer—and it's time we stop calling him a kidnapper—knew both women."

"Then how did *the killer* meet his victims? We compared their online connections and found nothing."

"Not everyone uses social media. Lance Weir doesn't."

"Okay. So maybe we're searching for an acquaintance who doesn't use Facebook, Twitter, and Instagram. What now?"

"Here's an idea," Raven said. "The killer disposed of Alena in a pond near Wolf Lake, close to where Karley lived. That tells me the killer is from Nightshade County, perhaps Wolf Lake."

"That's comforting," Scout said, rubbing the goosebumps off her arms.

"Unless he enjoys long commutes, that means he probably works nearby. We need to find business connections, not social."

"I'll get on board with that," Chelsey said.

Before Raven finished her thought, the door opened, and a pair of footsteps thudded down the hallway. LeVar, in full uniform, entered the office with Thomas.

"Saved by the bell," Raven said. "It's Sheriff Shepherd and the county's dapper new deputy."

"I can arrest you for taunting an officer of the law," said LeVar.

"That wouldn't hold up in court," Thomas said.

"Sit," Chelsey told them. "Especially you, Thomas. You slept less than I did."

"How did it go last night?" asked Raven.

Thomas fell into a chair and removed his hat, then pushed his hair back. "It was a nightmare. The detective working Alena's case joined me to notify the parents. The looks on their faces when we told them Alena was dead . . ."

"I'm sorry."

"It could have been worse. Don't ask me how they learned about the murder, but the press almost beat us to the scene. Two Syracuse PD officers needed to hold back the reporters. They wanted the parents' reactions, and we hadn't told them about Alena yet."

"It amazes me how callous the media acts when tragedy strikes. All they care about is being first with the story."

"Fortunately, we drove them off before they caused a scene. I made it back to the office at two. Then I filed the report."

"Did you eat breakfast?" Chelsey asked, concern creasing her forehead.

"I got something out of the machine at the office."

"The vending machine? No, that won't do. I'll make you something healthy."

"Chelsey, you don't have to."

She held up a hand, cutting off his protest. "I have a refrigerator full of food. How about an omelet? We're out of bread, but I can make—"

"Say no more," said Raven. "I'll run out and grab bagels at The Broken Yolk."

"You're doing too much," Thomas said. "Both of you."

"No sense arguing, Thomas," Scout said. "She cooks the best omelets in the county."

Thomas threw up his hands. "Fine."

Raven removed her wallet from her desk and hurried out of the office.

"What about you, LeVar?" Chelsey asked. "I've never known you to turn down breakfast."

"I ate before work," said LeVar.

"And you're probably hungry again."

"Not gonna lie. I'll never say no to an extra breakfast."

Chelsey whipped up two omelets and served them to Thomas and LeVar, who ate inside the office while the others worked.

Sipping coffee, Chelsey called up Alena Robinson's background file. "Alena worked as a workers' compensation adjuster in Syracuse. City Confidential. It's a non-profit organization."

"Any chance someone at Bryant Media Group filed a claim?" LeVar asked, sawing through the omelet with a fork.

"Good question."

Scout's fingers flew across her keyboard. "I'll check." A few mouse clicks later, a list of claims filled the teenager's monitor. "I got a hit."

Thomas set his plate down and read the screen over Scout's shoulder. "How long ago?"

"Last November. The claim went through City Confidential."

"Who handled the claim?"

"Hold on." Scout opened the report and scanned the details. "Oh, wow. Alena Robinson."

"Did the employee win?" asked Chelsey, pulling up a chair.

"The claimant received a payout if that's what you mean." Scout lifted an eyebrow. "The case took two or three times longer than normal. It appears Wallace Bryant fought it tooth and nail. We don't have access to the claimant's name."

"So much for Bryant putting his employees first," Thomas said.

"We already established Wallace Bryant knew Karley Weir through her husband," LeVar said, folding his hands over a stuffed belly. "This proves he also met Alena Robinson."

"And it might have been a volatile relationship. Sounds like Wallace Bryant wanted to pinch pennies."

"Don't forget Lance Weir. Chances are he came across Alena while she visited the office."

Thomas glanced at LeVar. "We should pay Weir another visit this morning. I'd like to know where he was last night when we dragged Alena out of the pond."

"While you interview Weir," Chelsey said, "I'll drive to Syracuse and speak with City Confidential."

"Contact us if you learn anything interesting." Thomas wiped his mouth with a napkin. "Tell Raven to save two bagels for me and LeVar."

"Make it four," LeVar said.

The sheriff placed his hands on his hips. "LeVar, where do you store all this food?"

"A growing boy needs his breakfast, Shep Dawg."

Chelsey slung her bag strap over one shoulder as Thomas and LeVar washed dishes in the kitchen. "Scout, can you hold down the fort until Raven returns?"

Scout typed at her workstation without looking up. "No problem."

"She should be back in twenty minutes."

LeVar followed Thomas out of the building. Chelsey paused in the doorway as the cruiser pulled out of the parking lot, a tingle of apprehension raising the hair behind her neck. She questioned her decision to leave Scout alone. The teenage intern was perfectly capable of answering phone calls, and the girl had Jack to guard the office if anything happened.

But what could happen? Finding Alena Robinson's dead body had left Chelsey paranoid.

Still, she kept shooting glances at the office as she climbed into the Honda Civic. What was making her so nervous?

30

With every Main Street parking space occupied on a busy Saturday morning, Raven stopped in the municipal lot a block away from The Broken Yolk. The chill had teeth this morning, and though the forecast called for a comfortable sunny afternoon, she shivered in a sweatshirt and jacket. On her way down the sidewalk, Raven dialed her mother. Again, she landed in her mother's voicemail. Since the argument at the cabin—or more accurately, the scolding—Serena had ghosted Raven, refusing to answer calls.

"Come on, Mom," she grumbled at the phone while she dialed a second time. After the message played, she sighed. "Will you please talk to me? I'm sorry about what happened. Call me. We can work this out."

Remembering the betrayal tightened Raven's throat. She was headstrong and pig-headed, even when she had the best intentions. Why had she prejudged Buck Benson and violated the man's privacy?

Raven pocketed the phone and lowered her head, teeth chattering as she jogged, hoping the exercise would thaw her bones. The scents of baked treats and coffee reached her before the cafe came into view. Her mouth watered. Maybe she'd buy an extra bagel for herself. Or a raspberry tart. Ruth Sims, the cafe's proprietor, baked some of the best treats in all of New York, second only to Naomi Mourning and Raven's mother.

The welcome warmth of The Broken Yolk enveloped Raven in the doorway. The checkout line stretched back to the seating area, where longtime customers mingled with the college crowd, sipping lattes and munching delectable desserts over the din of conversation. Raven checked her watch. Though she'd promised the staff breakfast, she worried the trip was taking too long. The priority was catching Alena Robinson's killer and locating Karley Weir before the woman's body showed up in the woods outside Wolf Lake.

A teenage girl worked behind the counter while Ruth juggled multiple orders in the back. Raven asked for a dozen bagels, resisting the tarts and pies under the glass case. She salivated like Jack whenever Thomas grilled filet mignon. Ruth glanced up in time to spot Raven before she left. The cafe owner smiled and waved, mouthing, "Tell your mom I need more pies."

Raven raised a thumb.

If only Mom would answer my calls.

The girl handed her a paper bag. Raven turned to leave and walked into Buck Benson. He backed up a step and raised his hands, giving her room.

"Ms. Hopkins," he said, barely acknowledging her before he turned his attention to the menu.

"My bad," she said. "I should watch where I'm going."

She weaved around Benson and stopped at the door. When she looked at Benson, his back was to her, the man's hands stuffed inside his pockets.

Raven pressed her lips together. This was ridiculous.

She swallowed the lump in her throat and returned to him.

The woman standing in line behind Benson stared knives into Raven for cutting in front of her.

"Mr. Benson, would you allow me to treat for breakfast?"

"I can order my own food, thank you."

"There's an open table in the back. If you'll join me—"

"I'm unsure why you'd share a table with a no-good racist like me, Ms. Hopkins."

"Please, I'd like to talk to you." He stared pointedly at the menu. "I was wrong."

"Don't know what you're talking about."

"I can't blame you for wanting me to suffer. But my mother is caught in the middle of this. Nobody is more upset than Mom. If only for her sake, give me a chance to apologize."

Benson regarded her as though expecting a trick, but he stepped out of line and followed Raven to the rear of the cafe, past the crowd, and sat across from her beside the window. Two college-age boys scoffed at Benson. One made a comment about his flannel shirt and work boots. Raven locked eyes with the boys until they turned away.

"Well, we're here," he said. "Talk if you want to talk."

She opened the bag and passed him a bagel. One thing Raven had learned over the years—toasting Ruth Sims's bagels was unnecessary, and slathering them with butter, cream cheese, or jelly was almost criminal. The taste held up without added flavor.

"I want to apologize for snooping," she said, clasping her hands on the table. "I had no right to search through your belongings. You invited me inside and gave me the benefit of the doubt, and I violated your trust."

He didn't reply, just stared at Raven.

"I peeled back the sheet because I'm overprotective of my mother. I feared the worst and wanted to find out what you were hiding."

"What did it accomplish?"

"I learned you're an amazing artist."

Benson's cheeks colored, and he dropped his gaze to the table.

"I mean it," she said, wanting to reach across the table and touch his arm. She held back. "It made me think of something you said."

"And what would that be?"

"The model car you built when you were a child. The Dukes of Hazzard. You said that was the one creation your father didn't laugh at."

"In his defense, I couldn't draw a stick figure without someone directing me."

"I doubt that's true. A father shouldn't belittle his son. That's not how you encourage a child."

"Water under the bridge," he said, looking out the window, his eyes remembering.

"But I'm not just apologizing for breaking your trust. I prejudged you, Mr. Benson, as though I haven't experienced enough prejudice throughout my life to learn better. All that time we were neighbors, I assumed the worst about you. I saw your flag and wanted to believe you were nothing but a—"

"Beer-swilling redneck?"

"Something like that. Ever since I left Harmon and moved to Wolf Lake, I've looked out the corner of my eye at everybody. Small town, mostly white, a lot more money than we ever saw growing up. I'm ashamed to admit I look for trouble, even when there's none to be found."

A vein pulsed in Benson's temple. She prepared for an outburst. Instead, he brushed a hand through his hair.

"You and I ain't so different. I grew up fifty miles east of here in a town a lot smaller than Wolf Lake. Doubt I met anybody who wasn't white until I hit my teenage years, and that was a dark-skinned Italian girl who'd transferred to my high school from Rochester. Most of my family lived between Alabama and South Carolina, and those were the places I visited on location. The Confederate flag flew everywhere, and to me, it was about the South holding on to its way of life. Southern pride shouldn't mean anything to a kid growing up in New York, but it did. I'm ignorant of a lot of things, Ms. Hopkins. Have been for as long as I can remember. But I'm trying."

"I can see that." Raven took his hand. "And so am I."

He sheepishly pulled his hand out of her grip and chewed a nail.

"Your painting took my breath away," she said. "It belongs on the wall, not hidden beneath a bedsheet."

"It's a lousy drawing."

"That's my mother's portrait you're talking about."

"You know what I mean."

"Did you intend to surprise my mother with the painting?"

Benson scratched his chin. After considering, he shook his head. "I don't want her to see it."

"Then why paint her portrait?"

"Because . . . I don't know why I chose your mother as a subject, okay? It was just something that came to mind."

"I don't believe you." His gaze shot to hers. "She's special to you. That's why."

"It don't matter. She'll never see the portrait, and I'll thank you for never telling her."

"Why? Because you're afraid she'll laugh at you the way your father did?"

"You don't know anything about my father."

"You'd be surprised," she said. "At least you had a father. Ours walked out when I was a child. LeVar was too young to remember him."

"That's a tough row to hoe, but my father wasn't wrong. I'm not an artist."

"I say otherwise." Unable to break the ice between them, Raven released a breath. "Please don't throw my mother out of your life because of my transgression. She hasn't been this upset in a long time. Whether she forgives me or lets me back into her life, she deserves happiness, and you provide her with some."

Benson wiped his eyes on his sleeve. "Not much I did except give her company."

"She cares for you."

"And I, her. Your mother is a beautiful woman. Inside and out."

"Then knock on her door and work through your problems. Don't pretend you don't want to. And for goodness' sake, show her the painting."

"You really think she'll like it?" Benson asked.

"She'll love it."

"I'm not sure."

"If you don't show her the darn painting, I'll hound you day and night," she said.

His lips quirked into a grin. "You would, wouldn't you?"

"You had better believe it."

"Then I suppose I have no choice." He leaned back in his chair and chewed his bagel. "Still warm. These are damn good. Awfully kind of you to buy me breakfast."

"Those pies under the glass?"

"The blackberry and apple pies?" he asked.

"My mother baked those. And our friend, Naomi. The best baking team this side of the Mississippi."

"Is that so? I reckon I should pick one up before I go."

"Are we okay now?"

"We understand each other," Benson said. "And I'll forgive

you for peeking at the painting if you forgive me for sticking that damn flag in your face."

"Done."

Raven held out a hand, and he shook it.

"We were never proper neighbors," he said, "but perhaps we can be friends."

31

"I wish I could get my hands on that workers' compensation claim," Thomas said, turning away from the village center and driving toward the Weir residence.

"Can't you ask the court for the claimant's name?" asked LeVar.

"I can, but there's no point unless I provide evidence the claim has anything to do with our murder investigation. We'll convince Lance Weir to talk. If that fails, there's always Wallace Bryant, though I suspect he'll slam the door in our faces."

Thomas didn't expect to find Weir home, but his vehicle was in the driveway and the curtains hung open, inviting sunshine into the living room. The sheriff stopped the cruiser out front. Before he stepped out, LeVar tapped his arm.

"Shep, check it out."

Thomas followed LeVar's gaze to the walkway, where dirt clumps covered the concrete, leading between the driveway and the front door.

"Interesting."

"He could have picked up dirt on his sneakers walking

through the forest. How long did the medical examiner say Alena Robinson spent in the water?"

"At least three or four days," said Thomas. "But those tracks weren't here the last time I spoke to Weir."

"He could have returned to the scene of the crime."

"That's one possibility."

"Either that, or Alena isn't the only victim Weir hid in the forest. We still haven't found his wife."

Thomas bit his lip. LeVar had jumped to a morbid conclusion, but the sheriff couldn't argue against the possibility, especially after the nonchalant attitude Weir had displayed on the day Thomas searched the upstairs.

"Follow my lead," Thomas said, opening the door.

They stepped over the curb. Thomas knelt on the sidewalk. Another dirty tread mark lay beside his feet. The sheriff reached into his pocket and removed an evidence bag. As he collected the dirt, Weir walked out of the house and stared at Thomas and LeVar.

"Snap a picture with your phone," Thomas said to LeVar.

"Can you prove the soil came from the forest?"

"Doubtful, but I'll send it to the lab."

"You can't do that," Weir said, stomping down the walkway.

Thomas stood. "The walkway is public property, Mr. Weir."

"What are you trying to prove? My wife has been missing since Tuesday evening, and you're cleaning up the sidewalk. No wonder you haven't found Karley."

"Mr. Weir, where were you last evening between the hours of six and ten?"

"Right here."

"Not working?"

"Mr. Bryant gave me the week off. He told me to focus on finding Karley and not to worry about my job."

Thomas stepped closer to Weir. "I don't suppose you can prove you were home."

"Without my wife here, no. What are you up to, sweeping dirt into an evidence bag?"

"You ever visit the forest off County Route 26 between Wolf Lake and Kane Grove?"

"Why the hell would I enter the forest?"

"Please answer the question."

"No, of course not."

Thomas eyed the tracks. "How did you get your sneakers so dirty?"

Weir shot Thomas an incredulous glare. "I worked in the yard all morning. Someone has to. The yard won't clean itself."

"Your clothes aren't dirty," LeVar said.

"I showered and changed," Weir said, his tone implying LeVar was a simpleton. "Would you care to sniff me for body odor while you're at it?"

"If someone close to me vanished," said Thomas, "I would search for her day and night. Yard work would be my lowest priority."

"Working keeps my mind off my wife," Weir said, scratching his nose. "I didn't sleep a wink last night. Not after I saw the news."

"What news?"

"That dead woman you found. It's all over the television. That's why you asked me about the forest, isn't it?"

"Her name is Alena Robinson." Thomas produced the woman's picture. "You knew her, correct?"

Weir lowered his head and scuffed the toe of his sneaker against the concrete. Thomas noted the dirt trapped inside Weir's treads.

"Mr. Weir?"

"Yes, yes. She's a workers' compensation adjuster or something. I remember her from the office, but I don't know her."

"Are you certain? You never spoke, not once?"

"We passed in the eatery, but it was nothing more than a greeting. Why? Are you saying I had something to do with her murder?"

"Did you?"

"No. That's a preposterous question."

"Who filed the workers' compensation claim, Mr. Weir?" asked Thomas. "Was it you?"

"Another ridiculous question, and one I'm not obligated to answer."

"We understand your wife did most of the yard work," said LeVar. "Perhaps because you injured yourself at the office?"

"I had nothing to do with Alena Robinson's death. It's a shame what happened to her, but there's nothing I can tell you."

Thomas glanced down at Lance Weir's sneakers. "You wear about a size-ten sneaker, correct?"

"Yeah, so?"

"I notice your treads are clogged with dirt."

"From working in the yard," Weir said. "How many times do I need to tell you?"

After they finished with Weir, Thomas and LeVar knocked on the neighbor's door. Supporting himself with a cane, the elderly man confirmed Weir had spent the morning in the backyard, mowing, trimming branches, and bagging brush. The man had only taken note because it was the first time he'd witnessed Weir lift a hand outside.

On their way to Bryant Media Group, Thomas and LeVar took the scenic route past the lake to avoid a road construction project.

"You asked Weir about Alena Robinson," said LeVar, "and not once did he express worry over his wife."

"I noticed. All he did was defend himself."

"If he injured himself at work, why wouldn't he tell us?"

Thomas scowled. "I can't find anything trustworthy about Lance Weir. Karley's parents were right to doubt his sincerity."

"Do you think Wallace Bryant will tell us anything useful?"

"Based on my last conversation with Bryant, I doubt it."

The security guard at Bryant Media Group questioned Thomas, as if he'd never seen the sheriff before. The man showed more interest in denying Thomas entry because he hadn't made an appointment than allowing a county official to investigate a murder. Rosa Fernandez, the friendly administrative assistant, convinced the guard to let the sheriff and his deputy enter the building.

"Mr. Bryant is on a conference call right now," Fernandez said, walking them to the elevator, where another security guard eyed Thomas and LeVar. "I'll let him know you're here."

On the second floor, Fernandez walked them past the cubicles to the waiting room. Snacks sat beside the microwave.

"Help yourself to coffee and donuts," she said. "Mr. Bryant will be with you in a moment."

The door closed, and LeVar turned to Thomas. "Do you mind?"

"You really want a donut? Raven promised us bagels, remember?"

"But she didn't make it back to the office in time."

Thomas raised his palms. "Help yourself."

LeVar returned with two donuts—one glazed, another with raspberry filling.

"Want one?" LeVar asked, holding out the donuts.

As much as Thomas loved glazed donuts, he was full from the omelet. He wondered if LeVar had a hundred-foot tapeworm or something.

"No, thanks."

"More for me, then."

LeVar wolfed down both donuts in record time. Thomas patted the deputy's belly.

"Must be a joy to have a young person's metabolism, LeVar. Wait until you hit your thirties. Didn't you go out for ice cream with Scout and her mother the other night?"

"Like I said, Shep Dawg, a—"

"—growing boy needs his food. Yes, I remember."

LeVar looked ready to return for more when a tall man in khakis and a button-down entered the room. He gave Thomas and LeVar a curious look before turning his attention to the array of snacks.

"Here to see Mr. Bryant?" the man asked.

"That's right," Thomas replied.

The tall man nodded and held out a hand. "Gene Digby. I'm an account manager at Bryant Media Group. Mr. Wallace isn't in any kind of trouble, is he?"

"We just need to speak with him." Gene Digby. Where had Thomas heard that name before? Then he remembered—Wallace Bryant claimed he had filled in for Digby on the night Karley Weir disappeared. "Perhaps you can help me."

"Oh? I'll do my best."

"Wallace Bryant says he worked your shift Tuesday evening. Something about you leaving town for a family emergency."

"My sister, yes. She was in a car accident."

"I hope everything is okay," said Thomas.

"It is now." Digby shuffled his feet. "She fractured her arm, but it could have been a lot worse. Drunk driver. The other driver, not my sister."

"I'm sorry."

"Appreciate it."

"Do you know if Mr. Bryant actually worked your shift?"

Digby's forehead creased. "Well, I suppose so. When I

returned to the office Thursday, the monthly reports were finished. Why?"

"We're just trying to establish his whereabouts on Tuesday evening."

"Like I said, I left town for my sister, so I wasn't here to verify Mr. Bryant was in the office. I suppose he must have been because I saw the reports."

"Thank you for verifying that information," said Thomas.

"Happy to help." Digby grabbed a donut and stopped at the door. "You know, he could have asked someone to fill in for me. Mr. Bryant, that is."

"Who would he ask?"

Digby shrugged. "Lance Weir. Bradley Andrews. Any senior members of the team could have covered my shift and completed the monthlies. I doubt Mr. Bryant asked Lance Weir with his wife missing."

"Do you know his wife?"

"Not really. She stopped by the office once or twice. Might have said hello to me, but nothing more." Digby glanced at his watch. "I'd better get back to my desk. Mr. Bryant doesn't like it when we take long breaks."

"Thank you, Mr. Digby."

After the door closed, LeVar turned to Thomas. "That wasn't a ringing endorsement for Wallace Bryant. Digby backtracked on his certainty that Bryant worked Tuesday night."

"And without anyone at the office to back up Bryant's story—"

A knock on the door brought Thomas's head up. Wallace Bryant, wearing blue jeans and an open black knit jacket over a white button down, poked his head into the room.

"Sheriff, I can see you now."

They followed Bryant to his office. The man set his feet upon his desk and leaned back in his chair.

"My apologies for keeping you," said Bryant. "I couldn't break away from my conference call. What can I do for you?"

Thomas slid Alena Robinson's photograph across the desk. "City Confidential sent a claims adjuster named Alena Robinson to follow up on a workers' compensation case."

"Yes, I recall Ms. Robinson," Bryant said, twisting his mouth, as though he'd bitten a lemon.

"What can you tell me about her?"

"She was driven, that's for certain. Thorough and persistent."

"But you didn't like her."

"It's not that I disliked her, but she tried to take money from my company."

"By awarding money to an employee who injured himself on the job," Thomas said. "What did the claim involve?"

"That's not your business. Why are you asking about Alena Robinson? Is she reopening the case?"

"She's dead."

Bryant paused and composed himself before replying. "Dead. How?"

"Someone murdered Alena and dropped her body into a pond outside Wolf Lake."

Wallace Bryant pinched his thumb and forefinger against his eyes. "Wait, someone murdered her? Why would anyone do such a thing?"

"You weren't aware? The news has been all over the television and radio since last night."

"I assure you, Sheriff, I don't have time for television." Bryant leaned forward and rubbed his forehead. "Murdered. I'm stunned."

"You said she was driven," LeVar said.

"That's right."

"*Was* driven. You spoke of her in the past tense."

Bryant stammered. "The claim occurred in the past, so that's how I referred to her. I haven't seen her since."

"Where were you last evening?" asked Thomas.

"Home, working on monthly reports."

"You live alone, correct?"

"Yes."

"Can anyone verify you were at home?"

"No," said Bryant. "I hope you aren't implying I murdered Ms. Robinson. If you are, I suggest you contact my legal team."

"Who filed the workers' compensation claim?"

"That's privileged information."

"Was it Lance Weir?"

"I can't answer that. Doing so would violate confidentiality. If you want that information, get a warrant."

"You understand our need to know, don't you? Someone in your office worked with Alena on the claim, and now she's dead."

"Nobody in my office killed Ms. Robinson, Sheriff. You're way off base."

"So far, the only person I can link to Robinson at Bryant Media Group is you. It's in your interest to tell us who filed the claim."

"I could be sued if I divulged confidential information. Forget it."

Bryant punched the call button on his desk. A gruff voice answered.

"Yes, Mr. Bryant?"

"Tim, the sheriff and his deputy are leaving now. Would you kindly escort them from the building?"

"Right away."

Wallace Bryant stared at the sheriff, making it clear there would be no more questions. Tim, the security guard from the entryway, rapped on the door and motioned at Thomas and LeVar to follow.

One thing was for certain: They would get nowhere by questioning Wallace Bryant.

Did Bryant have something to hide?

32

Chelsey left the interstate and followed County Route 26 toward Wolf Lake. She'd struck out at City Confidential, running into another brick wall, learning nothing except everyone liked Alena Robinson. Nobody sought revenge over a claim.

Using the Honda Civic's calling feature, she contacted Thomas, who was heading to Bryant Media Group with LeVar when last she'd heard.

"How did it go in Syracuse?" Thomas asked.

She muttered an expletive. "They wouldn't give me any details about the workers' compensation claim, other than Alena worked the case."

"Sounds like you had as much success as we did."

"That bad?"

"Wallace Bryant ordered security to toss us out of the building."

"Goodness, Thomas. What did you do?"

"LeVar ate all their donuts and refused to reimburse the company."

"Untrue," LeVar said in the background.

Thomas chuckled. "Bryant wouldn't tell us who filed the claim."

"Now what?"

"We keep digging. Wallace Bryant knew Alena and Karley, and so did Lance Weir. Someone is hiding the truth. I need to follow up with Syracuse PD when I get back to Wolf Lake. Hopefully, the detective working the murder can connect a few dots. Where are you?"

"Driving back to my office, but not until I stop for a sandwich. All this talk of donuts is making me hungry for lunch."

"Eat something healthy. No donuts. I'll call you if I learn anything."

Chelsey pushed her hair off her shoulders. A pulse of anxiety made her heart thump when she remembered Scout alone at the office. Raven had driven straight from The Broken Yolk to the state park. A hiker had broken his leg after he left the trail and tromped through the forest. Darren needed help to carry the injured man up the hill.

Chelsey was deciding what to buy for lunch when the supermarket appeared up the road. This was the last place anyone had seen Karley Weir, and Chelsey figured she could purchase food while checking out the store and parking lot.

As Thomas and Aguilar had learned, the security cameras over the entry doors covered the front of the parking lot and not much else. The camera inside the nail salon on the far side of the lot covered even less territory and wouldn't capture the parking spaces outside the supermarket. So where was Karley? No proof existed that someone had abducted the woman outside the store, but Chelsey's instincts rarely misled her.

The automatic doors whooshed open. Inside, the store smelled of baked goods and disinfectant, and long lines of shoppers waited at each checkout counter. Not finding anything worth eating in the sports nutrition aisle, Chelsey entered the bakery and surveyed the pre-made sandwiches, just as Karley had done Tuesday evening. A shadow drifted over her back, and she turned to find Urban Hammond several steps behind her. The ex-con leered, his face still bruised from the fight.

Chelsey spun around and pretended she hadn't seen Hammond. She felt his ice-cold stare as she picked through the sandwiches. Suddenly, she lost her appetite.

Lowering her head, she grabbed a shopping basket and glanced out of the corner of her eye toward Hammond. He was gone. She searched between the rows of bread and rolls but didn't see him.

Chelsey released a breath and hurried to the rear of the supermarket, where meat, poultry, and fish lay in refrigerated compartments. She checked each aisle as she walked, forcing herself not to hurry and draw attention. Hammond was nowhere to be found.

Was the psycho crazy enough to assault Chelsey in public? She didn't wish to find out.

The exit doors appeared, and Chelsey walked faster, shooting looks over her shoulder to ensure Hammond wasn't following. Her skin prickled, warning her he was watching. But from where?

When she reached the car, she locked the doors and turned the Civic onto County Route 26. A check of the mirrors revealed an empty road. The tension melted out of her neck and shoulders.

Until an engine roared behind her bumper. The black Toyota Tundra materialized out of nowhere, racing so close to Chelsey's car that she couldn't see the lower half of the truck. The Tundra fell back, then jumped forward, Hammond threatening to smash her from behind.

What would he do next? With a lunatic like Hammond, all possibilities were on the table. He could kill Chelsey and throw her in the woods. On this desolate stretch of road, it might be weeks before someone found her body.

The Tundra swerved across the double-striped dividing line into the left lane. The many curves in the road prevented Chelsey from knowing if another vehicle was speeding headlong toward the truck, but Hammond didn't care. When Hammond's truck ran neck-and-neck with the Civic, he grinned at Chelsey from across the cab.

Hammond yanked the wheel to the right. Chelsey anticipated the move and slammed the brakes before he could run her into the ditch. The Tundra raced in front of her and braked.

For several heartbeats, the two vehicles stood unmoving on the road, Hammond's truck in front of her and blocking the way forward. The Tundra's taillights were angry eyes.

Tires squealed, and Chelsey gripped the steering wheel. Instead of backing up and ramming the car, Hammond sped away and vanished around the curve. Chelsey fought to control her breath as her pulse hammered in her ears.

Remembering Thomas was on the other side of the county, Chelsey picked up her phone with a shaking hand. She expected the Tundra to return. It didn't. On the first ring, Raven answered.

"Urban Hammond tried to run me off the road," she said, breathless.

"Are you hurt?"

Chelsey heard chirping birds and voices in the background. Raven must still be at the state park with Darren, waiting for the paramedic to load the injured man into the ambulance.

"I'm uninjured, just shaken up."

"Chelsey, where are you?"

"A mile south of the supermarket on CR-26. Hammond must have spotted my car and followed me to the store."

"Either that, or he's been watching you the whole time. Are

you okay to drive, Chelsey? Say the word, and Darren and I will come get you."

"I can drive." Ice formed in Chelsey's chest. Hammond might be stalking the Wolf Lake Consulting staff. "Oh my God, Raven. What if Hammond is going after all of us?"

"He wouldn't dare."

"Are you sure? Scout is alone at the office, and Hammond has a thing for teenage girls."

Raven fell silent. After a pause, she lowered the phone and said something to Darren.

"Chelsey, we're heading to the office now. Darren will call the sheriff's department."

"Hurry, Raven. I'm on my way."

33

Scout found it impossible to concentrate. She sat before her computer, the office's many windows drawing her eyes as she waited for Urban Hammond's black truck to squeal into the parking lot. Darren and Raven wouldn't reach Wolf Lake Consulting for another fifteen minutes. Thomas and LeVar might arrive sooner, except a village road-construction project had forced them to take the long way back to the office.

The sidewalk should have been filled with shoppers, but everyone had decided the chilly wind was too much to bear and headed home. Inside the converted house, a preternatural silence traveled down the hallway from the many shadowed rooms. The unseen seemed to creep up on her.

Only the hums of the computer fans broke the quiet. The parking lot lay empty, and the branches rocking by the side window gave the impression of a monster about to shatter the glass and snatch her up. In the corner, Tigger slumbered beside Jack. But the enormous dog didn't sleep. His eyes peered out from inside the cone and studied Scout. The dog sensed her anxiousness and remained alert.

Scout busied herself researching the Alena Robinson and

Karley Weir investigations, hoping to put her mind at ease. It didn't work. Her eyes kept flicking to the windows. Logic told Scout even a psycho like Urban Hammond wouldn't attack her in the middle of the day. But the deep recesses of her lizard brain, the primitive side that ruled emotion during times of high stress, refused to believe she was safe.

She picked up the desk phone to call her mother. Not that her mother could reach Wolf Lake Consulting before Darren and Raven. Scout just wanted to hear Mom's voice. The phone crackled instead of emitting a dial tone. Had the wind taken a line down? Or had someone crept outside the office and sliced the cord?

Scout reached for her mobile phone.

And stopped when the hallway floor creaked.

Just the wind, she told herself.

Then why can't I stop my body from shaking?

The teenager opened the desk and searched for something . . . anything . . . to defend herself with. Except for a letter opener, there wasn't much to choose from. She stood with one hand curled around the cool stainless steel of the letter opener as Jack scrambled up and locked his gaze on the girl. When she crossed the office to the hall, he trotted alongside. His fur stood rigid.

Scout didn't dare turn the corner. Standing with her back against the frame, she breathed in through her nose, out through her mouth. Her heart thundered in her ears. Jack cocked his head, as though to ask what she was afraid of. Answering would only give away her position if someone was inside the building.

Jack made the first move. Before she grabbed his collar, he padded into the hall and looked left and right. Scout followed the dog. Darkness spilled out of the rooms at each end of the hall, as though it were midnight and not noon.

It's only because of the blackout curtains over the bedroom windows.

To Scout, those black pools beyond the doorways concealed every monster, every unspeakable evil that had haunted her childhood nightmares.

"Hello?" she muttered, surprised she'd spoken.

Stupid. She might as well announce she was alone to the madman hiding down the hallway.

Silence. No misshapen devils lumbered out of hiding. The danger only existed in her head.

She pressed a palm to her forehead and leaned against the wall, exasperated that she was afraid of her own shadow. How would she hunt serial killers as an FBI profiler if she couldn't get over her fear of the dark? There was nothing to be afraid of, and soon Thomas and LeVar—

The bedroom door at the end of the corridor creaked open. By itself.

Scout's breath whistled out of her lungs. Terror nearly made her lose consciousness as she grabbed the wall to keep her footing. Her stomach had become a cinder block. Who had pushed the door open?

Jack lunged in front of the teenager and shielded her with his frame. She didn't have time to think if the dog could defend itself—or her—with the restrictive cone extending down his snout. He barked and moved a half-step toward the unknown. His paws scurried across the bare wood floor. The dog jumped forward and back, warning the unseen attacker to flee, but refusing to leave Scout's side.

She waited for Urban Hammond to turn the corner. What if he had a gun?

But no one emerged from the bedroom.

There's nobody in the office.

Except there might be. And if it was Urban Hammond, he would murder Scout before help arrived.

She could run for the exit, but not without Jack and Tigger. Even if she coaxed the pets to escape with her, she feared she would throw the front door open and find Urban Hammond waiting outside the entrance.

Then the thumps of footsteps.

Amid Jack's barking, she couldn't determine if the steps came from inside or outside. A shudder rolled through her body, and she took an involuntary step toward the exit.

"Come, Jack. It's time to go, boy."

Over the snarling growls, a shrill scream arose. Like a poltergeist swooping down on the house.

It took Scout another breath before she identified the sound as an approaching siren. Thomas and LeVar.

Buoyed, she hauled Jack away from the bedroom and turned toward the front door. A shadow drifted across the window and stopped her dead, even as the siren grew closer.

The knob jiggled and the door shook as the intruder tried to yank it off its hinges. The pane wouldn't stop him from punching through the window and twisting the lock.

Jack escaped Scout's grip and threw himself at the door, snapping and growling. The knob stopped twisting. Seconds after, boots stomped across the parking lot before a vehicle door slammed. Scout had just enough time to reach the window and glimpse a black truck turning the corner.

She covered her face and wept. The sheriff's cruiser pulled into the lot with Raven's Nissan Rogue a heartbeat behind.

34

Thomas knelt before the trembling teenager, the girl's sweaty hand sandwiched between his. Jack, who'd somehow shaken loose of the cone, guarded Scout and wouldn't leave her side.

"Did you read the license plate or get the make and model of the truck?"

"All I saw was a black truck. It turned out of the parking lot before I read the plate. I'm sorry, Sheriff."

Scout never called him *Sheriff*. They had been on a first-name basis for over a year, and Thomas even bristled when she referred to him as *Mr. Shepherd*.

"Scout didn't identify Hammond's truck," said Chelsey, "but I got a clear view of him at the supermarket and on County Route 26. He tried to run me into the ditch."

"I put out an APB on Hammond," Thomas said, rising to his feet. "He's on the run now. Even his lawyer can't keep him out of jail this time. You did well, Scout. The important thing is you're safe."

Chelsey pressed her lips against the top of Scout's head and brushed the girl's hair back. "It's over now. I never should have left you alone."

"No worries," said Scout. "Jack kept me safe."

"This is all my fault," Raven said. "I promised to return to the office after I drove to the cafe."

Darren opened his mouth to steal the blame from everyone, but Scout cut him off.

"I'm not a child. Mom leaves me home by myself all the time. It's not like any of you could have predicted Urban Hammond would attack the office."

At the sheriff's side, LeVar coiled like a rattlesnake ready to strike. Anger heated the deputy's eyes. Urban Hammond was lucky Thomas and LeVar hadn't arrived a minute sooner.

"I see the revenge in your eyes, LeVar," said Thomas. "Focus. We'll catch Hammond."

"Hammond is losing control," Darren said, sitting beside Raven. "Have we ruled him out as a suspect in the Karley Weir and Alena Robinson cases?"

"I'm not taking him off the list, though I can only link him to Karley."

"Just in case he's holding Karley inside his house, you should obtain a search warrant."

"Getting a warrant shouldn't be an issue now that he's on the run. I also want to speak with the girl who lived in his house, Holly Doyle. She'll recognize Alena or Karley if he ever brought them home."

"If he kidnapped Karley and locked her inside his house, Holly won't admit to seeing her," Raven said. "She'll worry about being considered an accomplice."

"I'll visit the family while I wait for approval on the warrant. Then LeVar and I will search Hammond's property." Thomas folded his arms and leaned against Chelsey's desk. "In the meantime, you're all targets. Hammond is going after Wolf Lake Consulting investigators, and he's not afraid to break into the office in broad daylight. It's unsafe for you to work here. Unfortunately, the sheriff's department can't watch your office day and night."

"We have jobs to do," Chelsey said. "I can't turn my back on clients just because one sicko is threatening us."

"There's another way," said Darren. "Chelsey, can you run the business remotely?"

Chelsey scrunched her brow. "The travel laptop connects to our online database. I suppose I could work from home, but I have a staff to think about."

"What if we temporarily combine operations? Wolf Lake Consulting and our unofficial investigation group."

"We've done it before," Scout said when Chelsey opened her mouth to balk at the idea.

"I can host operations from the guest house," said LeVar.

"Or we can work at the ranger's cabin," Raven said. "What do you think, Chelsey?"

Chelsey shook her head. "It won't be easy. We'll need a location for eight to twelve hours per day. I feel like we're invading LeVar's privacy, as well as yours."

"Better than worrying about a psycho showing up."

Realizing Chelsey wasn't convinced, LeVar said, "This plan might be the best way to catch Hammond. Arming Wolf Lake Consulting with security cameras is long overdue. Send the feed over the internet, and we can monitor the office 24/7. When Hammond shows his face, we'll see him on camera."

"The state park is the best location," Darren said. "I have eight open cabins. We can move everyone to the campgrounds and watch each other's backs."

"Can one cabin serve as headquarters?" asked Chelsey.

"Definitely."

"All right. We did something similar last year, and it worked out. Can we convince everyone to come? Scout?"

"I'm down," Scout said. "Mom will treat it as a free camping vacation. You can count us in."

"What about your mother, Raven? It's doubtful Hammond will go after Serena, but there's no sense in taking chances."

Raven stuffed her hands into her pockets. "It might be best if someone else asks. She kinda isn't accepting my calls these days."

"I'll talk to her," Darren said.

Thomas knew Raven and Serena had been at odds, but he didn't realize they weren't talking.

"Then it's settled," said Thomas. "Wolf Lake Consulting will move to the state park until further notice."

Darren snapped his fingers. "We should place a bait for Hammond."

"I'm listening."

"Park an investigator's vehicle in the lot and set the lights on timers. Make it appear as if someone is here. How about Raven's Rogue? She can drive my Silverado."

"That works. I suggest switching vehicles once per day, in case Hammond is monitoring the office."

With everyone in agreement, Thomas breathed a sigh of relief. Today's attacks had proved how vulnerable his friends were, and he didn't want Scout alone with a sexual predator loose. The plan was coming together.

Now he needed Hammond to take the bait.

35

The Doyle family lived in a two-story house at the end of a cul-de-sac three miles from the village center. Blue shutters complimented the yellow siding, and two dormer windows poked out of a steep roof. Curtains covered the windows while a gated privacy fence circled the yard and connected with the garage.

Thomas checked his phone as he approached the porch. A message arrived from LeVar—they'd loaded Darren's truck with everything Chelsey needed to run Wolf Lake Consulting from the cabins. So far, the judge hadn't approved the search warrant for Urban Hammond's house.

What was taking so long? Thomas hoped the attorney, Heath Elledge, hadn't called in a favor with the DA or judge.

Thomas pressed the doorbell, bouncing on the balls of his feet when the wind ripped his body heat away. After a long wait, the door opened to a mousy-looking man in a turtleneck sweater, dress pants, and loafers.

"Sheriff Shepherd," Franz Doyle said. "I didn't expect you."

"Sorry to intrude, Mr. Doyle, but I'd like to speak with Holly."

Doyle tugged at his sweater. "Holly is in her room. After what she did, her mother and I had no choice but to ground her. She isn't to leave her bedroom without supervision. Kids today need more discipline than we did. They don't have the fear of war hanging over their heads. There are no positive influences outside the home to keep them on the straight and narrow. Even their teachers are hamstrung and unable to punish disruptive students for fear of lawsuits. This generation has strayed from the path. Look what happened to our family. We turned our backs for one moment, and Holly ran off and moved in with a reprobate. No, it's important Holly remain in her room and think about the consequences of her actions."

"I appreciate your need to discipline and monitor your daughter, but it's imperative I talk to her."

"Is this about that child molester she was living with?"

"Urban Hammond, yes."

Doyle thought it over and shook his head. "We put Mr. Hammond behind us, Sheriff. I see no reason to revisit the past."

When Doyle made to close the door, Thomas put his hand out. "Please. Holly can help us save a woman's life."

The man lowered his brow in confusion, then stepped back from the door. "If this is a matter of life and death, I won't turn you away. But you will be brief with your questions. My wife is at her sister's, but you're welcome to wait inside. I'll get Holly."

While Doyle retrieved his daughter, Thomas sat upon a couch with a slipcover. There wasn't a speck of dust to be found on the furniture, and the polished tables gleamed. A framed photograph showed Doyle and his wife with a much younger Holly. Thomas searched for a more recent photograph of the girl and couldn't find one.

Raised voices traveled from down the hallway. After a minute, Holly skulked into the living room with her head lowered, her cheeks chapped from crying.

Thomas rose. "Holly, I'm Sheriff Shepherd. Do you remember me?"

Holly nodded without speaking. Her hands cupped her elbows.

"Are you too simple to answer the sheriff?" Doyle asked. "Use words. Show respect for your elders."

Thomas raised a hand. "Please, Mr. Doyle. Holly, if I may have a moment of your time."

The teenager slumped into a lounge chair across from the couch. There was no television, no stereo, just two chairs, a couch, and shining end tables that appeared to have never held drink or food. Holly shivered, and for the first time, Thomas noticed how cold it was inside the house. His eyes moved to the thermostat, which was set at 60 degrees. The chill merged with the dark and sapped his will, as though the home was a vampire leeching his soul.

"I tried to tell you," Holly said, muttering.

"Tell me what?"

"Remove the marbles from your mouth and speak like an adult," Doyle snapped.

"This," the girl said, motioning to the room. "It's like a prison. They won't even let me breathe without permission."

"Nonsense. You exaggerate, Holly."

"Do I?"

"Perhaps you wish to return to your room so you can think about the disrespect you've shown."

Thomas glared at the father. "Mr. Doyle, if I may question Holly . . ."

Doyle drew himself up. "Yes, fine. Ask your questions, Sheriff. My daughter will answer truthfully, or I will add another month to her grounding."

The sheriff composed himself. He wanted to ban the father

from the room, but this was Doyle's house, and he was under no obligation to make Holly available.

"I'll get right to the point. While you stayed with Urban Hammond, did he ever bring women to the house?" Thomas asked.

Doyle sniffled and wiped her nose. "No."

"Didn't that tip you off?" Doyle asked. "What kind of man shows no interest in women his age?"

"Please, Mr. Doyle," Thomas said. Doyle huffed. "I'm going to show you two photographs, Holly. Tell me if you recognize either woman."

Thomas passed Holly two pictures—one of Alena Robinson, the other of Karley Weir. Holly stared at Alena's picture and handed it back to Thomas.

"I've never seen this woman before. Like I told you, Mr. Hammond never—"

Her eyes locked on the photograph of Karley Weir.

"Holly? Does she look familiar?"

Doyle moved behind the chair and peered over Holly's shoulder.

"I've seen this woman before," Holly said.

"At Urban Hammond's house?"

She shook her head, swinging her hair back and forth. "On his phone. He took her picture. I saw it while he was tying the garbage."

"Did you ask Hammond about the woman?"

"He claims it was just someone he met, but I don't believe they were acquainted."

"Why?"

"Because she wasn't even looking at the camera."

"As if he took the woman's picture without her knowledge," said Thomas.

"Yes. I think she was shopping in a store."

"The hardware store where Hammond worked?"

Holly shrugged. "Maybe."

"And you never saw this woman again?"

"Never. Urban got upset when I asked who she was, so I didn't bring it up after that."

"Why didn't you leave him?" Doyle asked. "He's a sicko who photographs women without them knowing, and still you stayed."

"You've helped a great deal," Thomas said.

A hint of a smile formed on the girl's face, quickly extinguished when Doyle ordered Holly to return to her room, now that she'd answered the sheriff's questions.

Holly's departure left an uncomfortable void. Doyle dry-washed his hands.

"Well, my daughter told you everything she knows, Sheriff. If you don't mind, I have work to do."

Doyle led Thomas to the door. Thomas turned to Holly's father before he left.

"Perhaps this isn't my place, Mr. Doyle, but you need to be careful with your daughter."

"You don't know what you're talking about. Holly is a bright girl, but she's prone to poor decision making, which I blame her so-called friends for. If other parents raised their children as we do, Holly wouldn't succumb to bad influences."

"Teenagers need friends. The more you suffocate her, the more you stunt her development and increase the chance that she'll run away again."

"We are teaching her respect so she won't betray our family."

"No, all you're doing is threatening and intimidating Holly. I understand Child Services scheduled a follow-up visit with you and your wife next week. In the meantime, I will provide them with a description of what I witnessed today."

"You wouldn't dare," said Doyle.

"In three years, whether you approve or not, Holly will leave home and attend college, where she will need to make good decisions without your supervision. You can either send an emotionally undeveloped girl to school and let her friends teach her right from wrong, or you can give her space, allow her to grow, and leave home as a mature student with life experience. It's your choice. But I must warn you, Mr. Doyle—grip the reins too tightly, and you will be the one who falls."

36

Karley staggered into the bathroom and assessed her pallid complexion. Her shirt hung off her shoulder, torn where the kidnapper had ripped the cloth. Bloodshot eyes looked back from the mirror.

She clutched her stomach when hunger pains doubled her over. Twice she leaned over the toilet to vomit, but nothing emerged. If Karley didn't take a risk and eat the food he kept bringing her, she'd starve.

All day, the kidnapper had come and gone. Every few hours, the door slammed, and the man's vehicle pulled out of the driveway, only to return an hour later. Karley had given up. There was no getting past the bars, no escape. Minutes before, balanced on top of the toilet, she'd screamed at the bathroom window while the farmer drove his tractor across the neighboring field. All she'd gained was a hoarse voice, and now her throat was sore. Too bad she couldn't kill herself and end the torture. With nothing to slit her wrists and no pills to swallow, she remained his prisoner, his slave forever. She considered winding the blanket into a makeshift rope and tying it around the bars. If she could fashion a noose . . .

As though her thoughts had summoned him, the psycho returned. The windows rattled when the front door opened, and his steps trailed across the basement ceiling, stopping somewhere in the kitchen.

Karley turned back to the reflection. The mirror. Why hadn't she thought of it before?

Rage that she'd missed the obvious rippled through her body. The kidnapper hadn't removed all the weapons, after all.

Worried he would stomp down the basement stairs at any second, she rushed to the futon and grabbed the blanket. It followed her like a tail as she dragged it into the bathroom, where she wrapped one end around her fist. Would he hear when she broke the glass?

Karley gathered the rest of the blanket and laid it over the mirror to cushion the blow and mute the sound. Outside, the tractor rumbled and coughed, spitting out a cloud of black smoke and dust, making just enough noise to cover her escape attempt. She balled her hand into a fist and struck the mirror. Even with the blanket between her hand and the glass, the mirror sliced her knuckles. Several pieces fell and tinkled against the basin. She held her breath, certain he'd somehow heard the glass shatter over the cacophony outside.

Footsteps moved across the ceiling again. Coming toward the basement door.

Dropping the blanket, Karley sifted through the broken pieces and settled on a fist-sized piece of glass with a deadly point. She didn't know if she could hold the weapon without cutting herself. To protect her palm, she tore a strip off the edge of the blanket and wrapped the cloth around the glass. She ran to the futon.

At the top of the stairs, the door opened as Karley fell onto the cushion. She hid the glass beneath the blanket and regulated her breathing—almost impossible with his shadow growing along the staircase.

Karley curled on her side and faced the wall, eyes wide, her teeth clamping down on her lower lip. Her body trembled. It was now or never.

"I hope you learned your lesson," he said, standing over her. "Turn over and face me. I know you're awake."

She did as she was told. The kidnapper moved his eyes over her blanket-covered body.

"Are you ready to eat? You'll waste away if you don't accept my food. I would never poison you, Karley. You are my soulmate, my everything."

"Yes, I'm starving."

"Thank goodness. I worried you wouldn't—"

The words weren't out of his mouth before she sprang forward and slashed the shard across his face. The glass caught on the stocking, but not before blood welled between his flesh and the fabric. He cried out, more stunned than injured, and stumbled backward.

She threw herself at him, this time raking the glass across his arm when he lifted it to block the attack. He dropped to one knee. She jammed the jagged point into the soft flesh of his upper shoulder. The kidnapper fell to the floor and convulsed.

Karley hurdled his body. He reached up and snatched her ankle. With her free leg, she stomped his arm until he relinquished his grip.

Then she raced up the stairs, breathless, terrified, his guttural screams following her.

She burst into a kitchen. A wood table stood in the center of the room with a microwave on the counter. As she looked left and right, he started up the steps, bellowing like a monster out of a horror movie.

A hallway led to the living room and front door. Daylight

streamed through the windows and promised freedom. If only she escaped before he caught up.

Multiple locks secured the front door. She snapped one open as he crashed into the kitchen behind her. Another lock clicked open.

Karley twisted the knob and tugged, but the door refused to budge.

The deadbolt.

She pulled back on the deadbolt and threw the door open, his breath hot on her neck. His fingers touched her arm, and she whirled and drove the shard into his chest.

The kidnapper crashed against the steps and twitched, blood pouring from his body. She didn't recognize her surroundings. One dusty road extended into the distance. An ornamental windmill loomed in the psychopath's yard, squealing as it turned. There were two vehicles in the driveway—a pickup truck and a red sedan.

Karley didn't wait. She bolted toward the only other property in sight—the farmer's house across the field. The farmer was nowhere to be seen. His tractor slumbered beside the open doors of the barn.

The woman ran screaming. Behind her, the madman crawled to his feet and demanded she stop. Halfway across the field, Karley felt the icy hand of fear grip her chest. What if the farmer was aiding the kidnapper? If the man turned on Karley, she still had the shard to defend herself with.

She angled away from the house and toward the barn when something clanged inside the structure's shadowed depths. The farmer spun around in surprise as she sprinted through the opening. Sunburn tinted his weathered face, and the way his clothes hung off his wiry frame made him look more scarecrow than man. A pile of junk, including a two-foot pipe, lay in the corner.

"He wants to kill me! Please!"

Concern on his face, he glanced over her shoulder. Seeing no one, he held her arms with a strong grip.

"There's no one out there, miss."

The farmer squinted at Karley, as though he suspected she was high on something or out of her mind.

"You don't understand. It's the man next door, the man who—"

She didn't have time to scream before the psychopath slammed the pipe down on the farmer's head. The farmer's skull rang with a sickening crack. Blood spurted out of the gash. Then the farmer grasped at the air and fell backward. He landed on the hay-covered dirt. The madman raised the pipe again.

Karley ran. Guilt struck her heart when she entered the sunlit outdoors. But there was no helping the farmer—he was already dead.

Two choices beckoned: the dusty road at the front of the property and the forest behind the barn. The man would find her unless she hid. In his vehicle, he could drive faster than she could run.

She raced toward the trees. He was coming for her.

37

The pipe thundered down on the writhing farmer, the metal featherlight in the killer's grip. He was not a man, but a god with power over life and death.

The madman lifted the pipe with both hands. Spittle flew from his mouth as he screeched with rage. The blow split the old man's forehead and caved his skull into a grotesque Halloween mask. Something white and chunky mixed with blood dripped off the pipe.

He ripped the stocking from his head and stuffed it inside his pocket. The farmer didn't move, eyes open and lifeless. Like a fish's eyes.

The fury fled his body. Awareness of his cuts and bruises clenched his teeth. Where had Karley found a piece of glass? If she'd squeezed her arm past the bars and broken a window, he would have seen her on camera.

The bathroom mirror. Why hadn't he removed the mirror from the cabinet?

He sank to his knees beside the dead farmer and clutched his hair—Warren Shorts was the farmer's name, and all he did was run that damn tractor all season; Shorts never had a kind word for anyone, let alone his only neighbor.

"Idiot!"

He ripped the hair out of his scalp in clumps, the pain searing yet deserved. Karley was the only woman for him, and he'd allowed her to escape. He left Shorts to bleed on the hay and wandered outside. Which way? The forest or the road? It mattered little. The day grew old, and he knew every road between his house and Wolf Lake. Karley couldn't escape.

The man stared at the road, searching for a trail of dust that would give her away. There wasn't one. He turned toward the forest. Darkness as black as night waited beyond the tree line. She wouldn't get far if she chose the forest.

Karley wasn't the only person on the run. Now he was too. Before long, someone would call on Shorts and discover the body. It was time to flee, to escape before the sheriff and his deputies captured him. But he wouldn't leave without Karley. Not without the love of his life.

First, he needed to hide the farmer. He grabbed Shorts by the ankle, dragged his wiry body to the rear of the barn, and covered the farmer in hay. A winding blood streak marked where he'd pulled Shorts through the barn. He grabbed a rake off the wall and covered the bloody trail with more hay. Soon the insects would find Shorts, and if an animal caught the farmer's scent and dug him out of hiding, someone would notify the sheriff.

Though almost nobody used the road, the man checked for traffic before he emerged from the barn and crossed the field to his house. Inside his bedroom closet, he kept a bag with enough clothes to last a week, should he need to disappear. That time had come. After he retrieved the bag and set it in the entryway, his eyes landed on the open basement door. His heart clenched. An hour ago, he'd been the master of his universe, the proud husband of the most beautiful woman in the world. His life should be perfect, but Karley was no better than Alena. In the end, she'd betrayed him as so many had before.

No, that wasn't true. He believed in Karley. In the past, she'd put her trust in him. He needed to recapture that trust. Maybe that meant showing himself to her without the stocking covering his face. Had he made a terrible mistake by disguising his identity? Too many questions. Pointless second-guessing wouldn't bring back Karley. He needed to go get her.

With sadness, he descended the steps and ran his gaze over the cellar—the barred windows, the futon with its blanket bunched into a clump.

In a daze, he wandered into the bathroom and stared at the broken cabinet mirror. Despite creating an inescapable prison, he'd let her get away through sheer stupidity. Before he knew what he was doing, he swung a fist at what remained of the mirror and shattered the last shards of glass. Red poured from his slashed knuckles and colored the basin. He deserved pain.

The man climbed the stairs and grabbed his travel bag. Was there anything he'd forgotten? Returning home wouldn't be an option once the authorities found the farmer. He cast a dismal look across the downstairs. This might be the last time he'd ever see his home.

Then he stepped into the late-afternoon sunlight, the wind whipping his hair. He didn't feel the chill. He felt nothing except insatiable need. Two hours until sunset.

When he found Karley, he would make her pay for betraying him.

38

Raven chewed her lip as she watched Darren escort her mother into a vacant cabin with a light shining over the entrance. Mom still wasn't taking Raven's calls, but Darren must have worked his magic, for he'd only been gone a half hour before returning to the state park with Serena in tow. At least everyone was together and safe.

Raven turned back to the others, who gathered around a set of computer monitors set upon a table in cabin one. This was the temporary home of Wolf Lake Consulting, as well as the meeting place for their amateur investigation club. The monitors displayed four views of Wolf Lake Consulting in the center of the village, including the parking lot, in case Urban Hammond's truck appeared.

A large bowl of popcorn sat in front of the monitors. Scout and Naomi grabbed handfuls, while Chelsey removed tinfoil from a plate of hamburgers and hot dogs. Before the meeting began, Raven and Chelsey had cooked enough food on the charcoal grill outside to feed an army.

"What I'm trying to say is," Naomi said, positioned in front of one monitor, "just because Lance Weir is a creep doesn't make him a kidnapper or a murderer. Yes, he bothered me at Shepherd Systems, but I'm unconvinced he's dangerous, or that he killed Alena Robinson or kidnapped his wife."

"So you believe Urban Hammond is the killer?" Scout asked, tossing a piece of popcorn into the air and catching it in her mouth. "Or Wallace Bryant?"

"I'm not claiming either. You're the experts. I'm only giving you my opinion of Lance Weir."

Raven blew out a frustrated sigh when Darren emerged from the cabin without her mother. A minute ago, he'd helped her carry three bags inside. The lights were on in Mom's cabin, and Raven could see a silhouette over a curtained window. When Darren came inside, he helped Chelsey plate the food.

"So Mom isn't joining us?" asked Raven.

"She might later," Darren said, though the way he looked away told her Serena Hopkins wouldn't show her face with Raven around.

"She should eat something."

"I offered, but she claims she ate dinner two hours ago. It's almost seven, after all."

Outside the window, the trees blocked the setting sun and drew deepening shadows across the campgrounds. Raven cast another glance at her mother's cabin. Mom would come around eventually. At least Raven hoped she would. She never remembered her mother holding a grudge for so long.

Though she didn't have an appetite, Raven accepted a plate from Darren. A heaping pile of macaroni salad butted up against a cheeseburger and a side of potatoes. It wasn't health food, but Raven craved comfort while she dealt with this idiotic family feud. She felt like herself when Darren sat beside her. His casual, relaxed demeanor almost convinced Raven everything would work out in due time.

For the past hour, the team members had pored over Alena

Robinson's credit card history, fruitlessly searching for a clue that would implicate any of their suspects. Now they ate and made small talk, every eye shooting to the monitors whenever so much as a bird's shadow moved across the outside of Wolf Lake Consulting.

"The resolutions on these cameras are amazing." Scout used a keyboard to zoom the parking lot camera in and out. At its widest setting, the view captured the sidewalk and street outside the converted house. "We can watch for Hammond from the safety of the campgrounds, and he is none the wiser."

"I should have installed cameras years ago," Chelsey said. "Sooner or later, someone with a grudge would have vandalized the office or started trouble."

"Do that many people hold grudges against the investigators?" Naomi asked.

Naomi tried to appear easygoing, but Raven knew she worried about her teenage daughter getting caught in the crossfire.

"When you're tracking down unfaithful spouses and serving court papers every day, you're bound to make enemies," Chelsey said. She lowered her brow and leaned forward. "Scout, zoom in on the bedroom window on the far left." Scout did as she was asked. "Never mind. I thought the pane was cracked, but it's just the lighting."

"The sheriff's department can see all of this, right?" Darren asked.

"We shared the feed," Raven said. "If Urban Hammond shows his face, they'll see him as soon as we do."

"Pretty cool, isn't it?" Scout asked.

"Sure, unless someone trashes my SUV."

Raven's Nissan Rogue sat like an abandoned child in the center of the lot. Two lights shone inside the building, cycling on and off every hour to give the appearance of activity. Maybe they should have parked multiple vehicles outside the office. The same SUV in the parking lot all day and night might raise suspicion.

Before Raven finished her thought, a black truck flew past Wolf Lake Consulting.

"Was that him?" Chelsey set her food aside.

"The camera only caught the lower portion of the truck," Scout said. "Want me to widen the view?"

"Might as well, though I don't know why Hammond would pass without stopping."

Raven rubbed the back of her neck. "Unless he's canvassing the office. And if he thinks someone is alone inside . . ."

She didn't have time to finish the thought. The same truck returned. With the camera zoomed out, Raven saw it was a black Toyota Tundra. The driver paused outside the parking lot entrance, then yanked the wheel and thundered past her SUV.

"It's him," Chelsey said. "I'll call the sheriff's department."

Raven stood and pointed at the screen, horror lancing through her chest when the figure jumped down from the cab. "Chelsey, he has a gun."

"We see him on the video feed," said Thomas, watching the monitor over LeVar's shoulder.

"Do we have a cruiser nearby?" asked LeVar.

"Lambert is on the west side of the county, and the other deputies are near the lake." He snatched the keys out of his pocket. "Let's go."

Thomas hurried to his cruiser. Even running at top speed, he couldn't keep up with LeVar, who reached the passenger door with Thomas several steps behind. After Thomas caught up, he popped the trunk.

"Shep, we don't have time."

"We're not leaving until you put on a vest."

The deputy squeezed into a bulletproof Kevlar vest, while Thomas zipped his. This was the sheriff's greatest fear at work—bringing a rookie officer to a firefight. He wished he could leave LeVar behind and take Aguilar, but she was home. There hadn't been time to call his lead deputy into work.

As they raced out of the lot, Thomas glanced at LeVar. Would the green deputy lose his cool under pressure? He trusted LeVar's judgment, but the former gangster had wanted Urban Hammond's blood since the attack on the office, when Scout had been alone and terrified. Dispatch relayed Thomas's destination and ordered the closest available cruiser to rush to Wolf Lake Consulting. Urban Hammond was armed and dangerous. Thomas feared how the encounter would end.

"You got it together, LeVar?"

LeVar stared straight forward. "Why wouldn't I?"

"Remember, this isn't personal."

"I can compartmentalize my feelings and do my job."

Thomas prayed LeVar would.

When they arrived at the office, the front door stood ajar with shattered glass in the entryway. Thomas approached along one side of the building and ordered LeVar to follow. Even if he trusted the deputy not to take out his anger on Hammond, LeVar was still a rookie and unprepared for an armed hostile. At the edge of the doorway, Thomas placed his back against the wall with LeVar opposite him. Footsteps warned Thomas someone was coming. A heartbeat later, Urban Hammond burst out of the entryway, brandishing a revolver.

"Freeze, Hammond!"

Thomas tackled the convict from behind and grabbed his arm, wrestling for control of the gun. Hammond squeezed the trigger. A bullet ricocheted off the pavement.

Hammond was as impossible to control as a runaway bull. It was all the sheriff could do to hang on to the convict's arm and direct the weapon toward the ground, but he couldn't stop Hammond from firing the revolver.

In one motion, LeVar grabbed Hammond's legs and lifted the man. Driving his shoulder into the small of Hammond's back, LeVar took the convict down. The breath whooshed out of Hammond's lungs when he landed face down on the blacktop. The gun flew across the macadam. Impressed with his deputy's strength and poise under pressure, Thomas yanked Hammond's arms behind his back and cuffed the man's wrists, but it was LeVar keeping the convict in place.

Thomas read Hammond his rights as a second cruiser screeched to a halt in the parking lot. Beneath LeVar's weight, Hammond cursed.

"My lawyer will sue your department!"

Thomas ignored the threat as two deputies hurried to the sheriff's side.

"Secure the building," Thomas told a mustached deputy, who led his partner inside.

When Hammond stopped struggling, Thomas nodded at LeVar.

"Nice job, deputy."

LeVar, who'd somehow managed not to lose his hat during the struggle, touched the brim and smiled at Thomas.

"Right back at you, Sheriff. But that was for Scout."

39

Spencer Johansen slowed his hatchback when he rounded a curve. He didn't trust this stretch of CR-26, especially after dark on a Saturday night. If the teenagers weren't drag-racing through the country, there were the drunks leaving the bars in Kane Grove to worry about.

At sixty-two years of age, the lifelong Nightshade County resident had seen his share of wrecks on this road—hot rods on their roofs in ditches, vehicles wrapped around trees. People were crazy. He didn't so much care that they risked their own lives, but they put innocent people in danger. At any second, someone might shoot around the curve in the oncoming lane and slam into him at highway speeds.

As Johansen eased up on the gas, he gripped the wheel with sweaty hands. At night, obstacles appeared to lurch out of the forest, the headlights drawing disfigured shadows across the road. Even with the windows closed to wall away the chill, he could hear the insects rasping along the edge of the forest, which encroached on both sides of his vehicle.

Johansen reached for the radio and turned up the sound. A news channel out of Syracuse crackled and popped as the signal faded. One of these days, he'd bite the bullet and install a satellite radio.

He was about to switch to another channel when a ghostly figure lunged out of the forest and staggered across the road. The man slammed his brakes, heart pounding inside his chest. The hatchback fishtailed and swung around until the back bumper faced forward and Johansen stared back the way he'd come.

"What the hell was that?"

He glanced at the mirrors and didn't see anyone on the road. Had he imagined the figure? Perhaps the shadows had tricked him, and his imagination had—

A fist pounded the glass behind him. Johansen screamed and jolted in his seat. Before he could find the person in his mirror, footsteps circled the vehicle toward the driver's side door.

This was it. Some lunatic had tricked him into stopping and would hold him at gunpoint for money. Or steal his car.

He should have felt relief when the woman appeared outside the window. But she seemed more phantom than human, her pale complexion stark in the moonlight. Bloody streaks crisscrossed her face, and open wounds dripped along her arms and legs.

Crazed on drugs. That was his first thought. But the terror pouring out of her eyes convinced Johansen that something horrible had befallen the woman.

Before he could open the door, she collapsed to her knees. He stepped onto the centerline and gathered the woman into his arms, thinking again about the maniacs and drunks who treated the road like a racetrack. In the distance, a motor revved.

"You're all right," he said, supporting the woman. "Let's get you on your feet."

Already, her blood covered his hands. He didn't know where

to touch the woman; every bit of flesh looked chewed and torn, as though she'd run through a maze of razor blades.

"Where am I?" she asked.

He scrunched his brow. "As the crow flies, five miles outside of Wolf Lake."

She didn't know where she was? Maybe his initial worries about the woman being on drugs were justified.

"Where's your car?" he asked. "Did you break down on the road?"

Another motor gunned in the dark. Or perhaps it was the same vehicle Johansen had heard before. It was closer now, a mile or so behind them, and approaching fast. Which meant he needed to get the woman out of the road and turn his car around before someone drove around the bend and plastered the tiny hatchback.

"Help me," she said. "He's coming."

"Who's coming?"

"Get us out of here. Please, there's no time."

He swung the woman's arm over his shoulder and helped her up. Her knees kept buckling, and the strain on his back reminded Johansen he wasn't a young man anymore. Listening for the telltale signs of drag-racing teens—screeching tires and dueling motors—he discerned only one engine. It wasn't far off.

The woman limped faster when the engine grew near. He helped her into the passenger seat and winced. In the dome light's glow, he saw even more cuts and bruises up and down her body. She'd lost a lot of blood.

Johansen slid behind the wheel and shifted into drive. His hurried attempt at a three-point turn almost planted them in the ditch, and he felt his throat constrict when the tires spun on the deep gravel. The first illumination from the approaching vehicle lit the curve. He punched the gas pedal, and the hatchback swung around and started down the road.

The man exhaled. That was close. Two pinpricks of headlights lit his mirrors, but he had a comfortable lead on the other vehicle, too far back to worry him. The odd woman swung around and clutched the seat, staring through the rear windshield with dinner plates for eyes.

"I'll get you to a doctor," he said, but she didn't appear to be listening.

Why was she so fixated on the other vehicle?

A sign beside the road read, *Wolf Lake: four miles*. Soon he'd reach civilization and get the woman help. If she really was out of her mind on narcotics, the doctors would deal with her. The bloody lashes spoke to the bramble inside the forest. It made him wonder what she'd been doing in the woods at night. Was she lost? Regardless, she didn't respond to anything he said, and he was happy for it. The sooner the strange woman was safe and out of his car, the better.

Three miles to Wolf Lake. The vehicle was only a few hundred yards behind, and the high beams were on.

"Thanks a lot, buddy," he growled at the mirror.

Johansen picked up speed until the speedometer read sixty. That was as fast as he would push the hatchback on this road. Any faster was an invitation to disaster.

The vehicle behind them was a truck, one of those fancy new pickups with oversized engines and gleaming exteriors. Johansen swallowed. The truck had gained a hundred yards on the hatchback since last he'd checked.

"How far to the village?" she asked, frantic.

"A little over two miles. I can see the lights. Do you live in Wolf Lake?"

"Just get us there and call the police."

"I don't have a phone."

She gave him an incredulous look, then swung her gaze back to the pickup, which was almost on their bumper.

"That maniac must be driving ninety," Johansen grumbled. "I'll pull over and let him pass."

"No!"

"Miss, he can't pass us over the double line. If I don't pull over, he'll run us off the road."

The truck lunged forward like a predator. The brights lit the inside of Johansen's car like a thousand suns.

"Drive faster. You can't let him catch us."

It wasn't safe to drive at these speeds. Johansen caught his breath when he realized he was doing seventy. And the pickup was on top of them.

One mile to Wolf Lake.

One mile until this nightmare was over.

He could see the water now, the turnoff for the lake road just past the inlet. The lights of the village twinkled like distant stars. He just wanted to reach downtown before the drunken psychopath in the pickup truck killed all of them. A chilling thought gripped Johansen: the pickup driver didn't want to pass. He was chasing them.

No, that was insane. Or was it?

Johansen pushed his speed past eighty. The steering wheel trembled in protest. Just a little longer. Behind them, the pickup's horn blared like a leviathan.

The lake road appeared behind a stand of trees. Johansen tapped the brakes and yanked the wheel. In his mind, the hatchback rocketed over the ditch and crashed into the forest. Somehow, he kept the car on the road, even as his tires shrieked and the rear end pulled toward the shoulder.

Not expecting the turn, the pickup shot down CR-26. As Johansen motored down the lake road, he could see the pickup stop and reverse.

The village was within reach. For goodness' sake, Johansen hoped they would make it.

40

The security footage of Urban Hammond breaking into Wolf Lake Consulting left Heath Elledge without an argument. It didn't help that Hammond carried another unlicensed weapon. The attorney showed too much disgust over his client to put up a fight, and he left the sheriff's office despondent. While Thomas filled out the paperwork, Hammond sat in a holding cell in the back, but the sheriff was no closer to catching Alena Robinson's killer.

The judge had approved the search warrant for Urban Hammond's home, but Thomas's deputies had found nothing to prove the convict had abducted Alena Robinson and Karley Weir. The sheriff crossed one suspect off the list. His mind kept returning to Wallace Bryant and the workers' compensation claim over which Alena had presided. If he could find out who Alena worked with, he might further narrow the suspect list. Maybe the injured worker was Lance Weir. But why would the man abduct his own wife?

It was difficult to concentrate with a phone ringing somewhere in the office. Thomas was about to answer himself when

Deputy Lambert picked up the call. Lambert fell silent for a moment, then said, "Are you certain it's Karley Weir?"

Thomas sprang out of his chair. A thousand worst-case scenarios flew through his head, and he pictured Karley Weir's dead body in the forest or floating in the pond. He stood over Lambert's shoulder as the deputy scribbled a note. When the call ended, Lambert turned to Thomas.

"Karley Weir is at County General."

The news left the sheriff at a loss for words. "She's at the hospital?"

"A man named Spencer Johansen picked her up on CR-26. Said she stumbled out of the forest, all cut up and bleeding. Johansen claims she was delirious and not making sense. She kept saying someone was following her. Then a pickup truck almost ran Johansen off the road outside Wolf Lake."

"When did this happen?"

"About an hour ago."

Earlier that evening, such news would have convinced Thomas that Urban Hammond was the killer. But Hammond had been in the sheriff's custody while Johansen drove Karley to the hospital.

Thomas and Lambert arrived at County General fifteen minutes later. Karley was on the third floor, and the bespectacled doctor who met them outside the room only allowed Thomas to enter.

"Mrs. Weir has been through a terrible ordeal," the doctor said. "Meeting too many people at once will overwhelm her."

Lambert waited in the hallway. Thomas knocked just loudly enough to call the woman's attention. Cuts and abrasions covered Karley Weir's face and arms. She clutched a bedsheet to her chest, as though creating a wall between her and Thomas.

"Mrs. Weir, I'm Sheriff Shepherd with the Nightshade

County Sheriff's Department. Your parents are on the way to the hospital."

"No, no, no. I don't want them to see me like this. Where's Lance?"

"We've tried contacting your husband, but he isn't answering his phone."

Karley looked down at her hands. "He turns it off when he needs rest."

"There's a deputy driving to the house to notify your husband that you're here and recovering. While you wait for him to arrive, I'd like to ask you a few questions about what happened this evening."

Karley cowered and drew her knees up. She stared at Thomas the way an injured mouse would a feral cat. Thomas removed his hat and sat in a chair against the wall, giving the woman space.

"I can't imagine what you went through tonight, but you're all right now. Help me find who did this to you, and I'll ensure he never hurts anyone again."

The floodgates opened, and Karley sobbed. To Thomas, it seemed the woman had held her terror and pain inside until now. He waited for Karley to cry herself out, not moving the chair closer to the bed until the woman stopped trembling. He reached for a box of tissues and handed it to her. She wiped her eyes.

"Thank you," she said.

"Can you please tell me what happened? We've been searching for you since Tuesday night. Did you recognize the man who kidnapped you?"

She shook her head. "He wore a stocking over his face and disguised his voice."

Another crying fit threatened to overtake her. She bit her forefinger until she gained control of her emotions. As Thomas listened, Karley recounted a man kidnapping her outside the supermarket on CR-26. The abductor had jammed a needle into her neck, causing her to faint and collapse. She recalled waking up inside the trunk of a car, then having no memory until her eyes opened to a basement. Since the abduction, the man had repeatedly raped and abused Karley. She recognized Alena Robinson as the woman he'd kidnapped. The psycho even forced Karley to look at pictures of Alena tortured and terrorized. Somehow, Karley escaped by breaking the mirror on the bathroom cabinet and stabbing her abductor.

"Can you tell me anything about the house?" asked Thomas.

"It was in the middle of the country, and I noticed a windmill in the front yard."

"A windmill," Thomas repeated, writing the information.

"An ornamental windmill on a stand. It was about eight feet tall. I noticed two vehicles in the driveway. A red sedan and a pickup truck. He must have thrown me in his sedan the night he grabbed me."

"Any neighboring houses?"

"One. A farm across the field." Remembering drained the blood from Karley's face and brought on another round of crying. Thomas pulled his chair beside Karley's bed. "Oh, God. That poor man."

"The farmer?"

"He killed him. The farmer tried to help me. It was so awful. He beat him to death with a pipe, and I never helped. I ran like a coward."

"You're not a coward," said Thomas. "You're a survivor, but now I need you to help me catch this guy. Can you describe his house?"

Karley couldn't tell Thomas much. She'd spent all her time locked inside the basement, and nothing stood out about the two-story home except the windmill. Now Thomas had another murder on his hands, and he didn't even know where to find the dead farmer's body.

"Oh, and he locked the cellar with a reinforced door and covered the basement windows with bars," Karley said.

Thomas's heart caught in his throat. An unbidden memory came to him—Kenneth Wendel abducting Chelsey and locking her inside a home with bars over the windows. Only a few months had passed since Wendel's attack. The wounds were still fresh. Thomas wondered how Chelsey would react after she learned of Karley's similar ordeal.

There was little else Karley remembered. She'd fled for her life without observing her surroundings. But she gave Thomas a handful of clues that might help him catch the lunatic and bring him to justice. For one, Karley had spent three or four hours running through the woods before she staggered onto County Route 26. That narrowed the search radius and would help Thomas locate the killer's home. How many houses displayed ornamental windmills in the yard?

"We're placing an officer outside your door," Thomas said when he finished the interview. "Try to sleep. You're safe now."

But experience had taught the sheriff that Karley wouldn't be safe until he caught the killer.

41

At four in the morning, with the sky at its darkest before dawn peeked over the distant hills, Thomas stopped his F-150 in front of the Wolf Lake State Park welcome center. His friends' vehicles were lined up in a row, including Chelsey's Honda Civic. With Urban Hammond behind bars, it was safe to return to Wolf Lake Consulting, but the investigators hadn't wished to move at such a late hour. Besides, Thomas suspected they enjoyed the adventure of sleeping in cabins on the edge of the wilderness.

The sheriff walked through the grassy clearing, careful not to step upon a stick and wake everyone. The lights were off in all the cabins, save one. Chelsey's temporary home. He sighed. She hadn't slept a wink.

Thomas knocked before fitting the key into the lock, not wanting to frighten Chelsey. She looked up from the computer just long enough to acknowledge him. Dark patches circled her eyes. A pot of coffee brewed in the kitchenette. Jack padded to Thomas with a sleepy grin, sniffed his hand, and gave the sheriff one sloppy kiss before returning to the corner, where he lay on a cushion. Tigger opened one disinterested eye and fell back asleep.

"I brought you something," Thomas said, handing her a paper bag.

Thomas didn't bother chastising her for staying up late. She was as stubborn as a mule when an investigation consumed her.

Chelsey set the mouse aside and peeked into the bag.

"Sourdough bread and green tea?"

"They help you focus."

He didn't tell her sourdough bread and green tea helped combat anxiety, a helpful tip he'd picked up from Deputy Aguilar.

"I'll make you a sandwich and heat some water," he said.

"No sandwich, Thomas. I don't have the stomach for it. There's a toaster in the corner, if you don't mind."

"Just toast? I don't have butter or jelly."

"Dry toast would hit the spot right about now."

He carried the bag to the counter and plugged the toaster into an outlet that had seen better days. While the bread toasted, he dumped the coffee down the drain and heated water. Chelsey needed soothing energy, not a blast of caffeine. If the tea and bread had their desired effects and calmed her nerves, all the better. The toast popped up, and Thomas plucked the hot bread out of the slot and placed it on a paper plate. He brought it to her with a cup of tea.

"Thank you," she said, "but I don't need you worrying about me."

"I love you. It's what I do."

"And I love you and appreciate everything you do for me." She leaned her head against his chest, and he massaged the knots out of her shoulders. "But let's not avoid the elephant in the room. Yes, this case reminds me of Kenneth Wendel. Whenever I think about Karley Weir, I remember what happened. The bars over the windows, the mind games he played. But Kenny can't hurt me anymore. I can investigate this case without dredging up old ghosts."

"Are you sure? There's no shame in letting Raven lead your investigation."

She ate half the toast and set the plate down.

"That's unnecessary. Besides, I'm in too deep to leave the water."

Thomas moved his chair closer to the table. The laptop displayed a digital map of Nightshade County.

"What are you looking at?"

"Something doesn't add up." Chelsey tapped a nail against the screen. "Karley told you she ran for several hours before she found CR-26." She clicked the mouse and enlarged the map. "This is where Spencer Johansen picked up Karley, and here is the supermarket where the killer abducted her."

"The store is only three miles away."

"Which tells me the killer lives nearby. But the woods don't run that deep between CR-26 and the next road."

Thomas scrolled the map half a mile northward. "There's a two-mile stretch of woods here. That would have taken Karley a long time to fight through, especially in the dark. Maybe she turned herself around and lost her way."

"I thought of that, but notice where the forest ends. I see a country road like the one Karley described, but no farm, and the street view doesn't show a house with a windmill outside."

"Those pictures aren't always up to date." Thomas folded his arms. "Our killer could have installed the windmill after the photo was taken."

"But what about the farm? Those don't build themselves overnight."

Thomas scratched his head. "This case has me turning in circles. At least Karley is alive."

"Who does that leave? We can eliminate Urban Hammond as a suspect. Wallace Bryant?"

"I phoned Bryant at midnight. He wasn't pleased to hear from me. Said he worked late at his media group and was in the office from sunrise until eleven o'clock."

"Let me guess," Chelsey said. "No one can verify his whereabouts during the evening."

"Says he was alone after seven."

"Lance Weir?"

"He finally showed his face at the hospital. It took a deputy pounding on his door to wake him up. With his phone off, the jerk had no idea his wife was alive and recovering at County General."

"Weir didn't show concern for his missing wife. Where was he while someone tried to run Spencer Johansen and Karley off the road?"

"Alone at home, watching the news and supposedly worried sick over Karley."

"Another dead end."

"Yep."

Chelsey sipped her tea and leaned back in her chair. "Two men who knew Karley, and neither has a valid alibi for last evening. Could either be our killer?"

"Neither owns a sedan and a truck. I can't imagine Bryant would be caught dead in a pickup."

"Karley knew her kidnapper. I'm sure of it."

Overcome with exhaustion, Chelsey covered her mouth and yawned into her hand. Thomas closed the laptop.

"That's it. We're both going to sleep. The case can wait until morning."

"Thomas, it *is* morning."

"Not until you wake up. Don't argue because I won't take no for an answer."

Chelsey glanced at the window. "I have to admit, it is a little exciting to sleep at the state park. Makes me feel all rustic."

"You might change your mind the first time a spider as big as your hand crawls across the wall."

"They make spiders that big in the woods?"

"Don't worry, they only attack people who stay up late."

She jabbed his arm. "You had me going for a second. Thomas, I can't let Karley experience what I went through."

"You won't. But you can't help Karley if you're too tired to think straight." He stood and held out his hand. "Come to bed. We'll catch a killer as a team."

Chelsey pressed her lips against his. They held heat, and it wasn't just from the tea. Were it four hours earlier, he would have suggested they make love. Goodness knew he desired her. As he did whenever she entered the room.

He tried not to picture Chelsey as he'd found her inside Kenneth Wendel's house of horrors. That nightmare was over, and already another took its place.

A new madman stalked the women of Nightshade County, and Thomas felt no closer to catching him.

42

Chirping birds pulled Thomas awake at eight o'clock on Sunday morning. He sat up, confused over his surroundings, until he recognized the cabin. Jack was already sprawled across the foot of the bed. Tigger had burrowed beneath the covers and curled between them.

Thomas didn't mean to rouse Chelsey—she needed rest even more than he did—but her eyes popped open while he pulled his clothes on.

"What time is it?" she muttered.

"Too early. Go back to sleep."

But she didn't. Instead, she threw on sweatpants and a T-shirt and crawled into the chair, intent on studying the digital map again. Thomas couldn't blame her. New information often presented itself after a night of sleep, though he hardly considered a few hours of shuteye enough. Either way, there was no point in arguing after she made up her mind.

While Chelsey worked, Thomas took Jack outside. The other investigators were already up. Lights shone from the cabins, and the delectable smoky scent of grilled food tickled Thomas's nose. Darren waved from behind a grill across the clearing. The ranger was busy cooking eggs and home fries in a cast iron pan over an open flame.

LeVar and Raven emerged moments after, the rookie deputy rubbing his eyes after the late night. Serena joined them, though the woman kept her distance from her daughter as she spoke with the others. Next came Naomi and Scout, the latter in shorts, slippers, and an extra-large sweatshirt despite a start to the day that was chilly enough for Thomas to see his breath.

They ate breakfast inside the cabin that served as Wolf Lake Consulting's operations base. Nobody wanted to be far from the computers after last night's developments.

"If you ask me," Darren said, swallowing a piece of egg, "we should concentrate on Wallace Bryant. He knew Karley and Alena, and he didn't have an alibi for last night."

Raven nodded. "I concur. We already considered the unsub might own a second home, somewhere to hide his victims. Bryant owns multiple properties, including houses in Los Angeles, Miami, and New York City."

"What about in the Finger Lakes?" Chelsey asked.

"Besides his mansion in the village of Wolf Lake, Bryant owns a country home near the tip of Cayuga Lake. Check the map. There's a farm a few hundred yards down the road."

"This house wouldn't have a windmill out front, would it?"

Raven shrugged. "I'll check."

Serena walked her plate to the sink. "Did y'all give up on Lance Weir? The way he treats women tells me he isn't trustworthy."

"You make a valid point, Mom," Raven said, looking hopefully at her mother. Serena sniffed and rinsed her dish. Raven pursed her lips and turned to the team members. "Lance Weir didn't even leave his phone on after Karley disappeared."

LeVar pushed his dreadlocks back. "I never trusted that

creep, not since the day he reported his wife missing. What do you think, Scout?"

The teenage girl raised her head in surprise. "You want my opinion of who the killer is?"

"You're our FBI profiler in the making, so yes."

"Karley knew her attacker, and so did Alena. I'm more certain than ever that our kidnapper and killer are one and the same. But there's nothing to prove Wallace Bryant and Lance Weir are cold-blooded murderers. Alena and Karley ran in different social circles. The only link between them is Bryant Media Group."

"But Wallace Bryant won't talk about the workers' compensation claim," said Thomas, "and neither will City Confidential."

"Gene Digby seemed pretty talkative," LeVar offered. "Maybe we can convince him to tell us who Alena Robinson mediated for."

"Who is Gene Digby?" Darren asked.

"Bryant claims he covered for Digby on Tuesday evening, the night Karley disappeared."

Before anyone offered a dissenting opinion, Chelsey typed Gene Digby's name into her computer. "What do we know about this guy?"

"He's a senior account manager at Bryant Media Group," Thomas said.

"Didn't Bryant say he took Digby's shift because of a family emergency?"

"A drunk driver caused an accident with Digby's sister."

Driven by an idea she hadn't yet shared, Chelsey's fingers rattled the keys with blinding speed. She clicked the mouse and sat back with Digby's background information displayed on the screen.

"Gene Digby, age thirty-four. Graduated from Findlay University. Current resides at 2 Quail Road in Mineral Springs

Township. Parents are Bennett and Leandra Digby in Cincinnati, Ohio."

"Where the heck is Quail Road?" LeVar asked.

"About five or six miles outside of Wolf Lake," Darren said, leaning forward with growing interest. "The forest borders that road. Sounds promising."

"Tell me about Digby's sister," said Thomas.

Chelsey scrolled down the screen. "We have a problem. Gene Digby is an only child."

"LeVar, punch up a map of Quail Road. Switch to street view and tell me what you see outside Digby's house."

"Right away," said LeVar as Thomas eyed his phone. "Who are you calling?"

"Lance Weir."

LeVar gave Thomas a confused glance before he entered the map coordinates into the computer. Thomas tapped his foot and waited for Weir to pick up his phone.

"What's taking him so long?" Thomas muttered. Weir answered in a gruff voice. "Mr. Weir, this is Sheriff Shepherd."

"If you don't mind, Sheriff, I'm at the hospital with my wife. I don't have time to answer questions today. The doctors say she can come home this afternoon, and I intend to get her out of here."

Thomas gritted his teeth. The man was impossible. At least Weir was with his wife instead of sleeping on the couch while Karley lay in a hospital bed.

"How well do you know Gene Digby?"

"Gene? We've worked together at Bryant Media Group for years. What's your interest in Gene?"

"Did you have problems with Mr. Digby, or did he ever show too much interest in your wife?"

Weir huffed. "Gene used to drive by the house to check on Karley when I worked late. I didn't need to ask. He offered."

"Have you seen him in the last week?"

"Not since Mr. Bryant told me to take time off. Wait a second. I spoke to Bryant on the phone this morning, and he mentioned needing me to come back once we got Karley settled."

"Did he say why?"

"Yeah. Gene called in with a flu virus and said he needs time off."

"Mr. Weir," Thomas said, "if you see or hear from Gene Digby, I want you to call my department immediately."

"But—"

"Just do it."

Weir ended the call. The investigators had already sprung into action as Thomas turned to LeVar.

"Shep," LeVar said, "Gene Digby has one neighbor. Warren Shorts. He owns farmland two hundred yards down the road from Digby."

"This has to be our guy."

"There's more. Digby put an ornamental windmill in the front yard."

"And he owns a red Impala and a blue GMC Sierra," said Chelsey, checking vehicle registrations.

LeVar jumped up from his chair. "We can be there in twenty minutes."

"Get ready, LeVar. We're going after Digby now."

43

A blanket of gray clouds stifled the sky, and the first sprinkle of rain wet Thomas's face as he crossed the lawn in front of Gene Digby's home. A red Impala sat in the driveway. There was no sign of the blue Sierra. The sheriff motioned Deputy Lambert and another deputy around the back of the house, while Thomas ascended the porch beside Aguilar. Two state troopers accompanied LeVar, who investigated the neighboring farm.

One kick opened the front door. With the curtains drawn over the window, shadows covered the living room. A bang from the rear of the house announced Lambert had entered through the back. Aguilar and Thomas met Lambert in the kitchen. Having cleared the downstairs, Thomas sent his deputies to the second floor. Alone, he eyed the open basement door and the steps leading into the dark unknown. He flicked a wall switch and illuminated the cellar. Ever cautious, he descended the stairs with his gun angled toward the blind spot beside the stairway.

The basement lay vacant. A futon in the far corner served as a bed. Thick bars covered the windows, preventing escape. His shoe crunched on broken glass. He glanced down and found two more pieces trailing toward a half-bath.

Thomas peeked his head around the corner and spied the shattered mirror of the medicine cabinet.

"Smart woman," he said, admiring Karley for fighting back.

Another set of bars covered the window above the half-bath. From here, Karley could have seen the farm and planned her escape route.

"Sheriff?" Thomas jumped at Aguilar's voice. She stood on the bottom step while Lambert and his partner pawed around the futon. "There's nobody upstairs. It looks like Digby left in a hurry. The dresser is full of clothes, and we found a desktop computer in his study."

"I want that hard drive. Find everything that links Digby to Alena Robinson and Karley Weir."

"Will do."

"And, God forbid, any other women he might have murdered."

Aguilar pounded up the stairs.

Wearing gloves, Lambert picked a handful of photographs out of the blanket. "You'd better check these out."

Thomas was almost afraid to look. He expected pictures of Alena Robinson—Karley had told him about the photos at the hospital—but viewing the murdered woman, her eyes brimming with panic and horror, curdled the sheriff's stomach. While his deputies collected evidence and photographed the scene, Thomas radioed the department and issued an alert for Gene Digby and his GMC Sierra. The entire state was searching for the killer, and any sane man would flee while he had a chance. But Thomas sensed he was still out there, waiting to recapture Karley or abduct another woman.

Thomas and Lambert met Aguilar on the first floor. Her face was pale, and she held another stack of photographs. Without a word, she handed the pictures to Thomas. This was his worst fear. The photos showed a dozen women, some bound and pleading for mercy, others with lifeless eyes, mouths agape, spittle running from the corners of their mouths. How many victims had Digby murdered?

"The pictures on the bottom are from the forest. All the women appear dead. Thomas, I saw a pond in the background."

The sheriff's mouth went dry. "I'll get a forensics team out to the forest. Better call the medical examiner too. There was a mass grave beneath our feet, and we never knew."

While one deputy secured the house, Thomas, Lambert, and Aguilar crossed the field to the farm. Raised voices traveled from within the barn. When the sheriff entered the structure, he found LeVar kneeling beside a state trooper. A chewed-up leg jutted out of a pile of hay.

"Warren Shorts," LeVar said, rising. "It appears an animal found him overnight."

Another victim to add to the killer's body count.

Thomas's phone rang. He recognized Trooper Fitzgerald's number. The state trooper had worked many cases with Thomas over the last year.

"Thomas here."

"Sheriff, the hospital just released Karley Weir," said Fitzgerald. "Her husband is walking her out of the facility."

"I take it you're at the hospital now?"

"I am. Want me to follow them home?"

"Yes. Gene Digby is still on the loose, and I'm afraid he'll go after Karley once she's unguarded."

"I'll ensure a state trooper drives past the Weir house every hour."

"And I'll station a deputy outside. Until Digby is behind bars, we need to expect the unexpected."

44

Karley couldn't believe Gene Digby would kidnap her and murder an innocent woman. Though she'd never considered the man a friend, he seemed kind. She recalled the times he'd checked on her while Lance was tied up at the office. She hadn't thought the gesture strange because Lance maintained close relationships with his coworkers.

Through a parting in the curtains, Karley watched her parents drive away. They had wanted to stay and even offered to take her home with them, not trusting Lance to care for Karley the way a husband should. Lance must have said something to convince them to leave.

Now the house was silent. Just Karley and the husband she resented. She didn't wish to be in the same room with him. The overcast sky quickened nightfall's approach, skipping dusk and blackening the sky. Outside, just beyond a cherry tree, the Nightshade County Sheriff's cruiser parked in the shadows. She discerned the silhouette of a deputy in the driver's seat. He sipped from a thermos while he waited for something to happen.

"We need to talk."

Karley jumped out of her skin. She hadn't heard Lance enter the living room.

"You and I have nothing to talk about, Lance."

"But Karley—"

"Don't *but* me. You turned your phone off the night Gene grabbed me outside the grocery store. Didn't you worry something had happened?"

Lance stammered. "I swore I left my phone on."

"You watch every move I make, as if you don't trust me, but the minute I need you, you're nowhere to be found."

He touched her shoulder, and she pulled away. Anger flashed in his eyes. She flinched, remembering the psychopath who'd tortured her for days while her husband lounged in comfort.

"I screwed up. Karley, I'll make it up to you."

She sniffed and turned back to the window. Full dark descended on the neighborhood. Every time a siren rose in the distance, she worried Digby was coming after her.

Lance took Karley's hand and pulled her from the window. She resisted, but he was stronger and able to lead her to the couch despite her protests. He sat beside her, closer than she would have preferred. How had this happened? Once she'd loved this man and looked past his aloofness, making excuses for his brash behavior. She couldn't stomach another day with him.

"Let me make this right," he said.

"You can't."

"Dammit, Karley. I don't mean to be a dictator. All I want is to protect you . . . protect you from people like . . ."

"Gene Digby?"

"How was I to know? I figured he just wanted to make sure you were safe. We all help each other out at work. It's a family."

"Unlike our household."

"That's not fair. I give you everything. A home, a marriage—"

"Thanks so much for rescuing me," she said, her voice tainted with cynicism.

"What do you want from me?"

"Freedom? Someone to spend time with after I return from work? You sure as hell didn't give me a son or daughter."

He blanched, and she wished she could take her words back. No matter how furious Lance made Karley, it wasn't fair to throw his impotence in his face, as though he didn't want a child as much as she did.

"I'm sorry," she said.

"That was low."

"I didn't mean it."

"Yes, you did. I failed you, Karley. I failed to give you a proper family, just as I failed to protect you when you needed me."

He rose. She reached for his arm, but he put distance between them, pacing the living room floor like a rat in a cage.

"If you'd only let me help," he said, his voice squeaking.

She rubbed her arms. "Until the sheriff catches Gene, there isn't much anyone can do."

"You're scared he'll come."

She pressed her lips together.

"He won't get past me," Lance said. "Gene Digby will never touch you again. I'll kill him if he tries." He peeked between the curtains. "Anyhow, the deputy's cruiser is out front. No chance Gene will risk coming here."

"You can't guarantee he won't." Even with the deputy outside and Lance guarding the entryway, Karley couldn't imagine sleeping here. This wasn't her home anymore. She should have accepted her parents' offer. "I'll call Mom and Dad."

Lance rounded on Karley. "You won't. I'm your husband, dammit. I won't let you run back to your parents like a child.

The doctor prescribed you anti-anxiety medication. Have you taken it yet?"

"He said to swallow a pill before bed."

"Maybe you shouldn't wait." Lance nervously tapped a hand against his thigh. "Okay, if you aren't comfortable in our home, I'll drive you to a hotel."

"That's not a wise idea."

"Why not? Think, Karley. Even if Digby figures out that we're at the hotel, he won't know the room number, and he'll have to pass through a busy lobby."

Karley closed her eyes. As angry as Lance made her, his plan made sense. She would feel safer surrounded by people, especially if their room was near the top of the hotel. There would be no way for Digby to break in through the window.

"All right, Lance, but you'd better clear your plan with the sheriff's department."

Lance glowered. He stepped outside and approached the cruiser. The deputy lowered the window, and after a brief discussion and a lot of nodding, Lance jogged back to the house, his eyes shooting left and right, as though he expected an attack out of the darkness.

"The deputy will follow us to the hotel and set up surveillance. Gather what you need. I'm ready to roll."

Karley packed a travel bag. Five minutes later, they backed out of the driveway, and Lance turned up the road and headed toward the village center. Soon Karley would experience the safety of bright lights and people. Behind them, the deputy followed. Karley fiddled with her phone and sent her mother a message.

When they approached the train tracks, Lance accelerated. Karley looked up as the lights flashed, warning of an approaching train. Before she asked Lance what he was doing, their vehicle sped through the crossing a moment before the gates lowered. She had just enough time to swing her head around and see the deputy brake. He wasn't going to make it through.

"Lance, we lost the deputy. Stop and wait for—"

The black pickup truck roared out of hiding and slammed into the driver's side door.

45

The collision whipped Karley's head forward before the seatbelt yanked her back. Her head spun, and the scene beyond the windshield seemed to pitch and shift as two blinding lights heated her face. Somewhere, a bell chimed and a train roared, sending tremors through Karley's body.

She was aware of Lance moaning. Something wet dotted her arms. Blood. It wasn't hers.

Karley reached for Lance, but the truck slammed into them again. The black GMC Sierra reversed and set its sights on their disabled vehicle.

"Lance! Lance!"

Karley's husband didn't respond. The seatbelt was the only thing holding him upright. Blood gushed from his nose, and bits of safety glass covered his lap. It wasn't until then that Karley realized his window had shattered. The glass glittered on her thighs.

The pickup's door swung open. Gene Digby jumped down from the cab and stalked toward Karley. The light of the street-lamp caught his insane grin as he leaned toward the window. He rapped his knuckles on the glass.

"You shouldn't have run, Karley."

Digby yanked the handle before she could engage the locks. He cursed when the jammed door refused to budge. His fist slammed the glass. Karley jumped, her trembling fingers working to free her from the seatbelt.

The madman rounded the car and wrenched Lance's door open. It made a shuddering squeal and hung askew. Digby ripped Lance from the vehicle and tossed him to the pavement. Karley screamed when the killer raised a booted foot. It thundered down on Lance's head and split his skull. The psychopath reached across the seats and groped at Karley, who fought to open the jammed door. It gave way, and she tumbled onto the blacktop. With a growl, Digby raced around the front bumper and converged on her. She scurried onto her hands and knees. The killer had a knife.

He clutched Karley's hair and ripped her away from the vehicle. She stumbled and threw herself across the hood, but there was nothing to grab hold of. The madman dragged her toward the pickup truck. She struck his face and bloodied his lip, but he overpowered her. Hugging her against his body, Digby hauled the flailing woman across the road.

Karley knew she would never escape if he forced her into the truck. She gouged his eyes, and he shrieked and dropped her. Before he recovered, she turned and ran.

Whirling lights and a siren brought her to a stop. The sheriff's cruiser skidded to a halt in front of her. A door opened, and the deputy stepped out of the vehicle with his gun trained on Digby's truck. The murderer had crawled behind the wheel of the Sierra and fired the engine. Tires squealed, then the truck shot forward. Diving out of the way, the deputy rolled across the macadam seconds before the behemoth smashed into his cruiser and shoved it into the ditch. The siren died. With the cruiser flipped over, the emergency lights stopped spinning.

Karley limped to the deputy, who lay in a heap, his eyes glazed in shock. The truck's headlights zeroed in on Karley and the prone officer. Digby would crush them both.

Just as the truck lurched forward, a state police vehicle clipped its front bumper and spun the pickup around. This was the chance Karley needed. Beside her, the deputy found his footing. He swung his service weapon at the killer's pickup just as a second sheriff's cruiser stopped short of the wreckage.

THOMAS SLAMMED his brakes when the vehicles popped out of the darkness without warning. Carnage covered the road. A sheriff's cruiser lay on its top beyond the ditch. Steam billowed from under the hood of Trooper Fitzgerald's vehicle, and Gene Digby's GMC Sierra faced in the wrong direction, its bumper hanging like a broken jaw. Behind the wreckage, another vehicle had been sideswiped. The driver's side door buckled inward. Safety glass littered the road. There was a body amid all that glass. Lance Weir. He wasn't moving.

The sheriff's eyes swept across the mayhem. Thomas saw an injured deputy help Karley Weir out of the road.

The Sierra had stalled, but Digby was cranking the engine and trying to start the pickup. The killer intended to crush the cruisers.

Thomas jumped out. Digby opened his mouth in surprise when the sheriff aimed his weapon.

"Put down the knife and step out of the vehicle."

The killer lashed out with the knife, missing Thomas's face by inches. Grabbing his TASER, Thomas struck Digby, who jerked upright and lost control of his muscles. The sheriff wrestled the knife from the killer's hand and pulled him out of the cab. Across the road, Fitzgerald hurried to Lance Weir. Thomas knelt on the small of Digby's back and cuffed the man's hands behind him.

"No, you can't do this," Digby said, thrashing. "She's mine! Karley is mine!"

"Why did you kill Alena Robinson?"

"I had no choice. She tried to leave me. I gave her my love, and she turned on me."

"The forest off County Route 26: how many women did you bury there?"

Digby refused to answer, but his blank stare unraveled Thomas's nerves.

The madman had no respect for life. To Digby, the victims belonged to him, and any woman who didn't fall in love with her captor deserved a death sentence. How long had the killer led a double life?

"You shouldn't have murdered Warren Shorts."

"You've got it all wrong. Shorts wanted Karley for himself. That's the only reason he helped her. I saved Karley from Shorts. Who knows what he would have done to her if I hadn't arrived in time?"

Thomas shook his head. Digby was out of his mind.

Another cruiser stopped on the side of the road, and LeVar and Deputy Lambert emerged from the vehicle.

"Call an ambulance," Thomas told them. "We have multiple injuries, and Lance Weir isn't responding."

"He deserves to die," the killer said, wiggling beneath Thomas. "Lance doesn't love Karley the way I do. I cared for her while he worked at the office. She should be mine."

Thomas was at a loss for words. Digby had admitted his

crimes without regret. If there was any justice in the world, the man would serve a life sentence and never get out of prison.

In the distance, the mournful cry of a train whistle faded into the night.

Thomas read Digby his rights.

46

Hunched over with his hands on his knees, Thomas quivered until the nausea passed. LeVar had an arm around the sheriff's shoulder as Deputy Lambert and Trooper Fitzgerald looked on with concern. The deputy who'd cared for Karley had suffered minor cuts and abrasions. He would be fine. It was a miracle every responding law enforcement had escaped Gene Digby's wrath relatively unscathed. All around Thomas, the lights of Lambert's cruiser threw dizzying reds and blues across the pavement.

"You all right now, Sheriff?" asked Lambert.

"I'll be okay. You mind killing the emergency lights while I catch my breath?"

"Not a problem."

Often the lights gave Thomas sensory overload, but the disturbing images playing through his mind unsettled the sheriff most. Whenever he closed his eyes, he pictured Digby stomping Lance Weir's head. Karley had witnessed the attack. What if some maniac beat Thomas to death in front of Chelsey?

"Any word on Lance Weir?" Thomas asked LeVar.

"His wife rode with him in the ambulance. I know one of the paramedics from school. He's studying criminal justice. If you want, I'll text him. The ambulance should be at the hospital."

Now that the sheriff had his footing, LeVar strode away to make his phone call. As if Thomas's thoughts had summoned her, Chelsey arrived with Raven and Darren. She hurried to Thomas and threw her arms around his shoulders.

"Thank goodness you're all right," she said, stroking his hair. "The police band radio said something about an injured officer."

"The deputy is fine, and I was never in danger." Except for the knife that almost raked across his eyes. Thomas decided not to share that close call. "Karley is safe, and the state police have Digby. He won't harm anyone again."

"What about the husband?"

"LeVar will find out." Thomas pinched the bridge of his nose. "Uh-oh. I just realized Jack and Tigger have been locked inside the cabin all day. Let's hope they haven't eaten the computers."

"No worries. I stopped by to feed them and take Jack outside around dinnertime. No accidents, no computer parts scattered around the room. But it looked like someone tore a hole in the bedsheets."

"Lucky for us we know the park ranger."

"I'll forget it happened," Darren said. "But only if you buy the next pizza."

Thomas forced himself to grin. "That can be arranged."

Raven squeezed through the crowd and hugged Thomas. "Glad you made it through in one piece, Thomas. I was worried."

He whispered in her ear, "Keep an eye on Chelsey. This case pulled her back to the Kenneth Wendel abduction. I don't want her internalizing her fears and shutting everyone out again."

Raven nodded, pointedly averting her eyes from Chelsey.

"That's what friends are for."

He wanted to ask Raven if she'd made up with her mother, but LeVar ran back to them with an update from the hospital.

"Good news. Lance Weir regained consciousness inside the ambulance. The doctor is worried about a skull fracture, but he's responsive."

A weight rolled off the sheriff's shoulders. "Thank you for calling, deputy. My opinion of Lance Weir as a husband couldn't fall much lower, but he didn't deserve what happened to him. In the end, he tried to get Karley to safety. He almost died defending her."

While Chelsey walked to the curb with Darren and Raven, Deputy Lambert leaned toward Thomas.

"I heard from the medical examiner. Claire estimates the cadaver dogs found ten or more bodies buried near the pond. The team is still excavating bones at the site."

"Nightshade County doesn't have that many missing women."

"Digby may have traveled. Aguilar is looking into his trip records. Seems he spent a lot of time driving the interstate between Buffalo and Albany."

"So our victims may have come from all over the state."

"Possibly. I also took a call from Digby's old girlfriend after we released the BOLO. She lived at his house on Quail Road for two months a few years ago. Says she sneaked out in the middle of the night and left him when he started acting weird. His mood swings scared her. Over the next year, she claims he followed her around the village. Once he accused her of trying to leave town without his permission."

"It's safe to assume Gene Digby was the injured worker in Alena Robinson's compensation case."

"Wallace Bryant admitted as much. He also contacted the office after he saw the BOLO."

If only Bryant had acted sooner.

Thomas pulled his jacket tight to ward off the chill. His officers had survived, but it was too late to save Digby's victims.

47

On the last day of September, the unseasonable chill relented for one final day of sunshine. Boaters flocked to the lake, desperate to rekindle memories of summer before the cold returned. The season's first frost had withered the flowers outside the guest house, and leaves fell in variegated yellows and reds.

Though it wasn't warm enough for shorts and a T-shirt, Thomas felt comfortable in a light jacket as he tended the grill. He glanced up when a delightful aroma met his nose. With Scout's help, Naomi set a dish wrapped in aluminum foil on the picnic table.

"Is that sweet potato casserole?" Thomas asked.

"With marshmallows on top," said Scout.

"Your favorite," Naomi said. "We're lucky the weather broke in time for the cookout. By next week, I fear we'll have to take the party indoors."

Thomas flipped the burgers. "No more outdoor grilling until mid-April if the winter forecast is correct."

"Ugh. It's not supposed to be that bad this winter, is it?"

"That's what they say. Which reminds me, I need to service the snowblower."

"Bet winter makes you miss Los Angeles," Scout said, sitting on the table with her feet on the bench. A sea-blue headband pulled the girl's dark hair off her forehead.

"Now and then. But winter doesn't last forever, and it always gives you the promise of spring to look forward to."

In the yard, Darren, Raven, and LeVar tossed a football, while Jack ran back and forth, leaping to intercept the ball. If the dog got hold of the football, they'd never see it again. Chelsey descended the deck and set a salad beside the casserole. The deputies were due to arrive in the next fifteen minutes, but Thomas sensed the group wasn't complete. He set the spatula down and looked around.

"Where's Serena?"

"Still fighting with her daughter," Naomi muttered from the corner of her mouth.

"She wouldn't skip dinner, would she?"

"I hope not, but I have no intention of getting between Serena and Raven. They're worse than two tomcats warring over a mouse."

Thomas was happy to see Chelsey active and chatting with friends. On his recommendation, she'd doubled up on therapy appointments. Provided Chelsey kept the lines of communication open, she would pull through. Her resiliency never ceased to astound Thomas.

Scout asked, "Whatever happened to Holly Doyle?"

"The Doyle family is attending counseling together. Tragedy has a way of redefining what is important, and the Doyles almost lost their daughter. Hopefully they take my advice and let Holly breathe."

"I doubt all the counseling in the world could save Lance

Weir," Naomi added. "I bet Karley leaves him. She deserves better."

"Last I heard, Karley was living with her parents. After the horrors she endured, Karley will need their support."

"Hey, Scout. Look what I got."

They all turned when a teenage girl with curly blond hair hopped down from Scout and Naomi's porch. The teen had knocked on the door before spotting everyone.

Scout waved. "Liz, what are you doing here?"

"Check out what arrived in the mail." Liz beamed over two electronic devices. "A digital voice recorder and an EMF sensor."

"Where in the world did you find an EMF sensor?"

"On the internet. You can buy anything online." Liz noticed everyone looking at her. "Sorry, I didn't realize you were having dinner. I'll come back later and show you."

"This is Liz, by the way."

A chorus of greetings welcomed Scout's friend to the backyard. Thomas's heart warmed. After moving from Ithaca, Scout had struggled to meet classmates. Though she had her mother and the investigators to lean on, she needed friends among her peers.

"Liz," said Thomas, "do you like your burgers medium rare or well done?"

Liz scuffed a sneaker against the grass. "I don't want to impose."

"There's plenty of food to go around, and a friend of Scout is a friend of ours."

"Thank you. Sheriff Shepherd, right?"

"Call me Thomas."

"My father says you're the best thing that ever happened to Wolf Lake. If you step down, he swears he'll move the family to Alaska."

Thomas cleared his throat. "Well, the village did just fine

without me, but thank your father all the same. So you bought an EMF sensor. Are you a ghost hunter?"

"I wish." Liz laughed. "Every week, I record all the paranormal investigation shows and binge-watch them."

"Do those gadgets work, or are they all hype?"

"That's what I intend to find out."

"Okay, but if you find any spirits wandering around my yard, don't tell me. I don't want to know."

The girls walked to the shore. Liz looked across the yard at LeVar and giggled into Scout's ear. Thomas heard the word *cute* muttered. He stoked the coals before a truck stopped in front of the house and pulled his attention. It was Serena and a man who looked like . . . but couldn't be Buck Benson. The clean-shaven man wore casual shorts and flip-flops, both of which must have left him chilly. Raven turned her head after Darren threw the football, and the ball bounced off her shoulder. She didn't seem to notice.

Serena escorted her friend to the grill. "Thomas, this is my neighbor, Buck Benson. Would you mind if he joined us for dinner?"

"Not at all." Thomas shook Benson's hand. "Thomas Shepherd."

"Buck Benson," the man said, grinning sheepishly. "Thank you for having me over."

"I hope you like burgers, Buck."

"Can't beat them on a sunny day."

"That's what I always say. Why don't you join me? I bet you're no stranger to grilling."

Buck gave Thomas a good-natured laugh, and the sheriff slapped him on the back. As they discussed how best to grill a burger, Raven shuffled over with Darren and LeVar trailing behind. Introductions were made, but Serena and Raven ignored each other, the tension reminiscent of the moment before a storm rolled across the lake. It was Buck who broke the ice.

"If the two of you insist on fighting, I won't stand in the middle. But you're both acting stubborn, and I should know a thing or two about stubbornness. Serena, Raven and I made our peace. There's no reason to be angry with your daughter."

"Mom," Raven said, lowering her eyes, "I'm sorry I hurt you."

One moment, Serena stared daggers into her daughter. The next, she broke down crying and wrapped Raven in a hug.

Thomas glanced at Buck in amazement. Was this truly Mark Benson's second cousin? Perhaps he was just as guilty as Raven. Prejudice didn't only close the mind; it drowned the heart. There were more tears, more apologies, and enough laughter to warm the chilliest of days.

Chelsey came to Thomas and kissed his cheek. "Looks like the family is back together."

"And growing," he said, nodding at Buck and Liz. "I'd better buy a bigger house."

She smiled into his eyes. "Oh, Thomas, your heart could host an entire village."

GET A FREE BOOK!

I'm a pretty nice guy once you look past the grisly images in my head. Most of all, I love connecting with awesome readers like you.

Join my VIP Reader Group and get a FREE serial killer thriller for your Kindle.

Get My Free Book

www.danpadavona.com/thriller-readers-vip-group/

SHOW YOUR SUPPORT FOR INDIE AUTHORS

Did you enjoy this book? If so, please let other thriller fans know by leaving a short review. Positive reviews help spread the word about independent authors and their novels. Thank you.

Copyright Information

Published by Dan Padavona

Visit my website at www.danpadavona.com

Cover Design by Caroline Teagle Johnson

ACKNOWLEDGMENTS

No writer journeys alone. Special thanks are in order to my editor, C.B. Moore, for providing invaluable feedback, catching errors, and making my story shine. I also wish to thank my brilliant cover designer, Caroline Teagle Johnson. Your artwork never ceases to amaze me. I owe so much of my success to your hard work. Shout outs to my advance readers Susan Cuff, Donna Puscek, David Parker, Mary Arnold, Marcia Campbell, and Teresa Padavona for catching those final pesky typos and plot holes. Most of all, thank you to my readers for your loyalty and support. You changed my life, and I am forever grateful.

ABOUT THE AUTHOR

Dan Padavona is the author of the The Logan and Scarlett series, The Darkwater Cove series, The Scarlett Bell thriller series, *Her Shallow Grave*, The Dark Vanishings series, *Camp Slasher, Quilt, Crawlspace, The Face of Midnight, Storberry, Shadow Witch*, and the horror anthology, *The Island*. He lives in upstate New York with his beautiful wife, Terri, and their children, Joe, and Julia. Dan retired as a meteorologist with NOAA's National Weather Service. Besides writing, he enjoys visiting amusement parks, beach vacations, Renaissance fairs, gardening, playing with the family dogs, and eating too much ice cream.

Visit Dan at: www.danpadavona.com

Made in the USA
Middletown, DE
06 November 2023